RATTLESNAKE LAWYER

A Novel

by

Jonathan C. Miller

Cool Titles and
Jonathan Miller
proudly support the
Ingram Cancer Center

ABOUT RATTLESNAKE LAWYER

"Watch for Rattlesnakes" reads the sign at the first rest stop within New Mexico's "Fighting 14th" district. Young attorney Dan Shepard has been fired by his mother's prestigious Washington law firm, and now must make his home among the rattlesnakes. A failed stand-up comic forced into law to pay the bills, Dan finds nothing amusing about his first case. His client, Jesus Villalobos, faces a murder charge, but nothing is what it seems. . . . The State seems a little too eager to pin the charge on Jesus. Along the way, it is hard to tell who is the lawyer and who is the client.

There is no escape for Dan in a small town where everybody knows what's going on except him. Dan faces a unique dilemma when he constantly encounters his client's family and friends as they cut his hair and serve his food—how much should he tip them?

Rattlesnake Lawyer is a darkly comic tale of a young lawyer's coming of age in the outback of America, how he learns to overcome his own fears and prejudices. Dan can't even pronounce his client's name when he first arrives, and leaves the door to the jail open on the way out. But through his mentor, Pete Baca, who has a few secrets of his own, Dan learns how to practice law in a land of outlaws.

Dan also learns about love from his client. Jesus wants to marry his long time sweetheart Anna Maria, a love that transcends prison bars and perhaps time itself. Desperately lonely as the story begins, Dan meets the woman of his dreams, but is she using him to get to his client?

Rattlesnake Lawyer ends with an unforgettable trial and an even more unforgettable wedding.

Jonathan Miller has practiced law all over New Mexico, primarily representing juveniles accused of crimes. Several of his clients could be considered high profile. He currently is in private practice in Albuquerque, where he writes and stays active working for legal services providers helping out the poor.

Published by
Cool Titles
12121 Wilshire Blvd., Suite 1201
Los Angeles, CA90025
www.cooltitles.com

The Library of Congress Cataloging-in-Publication Data Applied For

Jonathan Miller—
Rattlesnake Lawyer

p. cm
ISBN 0-9673920-3-9

1. Mystery 2. American Southwest I. Title
2004

Printed in the United States of America

1 3 5 7 9 10 8 6 4 2

Book editing and design by Lisa Wysocky
Cover design by White Horse Enterprises, Inc.
Marketing by J.D. Haas: jdrocks@jdhe.com

For interviews or information regarding special discounts for bulk purchases,
please contact us at njohnson@jrllp.com

PART I

Chapter 1

One on One

"ONE ON ONE, TWO ON one." The door clicked open.

The brand new guard in an oversized tan uniform entered the multi-purpose room of the Aguilar County Detention Center. It was his first time for sure, probably his first job ever since graduating from the vocational program at Aguilar High. He gagged on the smell from the remnants of the evening's dinner of green chile enchiladas, then scanned the groups of residents waiting for the nightly head count.

"Fresh white meat," a particularly large resident muttered behind the guard's back.

I sat at a far table with Jesus Villalobos who laughed, "That's what we used to say about you when you came here."

I felt for the poor guy and called to him, "Yo buddy, you looking for us?"

We were the only ones in suits—blue double-breasted, crisp red ties—sitting alone at the furthest of the plastic mesh tables. He hurried over to our table.

"Jesus Villalobos, Dan Shepard?" he asked nervously. We nodded simultaneously.

"Jury's back."

Jesus and I stared at each other. There really wasn't anything more to be said. This was it.

The guard kept his eyes at the level of our Windsor knots as he took out both sets of handcuffs. "They told me to take you back to court."

He finally looked at each of us in the eye, unsure of something. He fiddled with both sets of handcuffs a few more times, as he scanned each of our faces.

"I'm sorry," he mumbled at last. "I'm not sure exactly who I'm supposed to cuff—isn't one of you supposed to be the lawyer?"

Chapter 2

Game Over

One Year Earlier

WHEN IT ALL BEGAN I was a lawyer alright, at least I thought I was. My mother's law firm of Shepard and Shepard gave me a plush but messy office off in a forgotten corner, a view onto the bustle of Washington's K street down below. A pile of unopened motions, memorandums and responses stacked my desk. "Litigating for Godot," I had named the pile in my monthly humor column for the local young lawyers' newsletter.

I didn't have the heart to subject myself to a thirty page motion too early in the morning, so I often played computer games to start my day, usually knock-offs of the Tomb Raider family. There was a loud knock on my door in the midst of a particularly gruesome tomb. I turned off the computer, picked up a large legal book, and pretended to read.

My mother entered with a look that could kill. At fifty, she was still the best dressed lawyer in Washington, and probably hadn't gained a pound or a wrinkle since Harvard. "We lost the case, Dan. The client's absolutely livid. They're leaving us."

"I'm sorry."

My mother hit the resume button on the computer, frowned when she saw the writhing creatures in the tomb on screen. She shook her head, took a very deep breath. "We're letting you go."

I smiled. "Yeah, right."

"I'm serious this time. We can't afford you if you're just going to sit around the office all day playing games. I work very hard—" She paused, as though continuing required too much effort in her defeated state.

I shrugged. She was right. She looked far more disappointed than I did.

"We hired you when no firm would, because. . . ." She didn't have to finish the sentence. "But you just don't seem that interested in municipal redevelopment bonds."

"When I bleed, I bleed municipal redevelopment bonds."

"You don't really seem to care about much of anything," she said wearily, as though she'd failed at more than her job. "Dan, you're twenty-seven years old. No more free ride."

I waited for her to change her mind, like she had done a dozen times before. She looked at the framed picture of our trip to Florida. Her face relaxed for a moment, as if she remembered how well I got along with those big Florida clients, "who always asked for you," but then she caught herself, tightened her features into a cold mask.

Oh my God. She really was serious this time. I started to reach for the pile of memos. "I'm sorry, Mom. I'll work harder. Give me another chance."

"You're going to have to start over, probably leave D.C.," she said. "What about that job interview in New Mexico you had? That's where you're admitted to practice, right?"

She said that with disdain. I had taken the relatively easy New Mexico exam to waive in and avoid the notoriously difficult D.C. bar. There had been a woman involved of course, but that was way over.

"New Mexico? Yeah right." I went with the first thing that flashed through my mind as a last ditch effort to stay here in the tomb—I mean womb. "Too many rattlesnakes."

Rattlesnakes wouldn't work. It was too late. She closed the door behind her. Game over.

Chapter 3

Jornada de los Muertos

October 7

I HAD TO FILL OUT some paperwork in the state labor office in Albuquerque the first night. The motel was called something like the Cheapo. My back was sore from the thin, lumpy mattress when I awoke early the next morning. My old girlfriend hadn't returned my call. Good old Mary Alice. She hadn't even offered me her sofa. She never let anything get the best of her, especially me. I climbed into my beat-up Escort, my college graduation gift that I had never managed to replace with my own money, and drove east on Central Avenue, the old Route 66, headed for Aguilar.

The sun rose over the 10,000 foot ridge of the Sandia Crest. I took one last look back at endless miles of fast food and prefab adobe subdivisions, then merged onto I-40 at the end of Central. Albuquerque came to an abrupt end. Within a few hundred yards, a deep canyon engulfed the freeway, separating the granite overthrust of the Sandias from the steep, shadowy Manzano Mountains to the south. Short, scraggly juniper trees and tall, stately piñons dotted the canyon walls.

I sped through the villages of Carnuel, Tijeras, and Zuzax, where rustic cabins clung precariously to the ridges flanking the freeway. As the sun slowly emerged over the canyon walls, the road suddenly entered a prairie that stretched all the way to Oklahoma. At the Moriarty exit, a billboard advertised the historic Salt Missions Trail. There weren't even hamlets any more, much less Salt Missions, whatever they were, just isolated gas stations and mobile homes at the exits for Wagon Wheel and Clines Corners.

At the exit for Hynes Crossing—gas, food, no lodging—I turned off onto the two lanes of US-667 and found myself stuck behind a truck doing forty for several miles. When it turned off onto a dirt road leading to a ranch, I was the only one on the road. According to my map, I was now in a thousand-mile stretch of wasteland the Spanish had named the Jornada de Los Muertos, the Journey of the Dead. To the east were the vast high plain drifts of the Llano Estacado; to the west, the teeth-like Manzano Mountains.

The road was flat for the next fifty miles. I gripped the steering wheel with my left hand, held the map with my right, and read the description of the Jornada on the side of the map. A party of conquistadors had died one by one coming across from Mexico, looking for the Seven Lost Cities of Cibola, cities supposedly made of gold.

Passing a series of table-like buttes, I saw a herd of giant tumbleweeds almost as big as my car floating along the mesa. One blew in front of me and hovered in the middle of the lane. I honked before swerving to avoid it.

Hours later, after several plastic bottles of citrus Gatorade, I pulled into a rest stop out in the mesa right at the Aguilar County line. The parking lot was empty; a few weeds pushed up through the cracks. The highway department sign out front said in big block letters:

WATCH FOR RATTLESNAKES

I took a quick look around. The coast was clear.

After taking care of business in the neglected restroom, I jumped back into the car and headed south on 667. Off to the left I saw a snow-capped mountain. Sierra Milagro, according to the map. As I came over a brief rise, I headed right for it, an iceberg in a pale brown sea. The last twenty miles were rusting oil derricks and squat concrete bunkers labeled "testing stations" behind barbed wire fences.

There was a stretch of farmland, fallow for the season, then some farmhouses and the omnipresent mobile homes. It was only October but there must have been an early frost because everything was a sickly brown.

Once in Aguilar, Route 667 sprouted a name—Santa Fe Street. As I drove down Santa Fe Street, I saw no natural grass or surface water. There were few trees, none higher than my car. There were no palm trees to suggest an oasis, although saber yuccas, with their thick trunks and sword-like stems, looked like mutated palms with a bad attitude. The adobe and cinderblock buildings looked battered by the elements. The town still belonged to the desert as far as nature was concerned.

Downtown Aguilar offered mostly vacant Victorian houses and

adobe storefronts. I consulted my scribbled notes and made a left on Oil Avenue. The public defender's office was two blocks down, a one-story Spanish ranch house with a few styleless additions and a scraggly cactus garden in front.

Opening the door, I heard a radio playing something like, "Hey, baby. Que paso?" in a smooth blend of country and mariachi.

A burly man with a long ponytail sat at the receptionist's chair in front of a computer screen that displayed an electronic chess game. On the table beside him—bullets, hairs, bloody rags—all in tightly sealed plastic baggies labeled "Defense Exhibit #__."

"You Dan Shepard?" The man had a slight Texas accent and the build of a linebacker. He was ruggedly handsome in his Western clothes, even his large brass cowboy belt buckle seemed to suit him. A brown clip-on tie lay neatly on top of a baggie containing a spent bullet.

"That's right."I stood in silence while he finished a chess move.

"I'm Pete Baca. Welcome to Aguilar, America."

"Thanks, I guess." I looked at all the baggies. "Are you the boss here?"

He finally looked up from his screen, took the tie from on top of the baggie, clipped it on. "I guess you can say that. You're the little Ivy Leaguer, right? Princeton?"

"No, Brown. Undergrad. American for law school."

"Why the hell did they send you down here? You couldn't get a job nowhere else?"

I wasn't about to go through the Shepard and Shepard saga. "I don't know," I said. "I got lucky, I guess."

"I wouldn't call this lucky," he said, his eyes back on the game.

I looked around. "Where's everybody else?"

"There's been some budget cuts. But we're getting another temp secretary soon. We go through 'em pretty quick around here. Right now, it's just you and me, kid."

Curious, I reached for one of the baggies, the one with the spent bullet, but he grabbed my wrist, squeezed it tight. He had a helluva grip. "Don't touch," he said. "Souvenirs from my last 'not guilty.'"

"Sorry."

"We should be getting some new ones too. Last night a kid got beat up real bad in the parking lot during a drug deal or something. Cop trying to break it up got shot. Don't know if either of them is going to make it. Details about the whole thing are still pretty sketchy."

"They got the people who did it?"

"They arrested a kid named Villalobos." His voice changed when he pronounced those syllables. He had the lilt of old Spain for that moment. Then abruptly, his syllables returned to deep in the heart of Texas. "All this ol' boy did was kick the guy, so they're charging him with ag bat. No big deal. Just a probation violation."

"What do you mean?"

"So long as nobody dies and they don't try to transfer him, all he's looking at is two years in the boys' school up in Springer. Shit, they're letting them out to reintegrate after only four months. The file's already on your desk."

"I'm getting the case?" Suddenly municipal redevelopment bonds didn't sound so bad.

"I don't do juvie cases," he said with disdain. "That's why they hired you. You gotta meet with the kid in the jail before lunch. His detention hearing is tomorrow."

"Isn't that kind of—"

"Don't worry. Detention hearings aren't shit. That's just whether he stays in jail. Trust me on this one: They'll keep him."

"Why's that?"

"He's a nasty little cholo. They were going to detain him anyway. You can do your first hearing without any pressure. It's before a special master, not even a judge."

"Do I have to call witnesses?"

"You don't get it. It's not even a real trial; it's just a hearing. Don't even worry about it. You'll lose. Normally, I'd have waived it already, but it sounds like you need the experience."

That was certainly true. "When do we go over to talk to him?"

"What's this 'we' shit? I got to wait here. Villalobos is all yours."

"I have to meet with this guy alone?"

"Yeah. I need to stay by the phone. In case the chotas arrest someone else today, and try to violate the constitution before lunchtime."

"What about the kid?" I asked. "My little aggravated batterer. What's he like?"

"Oh, you'll just love him. The next time he's arrested, he'll qualify for a frequent-flyer discount. But you gotta go meet with him before they lockdown for lunch." Pete Baca smiled. "Hurry back and we'll go to lunch. Your office is back over there."

He turned back to the game. I walked into the ten by ten box that was to be my office and dumped my things. There was a desk, a chair, a bookcase. Period. Instead of K Street, Sierra Milagro loomed at the other end of Junkyard.

"You gotta get over there!" Baca said from the other room.

I grabbed the lone manila file on my desk and headed back out the door. "Where's the jail?"

"Right across the street. Big ugly depressing building that looks like a jail. Can't miss it."

I looked down at the file. "Villalobo, right?"

"Close enough, Via-lobos. By the way, we have a rule around here: Once you get a client, he's yours for life."

"What's that mean?"

"Your life or his."

Chapter 4

Loves at First Sight

I WALKED OUT INTO BRIGHT sunshine and pulled my lapels close against the gusty wind. The Aguilar County Detention Center was behind the courthouse. A woman stood by the door holding a sign that read, "Jimmy, I Love You." Her flaming red hair matched the lettering on a very tight black T-shirt that said "Snakeskin Cowboy."

I avoided eye contact and hustled through the metal-grated door and into the cramped reception area. The receptionist, a young, well-dressed woman with short brown hair, had a picture ID badge reading "Veronica Arias." She had two textbooks on her desk. She reminded me of the receptionist back at my parents' firm who simultaneously worked, modeled, and studied for her masters in public policy at George Washington University. I wondered why the jail would need someone of her caliber. No one was going to leave if they didn't like the service.

"Hi. I'm Dan Shepherd, PD office. This is my first time here. What do I do?"

"You have to go through the steel gates into the visiting area."

"How do I do that?"

"To get past the first door, you say 'one on one.' To get past the second one, say 'two on one.'"

"Why do I say that?"

"I could give you a complicated explanation about the circuitry if you want," she said with a warm smile. She pointed to a well worn electrical engineering textbook.

"If you don't mind my saying so, Veronica, you don't seem the type I'd expect to find working at a jail. Aren't you scared?"

"No. Everybody inside knows me. Who are you here to see?"

"Some kid named, uh . . . Villalobos," I said, glancing at the file.

She smiled as if she was about to say something and then thought better of it. "You'll like him. He's a friend of mine."

A video camera scanned me as I pressed the button and said "one on one," then "two on one." Both doors magically clanged open and I walked down a short concrete corridor. Video cameras and uniformed guards stared at my crisp gray suit and red tie.

The smell hit me as soon as I got to the waiting area. Even frat house kitchens hadn't prepared me for bologna sandwiches, cheddar cheese, urine mixed with disinfectant from the mop in the corner, stale cigarette smoke, and something else I couldn't quite identify. Semen?

A large uniformed man with a white cowboy hat sat drinking a cup of coffee by himself near a small knot of officers. He stared at me.

"I'm here to see Villalobos," I told one of the younger guards. His badge read "Gardea." He was about my age, but was balder and heavier. Definitely a home-town guy.

Gardea looked up at a white board listing the names of the inmates in different colors.

"He's not up there. You sure he's here?"

I didn't know what to say. Of course I wasn't sure.

The man drinking coffee put down his cup, came over to the board. "You the new baby lawyer over at the public defender's office?"

I nodded. "Dan Shepard."

"I'm Delbert Clint. I'm the deputy sheriff in charge of the Aguilar County Detention Center." He sounded exactly like I'd expect the deputy sheriff with a big white hat in charge of a county detention center to sound. He shook my hand and squeezed it so tight it hurt. "Mr. Shepard, your client is in the juvenile wing—they're in a whole other part of the building."

He pointed to a separate list on another board that had a handful of names written in blue ink.

"Mr. Gardea," Clint said, "will you go over to the juvenile wing and fetch Mr. Shepard's new friend for him? I think he's in the kitchen right now. I'll stay here and brief Mr. Shepard on proper procedures."

Gardea rushed away. It was obvious who the boss was around here.

"We got rules in this jail, son," Clint said, "and when you come here, I expect you to follow them. We let you meet with them in that interview room over there." He pointed to an empty room with cinderblock walls. "We don't have to be so understanding," he said, "but we pride ourselves on the personal touch. If you screw up, I'll make you meet with your clients over the telephone, behind the glass up in the front. . . ."

That didn't sound so bad.

". . . in the same room as all their scummy little families and friends. Trust me, son. It's hard to play lawyer when you're in the same room as one of these fella's gals who hasn't been laid in six months."

He motioned me over to a black log book. I signed in my name, address, then paused at "reason for coming."

"What do I put there?" I asked.

"I don't know why the hell you're here, son. Leave it blank if you don't know."

Gardea came down with a teenager wearing a blue jumpsuit that said Aguilar County Detention Center on the back. My first client was short but muscular. Every inch of exposed skin was tattooed, the Virgin Mary in fiery chains on his right arm. A red devil with a pitchfork appeared to cut through the other. A spider web, complete with black widow, crawled up the left side of his neck.

Gardea pointed me out to his charge and I'm sure I heard Villalobos snarl. Was this a jail or an old decaying zoo, the kid in the blue jump suit one of the dangerous exhibits? If the guards were the zoo keepers, a lawyer would be some sort of trusted vet here to treat the wounded. I felt more like a little kid who'd stumbled into a lion's cage after dropping a lollipop.

And yet there was something about the prisoner's walk that belied that image. He kept his head up, his eyes straight ahead. He didn't have the bobbing gait I expected from watching old prison movies. He walked toward me like a law student on his way to an interview.

Clint made him initial the line on the black book, then ushered us into the cinderblock interview room and shut the door. I looked around, half expecting to see a surveillance camera, but the room was empty except for a hard metal table and two light metal chairs. The walls were pretty thick. If he wanted to, Jesus Villalobos could bring the chair down on my head before anyone outside could stop him. Gardea and Clint certainly wouldn't hurry in to rescue me.

He didn't shake my hand. I noticed the two teardrops tattooed in black beneath his left eye. Didn't that mean he'd killed someone or something? Upon closer look, one hadn't been filled in yet.

When I finally looked at him, I realized where I got the law student image. This hard-core recidivist wore horned-rimmed glasses identical to mine.

"You my new lawyer, right?"

He had a Spanish accent but there wasn't an ounce of lilt to it. His voice stayed as close to the ground as he did. But then again, my rapid-fire Ivy League by way of Maryland vernacular probably sounded like shit to him. I nodded.

"You look pretty young. You ever handled a case before?"

Should I tell him I had been in court once with my mother, that I actually got to sit behind the counsel table and take notes for her on an anti-trust case? Not what he wanted to hear.

He muttered a few words in Spanish. I was glad I couldn't understand. I waited.

"Ese, anyone ever tell you that you look like Clark Kent?" he said. "You know, the guy in the Superman comics?"

I smiled. "Yeah, but when I take my glasses off, I still look like Clark Kent."

He nodded. "I hate wearing fucking glasses."

Pleasantries over, I opened the file and read the one-paragraph police report to him. "Officer John Diamond positively identified Jee-zus Villalobos as being present at a fight occurring in the Aguilar High School parking lot. Officer Diamond has personal knowledge that Mr. Villalobos is on probation, and one of the conditions of his probation is that he remain under house arrest. Officer Diamond witnessed Jee-zus Villalobos kick Victor Slade in the head before the officer was shot by an unidentified figure. Jee-zus Villalobos was arrested at the residence of his girlfriend, Anna Maria Arias, approximately four hours later."

He grabbed the folder and flung it against the wall. "Hey, pendejo, how the fuck can you expect to be my lawyer if you can't even pronounce my fucking name?" He then banged on the door and had Gardea take him back into the depths of the jail.

I tried to open the doors to the outside before I remembered that I had to say the magic words, "one on one," then "two on one." As I dashed out into the sunlight I heard Veronica, the receptionist, call from behind me. "You're lucky Clint wasn't there. He'd totally kill you."

I turned around. "Why?"

"You left the jail door open on the way out."

Safe in the office, Pete Baca had his fists clenched in triumph over Chessmaster 3000. "Have fun with your new buddy?" he asked.

"It was okay." I looked down at my shoes. "I'm pretty hungry. Let's go eat."

"Mexican all right with you?"

"Sure. I might as well get used to it."

We walked down an alley slowly—Pete had a slight limp—to a small restaurant called Rosalita's. It was painted white and lime green with a red-tiled roof missing half the tiles. Three men wearing black hats, overcoats, and boots with spurs emerged and practically ran over us. They piled into a shiny new Range Rover parked halfway up on the sidewalk.

"They think they own the fucking town," said Pete.

"Who was that?"

"The 'Snakeskin Cowboys.'"

Inside, except for the gold and red Zia sun sign of the New Mexico state flag, the walls of Rosalita's were bare. No cow skulls, no howling pink coyote with turquoise bandannas. So much for my vision of Santa Fe style. A poster of three desperadoes staring into the sunset was Scotch-taped to the cigarette machine. Cattle-brand letters spelled out "The Last of the Snakeskin Cowboys."

One Hollywood-type chatted up the young waitress in a low cut dress, mumbling something about "next time you're in L.A. . . ." She rolled her eyes, politely excused herself and quickly gave us menus. She was about eighteen, dark and pretty enough to be a Snakeskin Cowgirl herself with her luminous brown eyes—but up close she still was the epitome of a "before" picture in those makeovers in the women's magazines. Her hair was too small-town fluffy, her make-up piled on a touch too thick for the big time. Her name badge read "Hello, my name is Anna Maria."

"Any news?" Anna Maria asked, forcing a shy smile as she led us to a table.

"Not yet," Pete said. "Victor's still up at St. Joseph's Hospital in Albuquerque, far as I know."

She nodded as if she was fighting off tears, then walked away. Moments later, her eyes dry, she returned with bowls of chips and salsa.

"Green chile or red?" she asked.

I said nothing, until Pete interrupted "Green, of course. But don't make it too hot for the gringo."

She looked at me and then at Pete, who winked.

"Even our green is pretty hot today," she said. A real smile this time. Maybe she could be a star after all.

"You can stay at my house until you find a place," Pete said to me after our second bowl of chips. "I call it the Rancho Encantado. An old girlfriend just got back into town. I'll just stay with her."

"You don't have to give up your house on my account."

He grinned. "Things can get pretty . . . loud."

Not wanting to press for details, I changed the subject. "You have your own uh . . . rancho?"

"It's my family's. I'm just taking care of it for awhile. I had some small chickens and rabbits but they sort of got all mutilated and shit. Teenage pranks. At least around here that's a prank. So keep an eye on things."

Living in a town where teenagers mutilate chickens for fun made me feel a little queasy. "Is it hard to find an apartment here?" I asked.

"You can probably stay at the Acequia Vista for a couple hundred a month. It's really the only apartment complex in town, other than the housing projects by the high school."

"Pretty nice place?"

"No, so enjoy the rancho while you can."

I delved into the chips, seriously hungry after my trip across the Llano. The first glob of salsa was so hot I had to wash it down with iced tea, but it was delicious. The waitress smiled each time she refilled my glass.

Concentrating on the shy waitress between the chips, I missed the beginning of Pete's story about one Guillermo Juarez, who had been caught robbing a bank a few years back.

"When you're suspected of half the illegal shit that goes on and your face is hanging in every bank and post office, it's not a good idea to rob the bank in your home town," he explained. "At least you should have the bandanna on all the way when you go into the bank, no? and don't be wearing a short-sleeved shirt so you could see your fucking name tattooed on your forearm."

I laughed.

Pete smiled for the first time. I knew that smile. I'd used it myself when I did stand-up and a crowd of drunk undergrads finally laughed at one of my jokes.

"When they caught him," Pete went on. "Guillermo tells the arresting officer, 'You can't pin the bank robbery on me. I was with Rito all day.' So Thompson goes up to Rito and asks him what they were doing that day. Rito says, 'Oh, me and Guillermo was robbing the bank.'"

"God, what a putz."

"Putz?"

Wrong word choice. "What an idiot."

He grinned. "Ol'Guillermo may be your client's only hope."

"You think that guy's involved with Jee-zus and the fight?"

"It's pronounced 'Hay-Zeus.' And, yeah, it was some kind of drug deal. If it involves drugs in Aguilar, Guillermo's usually right in the middle of it."

"So my guy has a chance?"

"Hard to say. I don't think the cops have figured out what the fuck is going on, much less what they want to do about it."

"Then why'd they arrest him so fast?"

"You'll have to ask them about that."

Our main course arrived. Pete dived into a bowl of a soup called menudo. The bowl was big enough to have an undertow. I looked away when something that looked like a tiny eel slithered around in his mouth. I was glad he'd ordered a green chile chicken enchilada for me.

My first bite was even spicier than the salsa. I kept the iced tea coming. My eyes watered and I thought my tongue would melt. I gritted my teeth and kept chowing.

"I'll tell you about Guillermo," Pete said, his mouth half full. "I've represented him a coupla times. Shit, when he was in the pen, he wanted me to handle his divorce. I told him I don't do civil law, but if he killed the bitch, I'd get him off."

He launched into a long description of his brilliant legal maneuvers on behalf of Guillermo. I watched Anna Maria gracefully refill my iced tea, smiling at me as if. . . .

"Anna Maria's not bad, no?" Pete said as she walked back to the counter, "though she's a little too skinny for me. Shit, man, I've had *Playboy* playmates, beauty queens, actresses—some you might of even heard of. But screw that. I'm out of that whole scene now that I'm here, especially with Dora coming back soon. This is the world's easiest town to get laid in."

If a man with a clip-on tie could win in the courtroom and in the bedroom, Aguilar couldn't be all that bad. He chewed a few more eels, smiled. "How was the action back East?"

I shook my head. "I've got standards, like the NCAA. I won't date someone who has less than a two-point-oh high school average and a least a twelve on the ACT."

"Fuck that," Pete said. "I'd never get laid."

Which made me remember why I'd quit the comedy circuit. My best jokes always went over their heads.

Pete motioned toward Anna Maria, who eyed me with those sad brown eyes. She pulled up a chair next to me.

"Can I talk to you?" she asked politely. "You're representing Jesus Villalobos?"

"I guess."

"Next time you leave the door open, make sure Jesus is standing nearby, okay?" She gave me that dazzling smile. "He's my boyfriend."

Pete left, took care of the check up front. Alone with Anna Maria, there was an urgency in her brown eyes. She wanted something. . . .

"Is there something you want me to tell him?" I asked.

Her boss, Rosalita, called her name from the kitchen, and Anna Maria had to get a big order-up of enchiladas. "Just tell him I love him."

Pete took a phone call when we got back—I couldn't tell whether he was talking to a client or a girlfriend, perhaps a little of both. I headed back to ACDC to try again with Jesus. For some reason, Anna Maria's request was hard to resist.

The woman with the red hair was still outside with the sign for Jimmy. She had been joined by another woman whose sign was for Sammy. After greeting Veronica and saying the password to get past the metal doors, I asked Officer Gardea to bring Jesus over from the juvenile wing, grateful that Clint was nowhere to be seen.

I signed the book and sat down in the interview room. After a few minutes Gardea led Jesus in. In their casual banter as they walked, Gardea sounded more like a friend to Jesus than a guard. He kept the door open for a moment, as if waiting to see what his friend Jesus wanted to do with me. . . .

"Sorry about this morning, Jesus," I said, emphasizing the "zeus."

Jesus grunted and sat down.

"Look, I apologized, okay?"

"Because of you, he's not going be allowed any visitors other than on legal business," Gardea said. "I'm sure he appreciates that. The only reason he agreed to see you is he's got pots and pans this week in the kitchen. It's you or the grease trap."

I sighed. Jesus nodded at him. Gardea nodded back, shut the door.

"I saw your girlfriend at lunch," I said.

He was a statue. Those tattooed tears looked chiseled in.

"Well, don't you want to know what she said?"

"Yeah."

"She loves you."

"Tell her I love her, too." He stared at me intently with that tattooed eye. "She say anything else?"

"No, just that."

As he relaxed his glare, I took out his file, which was thick, listing all of his encounters with the juvenile justice system. "We've got to get ready for your detention hearing tomorrow." I tensed my muscles and looked him in the eye. "I'll do whatever I can for you, but you got to help me out here."

He shrugged.

"How did you first get into trouble?"

Nothing.

"It's me or the grease trap."

He thought for a long minute. "Wait," he said. "You mean you want to know the first time I got in trouble or the first time I got thrown in this place?"

"This place."

"I was only thirteen, and these dudes with knives mad-dogged me, and—"

"Mad-dogged you?"

"Gave me a dirty look like they was gonna kill me."

"So what did you do?"

"Well, one of them dudes came at me so I pulled out my knife and cut his arm. But then the fucking knife broke. But anyway, some chotas came and broke it up."

"Chotas?"

He shook his head at my ignorance. "The cops."

"What happened? What was your sentence?"

"Consent Decree, then probation. Nada."

"It says here you violated probation."

"I talked back to a teacher. You fuckin' believe it?"

"What?"

"When you're on probation, one of the things you gotta do is obey your teachers and shit. This old guy, Mr. Lowe, made fun of my accent, so I got pissed off."

I could see where Jesus was coming from. Back in law school I'd locked horns with the esteemed Contracts Professor, Mr. Lipschitz.

"So what did you say?"

"I told him I didn't think my accent was funny."

"That's it?"

"Well, maybe I said, 'My accent isn't that funny, motherfucker.'"

When I'd said, 'Professor Lipschitz, I agree with Judge Cardozo's opinion in this case. He has a law school named after him and I don't recall there being a Lipschitz Law School,' I'd lost three extra credit points. For essentially the same crime, Jesus spent forty-five days at the Youth Development Diagnostic Center.

"How'd you do at YDDC?"

"It was weird, but I did okay. Even got high honors in English, but I kinda fucked up in math. I always seemed to, like, reverse numbers and shit. They said I was dyslixes-dyslexic-something like that. That's when I had to get these goddamn glasses."

"They look all right. Kind of artistic."

"Hey, really? 'Cause I'm best at drawing. If I didn't keep getting into shit, I'd probably be an artist. Here, watch." He took a piece of paper from my pad and in a few seconds produced a reasonable sketch of my lunch-time waitress. "That's like totally from memory. You should see it when Anna Maria poses and I have more time."

I nodded. He was good. "So what happened after that?"

"The diagnostic report said I should be in a drug treatment program, so the probation office tried to get me into an RTC."

"Which is?"

He muttered something in Spanish. "I think I know more about the system than you do, bro. It's a residential treatment center. You get treatment and counseling."

"Did you ever get in?"

"Not even. None of that shit would ever work out. I sent out like twenty applications to every program in the state; filled out the forms myself. Some programs were booked up. A few programs said I was too violent. One said I wasn't violent enough."

Most of my friends with abuse problems were working for big law firms. As for me, all of my fuck-ups had been accomplished without the help of substances. I didn't have an excuse.

"Did you get ever into a program?" I asked him.

"I was supposed to get into one, but I was like on standby."

"Wait-listed?"

"I guess that's what they called it."

I'd been waitlisted at Georgetown, Northwestern and Duke for law school. My mom used to tell me that I acted like I was still waiting for something. Maybe I was.

"The report say anything else?"

"Yeah, it said I had to go to the dentist." He pointed to a line on one of the reports: "Dental care as per medical report."

His teeth were indeed crooked and yellowed.

"They're not going to violate me for not going to the dentist, are they?"

I had to laugh. "Right now I'd say bad teeth are the least of your worries."

We both chuckled. Good, I was getting through to him. "So what finally happened?" I asked him.

He shrugged. "Well, this happened."

I turned to the file with the latest charges, the probation violation, the time he kicked, or I guess I should say allegedly kicked, this Victor Slade fellow. A lot of witnesses at a party had seen him follow several others into a parking lot for an alleged drug buy, then kick this Victor guy in the head for no apparent reason.

"This could be a tough case." I looked up from the file. "I guess we should probably plead and see what we can get. Pete said the worst you can expect is two years in the boys' school in Springer, which really amounts to only four months or so."

He put his head in his hands.

"Four months wouldn't be so bad, would it?" I asked.

"You ever do four months? Four months is like forever."

"If Pete thinks that's the best we can expect from the district attorney's office, I'd listen to him."

"You sure you're a lawyer?"

That hurt. I vaguely remembered Pete saying that once you defended a client, he was yours for life, so I might as well make the best of it. "Anyone else you want me to talk to?" I asked. "What really happened out there?"

"You really don't know shit about the law, do you? Rule Fucking One of the law is: never ask your client what happened."

I gulped. "Okay, we'll see . . . "

"Now get me out of jail at the detention hearing tomorrow. There's a lot of things I got to take care of."

"Pete said detention hearings are impossible to—"

"Shit, man, just do it."

That night I stayed in the small adobe ranch house Pete had wistfully named Rancho Encantado, while he went off with the allegedly noisy girlfriend. The "rancho" was five acres of grassland whose small herd of livestock consisted of two cats. I scanned the yard for any evidence of predators, teenage or otherwise, but found only a few patches of slightly blackened ground.

Pete's old football and rodeo trophies occupied a shelf in the living room. On his bulletin board were autographed pictures of a few actresses, some of whom I had indeed heard of. They were sentiments like: "Thanks for everything, Love you" scribbled across them in, what to me looked like a suspiciously masculine script.

The walk-in cooler was well stocked, especially with plastic-wrapped packages of something that looked like a newly dead buffalo.

During my meager dinner of mystery meat, I switched on the local news. After twenty minutes of Albuquerque stories, theme music vaguely reminiscent of the Lone Ranger followed a montage of cowboys, oil rigs, and police cars, under the heading "Channel 14 Aguilar's Local News."

As I got up to throw away the remains of my dinner, a female voice give a play by play just a touch too much emphasis on the verbs.

". . . in the parking lot of Aguilar High School as several unidentified individuals nearly ended a young man's life. Police have finally released some details. The suspects were identified as a middle-aged Hispanic man, a teenager with long blond hair, and another teenager with long black hair."

So my little probation violation made the big time. The screen showed three artist's sketches of an old man and two teenagers who could have been anyone.

"The teenage suspect with long blond hair allegedly threw Victor Slade down against the pavement, then the dark-haired suspect allegedly kicked him in the head, apparently causing his injuries."

Cut to a high school yearbook picture of Victor Slade in white football jersey (number 42), a good looking kid with the sort of bland forgettable features you find in airbrushed yearbook photos they use in the ads for the yearbook companies.

"Victor Slade was a young man who had turned his life around from deprivation and squalor," the voice said. "He was a straight A student at Aguilar High School and a wide receiver for the Golden Eagles football team. He was recently awarded an athletic scholarship to Eastern New Mexico University in Portales. And now he's fighting for his life in St. Joseph Hospital up in Albuquerque."

Wide shot of people milling in front of Victor's home, a small adobe house with a gravel front yard.

"Many of Victor's neighbors speculated that Victor was just a good boy who was in the wrong place at the wrong time. One person, a juvenile whose name has not been released yet, is already in custody on the charge of violating his probation in connection with the crime."

Cut to a close up of an obese policeman. "Officer John Diamond, who tried to break up the altercation, was shot as he approached."

Cut to a pale, sunken-eyed Diamond sitting in a hospital bed. "Officer Diamond lost a lot of blood and had to be airlifted to Albuquerque. He's been in and out of consciousness." Then cut to the prosecutor, Matt Merril, who had a Robert E. Lee beard and a military manner to go with it. "We're not going to proceed until all the details are in."

Close up of Merril, flashing an evil smile, his mouth a hole in a brush pile. "Now, we can't rush these things; we don't want to trample on anybody's constitutional rights, do we?"

Merril went on from there, but I stopped paying attention when I saw the reaction shot of the female reporter interviewing him. She definitely was not a local, she looked part Asian. Even on Pete's black and white screen I sensed a kinship with her. She had straight hair down to her shoulders, so much ambition it showed, and a lot of nervousness. Her microphone hand shook a little as Merril talked on and on.

Finally she signed off. "This is Amanda Finch, live from Aguilar."

Amanda live from Aguilar. What a name. It sounded a name for a young reporter on the go, a romance heroine, or maybe an exotic dancer.

Chapter 5

Day 2

WHEN I GOT TO THE office, Pete scanned a book of mugshots with the same intensity as others looked at pornography. He wore the same western shirt, which looked as if he'd slept in it.

"We're going on a little road trip to the scene of the crime," he said.

"What about the hearing?"

"This won't take long."

We got into Pete's pickup, a red Ford he called the Baca Beamer. The bumper sticker read:

MY CLIENT MOLESTED YOUR HONOR STUDENT
AT AGUILAR MIDDLE SCHOOL

"Nice truck," I said, trying to settle in amidst dirty laundry.

"Always spend more on your truck than your house." Pete took a swig of 7-11 coffee. "You can always sleep in a truck, but you can't cruise in your house on a Saturday night."

We drove up Santa Fe Avenue to Aguilar High School and parked in the lot, which was filled with aging muscle cars and pickups much like the Baca Beamer. It was quiet, except for the wind. School had already started. The trees had shed most of their leaves, the grass was dried up.

Pete walked away from the school toward an apartment complex just north of the high school, terra cotta concrete with a turquoise stripe about waist high and red swirling graffiti on the walls. "The Coven," were the only words in English that I could make out. On another wall, a mural—an eagle landing on Sierra Milagro—signed by none other than our own Jesus Villalobos.

A few young toughs on the second floor leaned out, stared at us. An infant crumpled some yellow crime scene tape into a ball.

Pete shouted something to them in Spanish and they laughed. I played straight man. "Do we got to show them badges or something?"

"We don't need no stinking badges," he said.

Someone stage-whispered, "Who's the pendejo?" I didn't turn around.

Pete walked to the edge of the property but did not cross over. There was no yard, just a lot with weeds, broken bottles, and a leashed dog of the junkyard variety.

"This is Rito Juarez's apartment," Pete said. He looked down at all the broken glass on the ground. "Pretty loco party, no?"

I tried to picture it: a boom box blasting, people drinking cheap beer, men in T-shirts and baseball hats, women in tight tank tops. Lots of food. Guys throwing their empty bottles down on the ground as the night wore on. . . .

I certainly didn't go to parties like that at DC. As a matter of fact, I didn't go to many parties, period.

Pete limped as we retraced our steps toward the high school, crunching glass and dried prickly weeds with his deep footprints. "Guillermo, Victor, and some others leave the party and walk back to the parking lot over here." The dog barked a few times. "Your little cholo, Jesus, follows the group . . . allegedly."

We stopped at the edge of the parking lot. Grass-less knolls and a maintenance building obscured our view of the street. There were some tangles of the yellow crime scene tape caught in the dried weeds.

Pete looked around until he saw a some spots on the pavement by the curb and flattened weeds on the embankment. "This is ground zero right here," he said.

I expected a chalk outline like in the movies, but then I remembered: Victor wasn't dead, yet . . .

"Guillermo and Victor have an argument about something, probably right here," Pete continued. He stooped over, made a stupid face, and nodded up and down as though he was the burnt-out, loco, ex-con Guillermo. He then flexed his muscles liked a football player to simulate Victor the high school golden boy. "Victor would be standing here, on the pavement. Meanwhile, somebody calls the cops and they pull into the parking lot over there." He pointed to the main entrance to the parking lot some fifty yards away. "Notice how far away the entrance is."

"Then what?"

"Somebody pushes Victor against the curb. A teenager with long blond hair is all we know so far." He pantomimed throwing down a body. I looked at Pete's massive arms. He didn't get those at law school. "From the medical reports, the point of impact is the left temple."

I looked at the dried bloodstains against the curb and a dusty imprint on the ground behind it. Victor must not have bled much before the cops came. "So what does Victor do?"

"He's hurt, bleeding a little, I'd guess. Supposedly he pulls out a gun, though it was never found. This is where our 'alleged perpetrator' comes in."

I stood behind him, right where Jesus (assuming he was the perp) probably had stood, and tried to picture the group of people who were arguing, who had watched as number 42 went down hard. I tried to picture the bloodstain on the curb as a person who has just been knocked down, a person who has just pulled out a gun. An enemy. . . .

Jesus was a tough little kid who'd never taken shit from anyone, especially if armed. He would have no compunction about kicking Victor in the head, especially if they already had a history. Did they?

I walked a few steps and practiced a kick, like kicking a soccer ball. "He shoots, he scores." The body is now totally limp against the curb.

I shuddered, planted my leg back down on solid earth, glanced over at Pete. "Then what happened?"

"Cops come running from over there, shouting, all hell breaks loose. Someone shoots at Diamond and hits him pretty good. Maybe with Victor's gun, maybe not. Our hero runs like hell. Jesus ends up at his girlfriend's house and gets arrested." He pointed at the stain. "As for Victor, he don't go nowhere."

We crunched back to the Baca Beamer and drove to the courthouse. As I got in the truck, I could see that Pete's eyes kept combing the scene for clues.

"I thought you said this was no big deal," I said.

"I lied."

The detention hearing convened in the court administrator's office in the annex to the courthouse. The annex was a converted appliance store, the hearing room itself must have been a converted storage room—it had cleaning items stored against the back and the aroma of a sour mop.

The last time I'd been in any type of courtroom was my mother's oral argument in the Supreme Court of course, which I'd watched from the gallery.

I sat down next to Jesus, who was already seated, his eyes impassive. I heard a strange rattling. I looked down. He wore leg chains and clanked them softly under the table. He took off his glasses and rubbed them with some tissues.

I grabbed some tissues and cleaned mine. I noticed a new mark under his eye. The outline of another tear that hadn't been filled in. Was that for Victor, or me?

"You ready?" he asked as we both put our glasses back on.

"I guess so."

Pete, who had rushed back to the office and grabbed a brown corduroy jacket and clip-on tie, ambled into the room. He sat down next to me and nudged me in the arm. "Hey, baby. Que paso?" he whispered.

"Nothing yet."

A woman sat down behind us. "Jesus's mother," Pete whispered.

She was tiny, with delicate hands, and must have had Jesus very early in life since she looked about thirty-five, or was it fifty-five? It was hard to tell, the lines on her face were deep but her eyes still shown bright. Her hair was streaked with gray but arranged stylishly. She also had two teardrop tattoos under her eyes.

"Do you have your questions for her?" Pete whispered.

"But you said—"

"She's not a real witness. You're just supposed to ask her whether her boy is a threat to the community."

"That's it?"

"That's it."

Anna Maria came in, sat down in a metal chair by one of the brooms. Still in her waitress outfit, her eyes looked puffy from another night of crying.

"Why are you here?" I asked her. "We didn't need you to testify."

"The prosecutor called," she said. "I got a subpoena right after you left."

I looked down at the file. In all the hours of reading and writing during my three years of law school and my one year at Shepard and Shepard, I had never been involved in a hearing, much less a real trial. Oh hell, how hard could it be, especially in a broom closet? And anyway, here came the judge. . . .

"Harry Lamb," Pete whispered. "He'll learn to read next week."

He was a tall man in his sixties, dressed not in a robe but in a brown suit and yellow striped tie. He looked like a football coach, not a judge. Behind him was the bearded Merril, the prosecutor I'd seen on the telecast, his blue blazer adorned with an eagle over the inscription "Fighting 14th."

Lamb told Jesus to stop rattling and then launched into a few introductory remarks. I wish I knew exactly what "stipulated" meant. Then Merril called Officer Thompson.

"Could you tell us, officer, what happened the night of the incident regarding the accused, Jesus Villalobos?" Merril was so tall, his deep resonant voice seemed to come from the ceiling.

"My partner, Officer Diamond, and I responded to a routine call," Thompson said.

"What did you see when you arrived?"

"Well, Diamond went up ahead and I stayed behind so I really didn't see what happened. My partner told me—"

"Objection! Hearsay, Your Honor." I knew that much from my second-year Evidence class. A witness couldn't repeat somebody else's statement.

Silence, except for a soft chuckle from Pete. Then Merril said, "Your Honor, you may wish to instruct defense counsel that hearsay is permitted in detention hearings."

"Got it, son?" Lamb smiled.

I nodded.

"Officer," Lamb said, "you may continue."

"Officer Diamond said that when he came upon the scene of the incident, he saw a group of people. He positively identified one of them as Jesus Villalobos, whose reputation for violence in the community is—"

"That motherfucker's lying!" Jesus shouted, rattling his leg chains.

"Mr. Shepard," Lamb said, "if that happens again, I will hold you in contempt and you'll be sharing a cell with your client."

"Officer," Merril said, "if you'll pardon the interruption and continue about this boy . . . with his reputation for violence in the community. Will you read this sheet for us?"

Thompson read Jesus's lengthy police record in a monotone.

"Thank you, officer. Now let's return to the night in question. What happened next?"

"Officer Diamond told me that after somebody knocked Victor Slade down, he saw Jesus Villalobos kick him in the head."

"And how did he know it was Jesus Villalobos?"

"He's arrested him before. So have I."

There was something wrong with that answer. I knew I should object, but couldn't think of the right one.

"Were you able to apprehend him?" Merril asked before my brain could kick into gear.

"He outran us," the officer replied. "He was picked up a few hours later at his girlfriend's house by another officer." The officer smiled "They were in the midst of . . . relations, when he was apprehended."

Jesus couldn't help but smile. Anna Maria blushed, hid her face beneath her hands and hair.

"And where is Victor Slade right now?"

"Still in the hospital."

"And his condition?"

"They don't know if he's going to make it."

"Thank you. No further questions."

It was time to cross-examine the officer like they do on TV. Begin by trying to prove a self-defense case, or mistaken identity. I leaned back in my chair and put my hands behind my head.

"You arrived after Victor Slade provoked my client, didn't you?"

"Objection! Assumes facts not in evidence," Merril said.

"Son, don't get ahead of yourself," Lamb said. "You got to ask him a question he can answer. And goddamnit, stand up in my courtroom."

I hastily stood up, tried again. "Do you know if Victor provoked him?" I glanced to the judge, who nodded.

"I don't know about the provocation," Thompson said, "but we got there in time for the murder . . . I mean the battery."

"Officer Thompson," I said, "do you know for sure it was my client?"

He didn't miss a beat. "Yeah. I'm sure."

I didn't know what else to say. "Are you sure?"

"Yep, I'm sure."

"Are you absolutely—"

Merril rose, smiling. "Objection. Asked and answered."

Lamb looked at me. "Any other questions, Mr. Shepard?"

I shook my head. Then Pete stood up. "Your Honor, with your permission, could I ask this witness a few questions?"

Merril was on his feet again, but before he could object, Lamb nodded. "Oh, what the heck. Haven't seen ol' Pete in action for a while."

Pete got up, walked with his stiff limp over to where the officer sat, and put his hand on the man's shoulder like they were old friends. "Officer, you didn't see what was going on in the parking lot prior to this occurrence, did you?"

"I did not."

"You have no idea how Jesus Villalobos got there, do you?"

"I just know that he's supposed to—"

"Sir, I asked you a yes or no question. So could you give me a shorter and better answer."

"No."

"No, you don't wish me to explain, or no, you don't know how Jesus got there?

"I don't know how Jesus got there."

"So you don't know if he had a legitimate reason for being there at all, do you? Assuming for the moment he was actually there."

"Uh . . . no."

Pete leaned forward. "And you yourself didn't actually see him up close, did you?"

"No, but Officer Diamond said—"

"You are not Officer Diamond, are you?"

Thompson was dazed. "Uh . . . no?"

"I asked you if you saw Jesus's face with your own eyes. Did you?"

"Well . . . no."

"Do you have any idea how many short Hispanic males between the ages of sixteen and twenty-four there are in Aguilar County, officer?"

"Uh . . . no."

"Would the word 'shitload' come to mind?"

"Pete, I'll pretend I didn't hear that," said Lamb, banging his gavel

"Let me rephrase that. As to the number of short Hispanic males in Aguilar County, would the words 'quite a few' come to mind?"

"Uh . . . I guess."

"And you, personally, are not able to identify anyone else who was there that night?"

"No. By the time I got there, Officer Diamond had been shot. He knows what was going on better than me."

"And he was still suffering from gunshot wounds when he talked to you, wasn't he?"

"Yeah. But he was still, uh . . . coherent."

"I didn't ask you that. You would have no expertise as to whether he was coherent or not. You're not a doctor, are you?"

"No."

"No further questions." Pete sat down and shrugged.

Merril got up. "Your Honor, this is merely a detention hearing, a detention hearing on a probation violation. Our job is merely to determine whether this boy meets the criteria to be detained, pending an adjudicatory hearing. Once Officer Diamond recovers, I'm sure he'll be able to give us a more complete account of what happened. As for now, I'd like to call Anna Maria Arias to the stand."

Anna Maria stood up. Lamb swore her in, then indicated that she could remain at her seat. Probably just as well, her darting eyes betrayed a bad case of stage fright.

"Jesus Villalobos was at your residence when the officer arrested him, wasn't he?" Merril asked.

"Yes, he was."

"I won't even ask what he was doing when he was apprehended." Anna Maria said nothing, looked downward, and Merril continued, "But merely establish one fact . . . he wasn't supposed to be there, according to the terms of his probation, was he?"

Anna Maria started crying. "I love him."

"Love's not an issue in this courtroom," Merril said with a smirk. "I didn't ask you how you feel about him, I asked you whether he was supposed to be there. Yes or no?"

"No."

"Thank you. Nothing further."

I started to rise, but I couldn't think of any questions to ask.

Anna Maria, crossed her arms over her chest, as if all the men in the room, including myself, scanned her body with x-ray eyes. I faced Lamb. "Nothing, Your Honor."

After the State rested, I called Jesus' mother to the stand. Pete looked at my notes, then wrote down the exact words I was to use in questioning.

"What is your son's reputation in the community for being a peaceable person?"

She swelled with pride. "No one ever takes advantage of my Jesus. He don't take no crap from no one."

"So if he was involved in this argument, he probably was acting in self-defense?"

Merril stood up but sat down without objecting. "Oh, what the heck, Your Honor. Let's hear the answer."

"My boy wouldn't kick no one who didn't have it coming."

After I sat, Merril swaggered up to within inches of her face. She began to cry. He handed her a tissue, waited patiently while she wiped away her tears. Then, softly he asked, "You have no control over your son, do you, ma'am?"

"Yes, I do. He loves me."

"And I know you love him, too. So much so that it's hard to stop him from scampering around town, kicking innocent people in the head. Love and control are two different things, aren't they?"

"Your Honor!" I yelled, already in the air, figuring that this had to be somehow objectionable. "He's . . . badgering the witness!"

"Badgering?" Merril said. "Not ferreting or rabitting or even ottering, but badgering? As Your Honor well knows, there is no such objection as 'badgering' a witness in a detention hearing."

Lamb looked at me. "Son, today is just not your day. Objection overruled."

By that time Clint had his handcuffs opened and was inching toward Jesus. I sat down.

"As to the charge of aggravated battery," Lamb intoned, "I find probable cause to believe that he is delinquent and has insufficient care and supervision. I will order his continued detention."

"Your Honor?" I stood up, yellow note pad clutched in one hand. "Don't you want to hear my closing argument?"

"If you insist, son. Now, do you want Officer Clint to take your boy back to the jail before or after you give your little speech?"

Before I could respond, Clint had Jesus out of the courtroom. Pete had beaten him to the door. Jesus looked at me for a moment before he was dragged out. "You know what the fuck you're doin'?" he asked.

Senora Villalobos looked at me, crying. Shit. Now I had disappointed someone else's mother.

When I dragged my butt back to the office, Pete stood over a couple of gory photos from one of his out-of-town murder trials that sprawled along his floor.

"Two words," he said, not looking up from a photograph of a badly crushed skull. "Banana and split."

I just cost a seventeen-year-old boy his liberty and all he could say is 'banana and split'?

"We've got a tradition here," he said, putting the pictures back in a file. "After your first hearing, the State of New Mexico, meaning the petty cash drawer of the office, buys you whatever you want at Dairy Queen. Your first real day in court is usually pretty depressing."

"No shit."

"Don't worry, it's just a detention hearing," Pete said, heading for the door. "You don't have to start worrying until the actual trial."

The pickup sputtered and balked, but Pete finally brought the aging engine to enough life to get us the few blocks down Oil Avenue to the Dairy Queen. I ordered a banana split. Pete ordered two.

"It ain't the Ivy League Debating Society out here, no?" he said. "Believe me, my first was that bad, too. I won my second one, of course. It was so quick one of the jurors asked the judge if they had to go back to the jury room to deliberate."

"What happened?" I asked, cringing as that cold mouthful of ice cream sent a jolt of pain between my eyes.

"The judge said they could deliberate right there in the box if they wanted to. A juror got up and said, 'I'll be foreman. Not guilty, right?' and the whole jury all agreed, just like that." He patted my shoulder. "You'll get there some day."

"Did I do anything right?"

"You've got a good speaking voice. Plus, you've got stage presence. You're articulate and shit, which is good."

"Articulate and shit?"

"You sound smart and educated, no? But watch it. Juries don't like people who talk down to them. It takes a while, if you've never done anything like this before. Lots of pressure."

"How do you handle it?"

"I get laid and play darts," Pete said. "Sex is an amazing stress buster."

He launched into a story about all the women at the district attorney's office in El Paso and the one who felt so left out that he had to rectify the situation immediately in the copy room.

When we got back, Pete handed me two more thick manila case files, an adult named Oswald Thomas and a juvie named Joey Lilly. I turned to Thomas first. He'd already pled guilty and I would be handling his sentencing at the next docket call. I wouldn't have to do anything on that one so I selected a few books on criminal law to mentally prepare for Jesus' trial before visiting him in jail.

When I got there, Veronica stopped me. "You can't go in there, they're filming," she said, looking up from *Tess of the D'urbervilles.*

"What kind of commercial are they doing? A promo for the jail? Nine out of ten convicts agree. . . . ?'"

She smiled. "With the way they pay salaries down here, it could be 'Aguilar County Detention Center—we pass the savings onto you.'"

Gardea laughed from across the room. "Ain't that the truth."

"Actually they're shooting a scene for *Snakeskin Cowboy* in the old holding cell," she said. "Billy the Kid was in there once."

"Oh, wow. So if I had a DWI I could request the Billy the Kid suite?"

She shook her head. "You'd have to commit a bigger crime than that."

Twenty or so people hauling cameras and other high-tech equipment burst through the jail doors. Several actors in period costumes came next, trailed by their personal assistants in hightops and Banana Republic shirts. All of them ignored Veronica and myself, so I headed off to see Jesus.

He was already in the waiting area, mopping up all the debris the movie people had left. The floor was filthy. Actors must disdain cleaning up after their own messes. Gardea made me wait a few minutes until Jesus had the floor spotless, then he ushered us into the interview room.

"Sorry about this morning," I said.

"Fuck it. You can never win one of those."

"Then why'd you think you were going to get out?"

"I wanted to see if you knew what you were doing."

I handed him my highlighted copies of several recent New Mexico Supreme Court cases on provocation and diminished capacity in aggravated battery.

He pushed them away. "Pendejo, you're not going to find the answer in the library."

"So what should I do?"

"Go to Wal-Mart and buy yourself a clue. You didn't sound like you knew shit at my hearing. Seriously, you got to talk to the witnesses."

"Sure. I'll do it as soon as I leave."

"Thanks a lot."

Before I opened the door, he asked, "You see the TV news last night?"

"You guys get TV in here?"

"That's all we got. You see the new chick they got on the news? Good looking girl, no? What's her name—"

I didn't even know her but I felt a twinge of jealousy. How dare this little hood!

"She got a little bit of an attitude," he said. "I'll just stick with Anna Maria. But who knows, maybe she'll go for a fancy lawyer like you, bro. I say go for it, ese."

Now I had to prove myself to my client about my sex life, too?

"You haven't talked to anyone else about the case, have you?" he asked.

"Just Pete Baca, and he hasn't told me shit."

Jesus thought for a moment. "Then it's time for you to talk to Joey. He can hook you up with Dora."

"Who are Joey and Dora?"

"Joey's a buddy of mine. Dora's his sister."

"How do I find them?"

"Joey will find you."

Back at the office, Pete headed out to visit a witness over in the Chaves County Detention Center in Roswell.

"I'm supposed to look out for some guy called Joe or Joey," I said. "Know him?"

"He's your next client," Pete said. "You meet him Monday. A paint sniffer. Want to call him?"

I shook my head. "If he's coming in on Monday, I'll just wait. How about Dora?"

"Everybody knows Dora. She's out of town again."

"Why didn't you tell me that?"

There are things you got to learn on your own around here. Now try the prosecutors.

My mind raced back to the time my parents hovered over my shoulder as I nervously dialed my grandmother to thank her for making me a sweater. "No allowance until you reach her," my dad's voice echoed in my ear. The fact that she was deaf and didn't always answer the phone did not always mitigate his anger.

Back in the present, I misdialed, then tried again. A woman answered.

"Could I speak to a prosecutor? It's Dan Shepard."

"Are you one of the victims in one of their cases? They're both busy. Can they call you back?"

"Uh, sure. I'm not a victim as far as I know. I'm a lawyer at the Public Defenders Office."

"Oh, the guy who left the jail door open."

Pete smiled. "You gotta learn to stop taking no for an answer."

Chapter 6

Acequia Vista

October 9

AFTER TWO NIGHTS WITH THE cats at Pete's rancho, I moved into the apartment complex he'd told me about—the Acequia Vista—a sprawling stucco complex on the far west end of Oil Avenue.

The landlady, a heavy-set Anglo woman with fossilized makeup and a blond version of Marge Simpson's hair, told me this was it, the only apartment complex other than subsidized housing in Aguilar. Its vista was the *Acequia Madre*, or "mother ditch," used for irrigation. Ditch View wouldn't cut it as a name, I suppose.

I signed the lease for only six months and transferred my few possessions from my car into the apartment. By way of furniture, I had six stylish chairs my mother had bought me at Ikea. I set them up in a semi-circle, then looked around the small, otherwise empty apartment. Where was I going to find six stylish friends in this town?

When I finished unpacking, I took a run to clear my head. After a few blocks of dodging broken glass and barking dogs, I circled back and ran onto the dirt path next to the *Acequia Madre*. The *Acequia* was dry. At the grate under the roadway, the ditch was jam-packed with lifeless brown weeds.

"Tumbleweed graveyard," I muttered as I crossed onto the deserted dirt road. It was a relief after running on the crowded bike paths along city streets back home in Rockville. The view to the west was amazing. Past the miles of weeds of the llano lay the white cone of Sierra Milagro and the aptly named outline of Pyramid Peak. After a few minutes I noticed a smell I couldn't quite identify, though at first it reminded me of the jail. The smell and my curiosity drew me onward, like someone straining to get a glimpse of a traffic accident.

A dark shape lay still in the middle of the road, a dead collie with flies buzzing all over it. It had no head. Blood had trickled down to the bottom of the ditch.

It was time to turn around. Jesus, I didn't even have the huevos to deal with a dead dog. I saw the dog's tag on the ground—"Elwood. Property of George Cloud."

I ran like hell back to the turn-off where a cop car waited on the side of the road, its engine idling. The car must have watched me the entire time. That hardly made me feel safe, especially when I saw that the driver was Thompson, the cop I had cross-examined.

"There's a beheaded dog out there in the mesa." I said.

"We saw it."

"But shouldn't somebody tell the owner?"

"He's one of the movie assholes likes letting his dog run. Serves him right."

Later that night I almost called this George Cloud fellow to offer my condolences, but I couldn't really think of anything to say. At midnight, there was a knock on my door. I opened it to find no one outside. I looked down to find a plastic dog bone smeared with blood.

By Sunday it was time to go to Wal-Mart and buy myself a clue. Well, a TV and a VCR. Down Santa Fe Avenue to the south was the great concrete mass of the Cortez Center. Under a banner by the main entrance, people waited in line to sign up as movie extras. One of the posse signed autographs at the front of the line.

"It's Sky Roberts up there!" yelled a young girl at the back of the crowd. She looked about ready to faint.

Sky Roberts, aging teen idol. He was the biggest thing to hit these parts since the aliens crashed in Roswell back in 1947.

I couldn't make him out of the other side of the crowd.

Scanning the scene, I realized how far I had traveled, both geographically and culturally. There were real cowboys, men dressed in ostrich boots and brushpopper shirts, and women in tight Wranglers and black and pink shirts with fringes.

One cowboy, a man in his twenties, wore a white T-shirt that said "Shut up, bitch." He had his arms around a pretty young cowgirl, a pair of pre-school twins dressed in matching cowboy suits at her side. The cocky look on the man's face matched his dreadful shirt. What would have happened to me if I'd worn a shirt like that as I walked by the Brown University Women's Forum? Still, Mr. Shut Up Bitch, was the one with an adoring family around him. I was the one with six stylish chairs for companionship.

Behind him, the character of the line shifted, not so much according to race as to money and age. Most of the teenage boys were dressed in black heavy metal T-shirts, while most of the girls wore their hair teased half a foot above their head.

I walked past a group of well-dressed young women heading into the one nice boutique in the mall. There were yuppies here after all, but as they walked past me, I felt invisible.

I shuffled into a bookstore to scan magazines and remind myself there was an outside world. Veronica stood on her tippy-toes way back in the "literature" section, loading volume after volume into the arms of a large tough-looking guy clad in Oakland Raiders garb. He carried her books like a Sherpa porter. He gave me a dirty look.

Why do the good girls always like the bad boys? Not really wanting to find out the answer, I turned back to find last month's edition of *Entertainment Weekly*.

A muscle-bound teenager with a long black trench coat and a San Jose Sharks hat stood in the corner by the motorcycle magazines. He looked nervously around, then took one of the magazines and slid it under his coat. He looked around again. The coast was clear.

Yet then, as if his mother had told him that it was wrong to steal, he put the magazine back on the rack where it belonged. He then took a wrestling magazine out of his coat and put that one back, too. He shrugged and walked out of the store. I stayed for a few minutes and tried in vain to find something I hadn't read already back home before I left. No such luck. So much for whiling away the afternoon. To make things worse, they didn't get *Playboy* and *Penthouse* in Aguilar.

Navigating my way toward Wal-Mart through the herd of delirious girls and their boyfriends, I found a short, narrow corridor that would take me quickly to the exit so I could enter the store from outside entrance. That's when I bumped into someone. Or maybe he bumped into me. On a basketball court the ref could have called it either way. In the mall, it was simple battery. I stared up at a young Anglo boy, the one who'd returned the magazine.

"I'm sorry," I said, about to tell him I applauded his display of conscience in the bookstore but he mad-dogged, a look that was pure intimidation. His hands were jammed deep in his pockets of the trenchcoat, poised to pull out a knife or a gun or God knows what. I stepped back.

"You ever visit me in the joint," he said, "make sure you leave the door open."

God, did everyone in this town know about my gaffe? By the looks of him, I probably would be visiting him someday.

"Sorry, " I said again.

He didn't respond, held his ground. We were all alone in the corridor.

Then it dawned on me: maybe this was the new client I was supposed to meet Monday. "Are you Joey? Jesus said you were looking for me."

Wrong question. "Jesus told you that someone named Joey was looking for you?"

"Uh . . . yeah."

"Well, I ain't Joey and you sure as fuck don't want me looking for you." He came forward, stuck his face in mine. "Victor was a friend of mine."

He pushed me back slightly. The smudges on his hands had a weird smell on them—fresh collie blood? "You're so fucking dead," he said.

I looked in his icy blue eyes—he was young, but he was totally serious.

He kept up his gaze, reached into his baggy pockets—I glanced down at the glimmer of something metallic and shiny in the red light of the exit sign.

Shit! This isn't the way I wanted to go. I looked around for escape routes. There weren't any. . . .

"Dan!" Pete's voice came from out in the mall.

"You're so fucking lucky," the boy said. "I could cut your neck like a—"

"Over here," I yelled before he could finish. "The corridor!"

Pete looked around the bend. I was about to say something, but stopped. The boy was gone. Almost like he had vanished into thin air.

Pete came up to me. I kept shaking.

"You look like you'd seen a ghost."

"This kid, he was in this long trenchcoat."

"Aryan Eddie, probably."

"You see him?"

"Nah . . . he's like that. He's the fucker whose probably been mutilating shit around here."

"Why don't they catch him?" I muttered. "Can't I get him on assault? He might have had a knife—"

"I didn't see no assault." He smiled at me. "Trust me, don't even bother taking this to the cops, shit like this happens every hour on the hour in Aguilar."

Pete didn't elaborate further, turned around headed out. "And don't count on me to fight all your battles for you."

Chapter 7

Courthouse Rock

October 12

After waiting all day Monday, Columbus Day, for the cable installer to connect me with the outside world, I went to court on Tuesday for my first docket call after grabbing a quick scrambled egg and chorizo breakfast burrito at Rosalita's. My client had already pled guilty so I simply had to monitor the sentencing. Now how hard could that be?

The Aguilar County District Courthouse was a three story adobe cube with long wooden vigas sticking out at right angles. The walls under the main entrance looked a solid two feet thick worth of adobe and there were assorted cattle brands on the sides. The courtroom was on the second floor—not the Supreme Court, but hardly a broom closet. The gallery could probably hold nearly a hundred on a particularly juicy case. On the wall, pictures of judges dating back to territorial days, every one of them wearing bolo ties and cowboy hats.

Up on the bench, the sitting District Court Judge Oscar Perez also wore a bolo under his robe as he finished the civil docket call, but he looked far more animated than his predecessors. When I entered, he was in the midst of confiscating a cellphone from an out-of-town lawyer who had the audacity to let it ring during the civil docket call.

"I'm God in this room," he said with only the slightest smile as he fingered with the lawyer's phone. "And God doesn't like being disrespected in his church."

There was literally a changing of the guard as the civil docket ended and the criminal docket began. The conservatively dressed civil lawyers didn't look much different than their counterparts in D.C. They got up, clutching their cellphones and laptops for dear life. The criminal lawyers—some wearing the latest styles, others wearing cowboy boots and corduroy—moved in to take their places at the long oaken tables.

I sat next to Pete and a few other lawyers at one table. The prosecutors took the other. Next to Merril, a middle-aged woman wet her finger and delicately touched the tabbed pages of each file. She had perfect posture, gray hair severely drawn back into a bun. Both of them wore blue blazers with the inscription "Fighting 14th" on them.

"Jovanka Smith," Pete said, "the bitch from beyond. She used to be a school teacher somewhere in Europe. One of those places behind the iron curtain. Married a local boy who was stationed over there." He pointed at a picture of one of the judges, a mild mannered man who looked more like a kindly old farmer. "That was her husband before he got whacked. I always thought she done it, but they blamed it on some kids. Never got caught anyone."

I looked at Jovanka again as she jotted down detailed notes with a ballpoint pen.

"I hope you know that this will go down on your permanent record," I whispered to myself, imitating my third grade teacher.

As the civil lawyers gingerly closed the doors behind them, the nicely dressed oil executives, store owners and divorcing couples sitting in the gallery followed them out. Their seats were quickly filled by the dregs of humanity—rednecks, bikers, and gang members of a variety of races. And those were just the families. . . .

In the jury box, Clint brought in the actual criminals—tough men and women in jump suits which were invariably too big, too small or too orange.

Judge Perez went through the cases one by one. Pete would go up to the podium and mumble a few simple phrases, then Merril and Jovanka Smith would mumble something back. Jovanka sometimes pounded the table to make a point in a few select cases, and recited her notes as if by memory. Somehow the judge made enough sense of it to determine whether the defendant should be tried, sentenced, or released on his own recognizance.

It was nearly two hours before Clint brought my client, Oswald Thomas, over from the jail. By then the green chiles in my breakfast burrito wanted to announce their presence. There was a bubble in my gut about to burst.

At forty, Oswald had been around the block a few times. Pete had already pled him guilty to attempted burglary, since Oswald was found asleep under the counter at the snack bar at Discount Mart with a few open packages of glazed apple pies around him. But Oswald was wide awake when I sat next to him, shook my hand anxiously with a sweaty grip. I instinctively wiped my hand on my pant leg. He frowned, but didn't say anything for moment as I opened his file, scanned the pages.

"I work with Jesus in the kitchen," he said before I could find the proper page. "He wants to know if you seen Joey yet?"

"Not yet," I pointed to the rows of defendants. "Is Joey in here now?"

"No. He kinda wanders around a lot."

He touched me on the shoulder. I tensed immediately as I felt the dampness of his touch through the fabric. "Hey man," he said, "you got to get me up to prison today."

"Why the hurry?"

"I don't want them to find out about my bitch."

"I don't get it," I said. "What's she got to do with this?"

When he started to laugh, Clint leaned over and said, "I don't mean to, ah, interrupt here, Mr. Shepard, but when your boy here says 'bitch,' he means the habitual offender, ah, enhancement. It's the extra time they tack on for a second or third offense."

Oswald stage-whispered to the convict next to him, a biker with a large cobra tattoo on his arm. "Hey man, baby lawyer here thinks my bitch is a lady."

The other convicts overheard, laughed uproariously until Clint stopped them cold with a hard glance.

With a sharp bang of the gavel, the judge called Oswald's case. Clutching my grumbling stomach, I went up to the bench, Merril and Jovanka Smith behind me. That's when it happened. Without going into detail, the atmosphere changed, literally. No one heard, but the silence was hardly golden.

I held my breath as the judge looked down at me with disdain. Merril and Smith retreated to the bailiff's station. Thank God, Pete was out of the courtroom talking with one of his aggravated batterers.

I recalled Sun Tzu and his famous treatise on *The Art of War*, although my only exposure to it was Charlie Sheen quoting it to Michael Douglas in *Wall Street*. Charlie had said something about utilizing your opponent's force against him. Or was it to use your own force?

When I started to breathe again, the surrounding air stopped me cold. But somehow, I kept talking. No one stopped me, obviously no one wanted the hearing to last any longer than necessary. Oswald got his wish, he was sent up that day. I guess I had succeeded in spite of myself. When he shook my hand again he thanked me profusely as if I had saved his life. Perhaps I had. I made it a point not to wipe off the dampness until he was out of the courtroom.

That's when I saw her . . . Amanda Finch, famous reporter in the flesh. Her red camera light was on. The back of my head would appear at six-twenty-two tonight on television screens throughout the southeastern New Mexico viewing area. Thank God I wasn't going bald back there yet. I hoped she didn't get me wiping my client's handshake off.

She smiled at me. Fresh highlights in her hair shimmered in the skylights, as if she was trying to look more American than Asian. She'd got it alright. After the courtroom cleared, she turned off the red light and put her camera down. "Excuse me, do you need a tissue?" She called from across the room. "Don't worry, that's not going to be my lead on the news tonight."

She was a little thinner off camera and wore a conservative blue suit with some kind of patch on the blazer that did not, Thank God, say "Fighting 14th."

I actually strutted a little when I walked over to her. "Hi. My name is Dan Shepard. I'm a lawyer." I took the tissue from her, wiped my hand, then shook hands with her.

"Amanda Finch, the new girl here in hell." She pointed to a tripod. "This is my cameraman, which constitutes the rest of my office."

"Glad to meet you both."

"Could you give me a hand with my equipment?" she asked. "We can talk a little, off the record."

I turned and couldn't help smiling a cocky smile at Merril.

We went outside to the crappy News 14 van. She fiddled with the keys for a few moments, swore slightly when she used the wrong one.

"I take it this assignment is not your first choice?" I jiggled the keys and forced the back door open.

"The job in Bermuda was already taken."

"Are you a native?"

"You must be kidding. Are you?"

"No. I'm from D.C., a little north of here if you head out on Santa Fe Street. Yourself?"

"A few miles west down Oil Avenue. A small town on the llano called Los Angeles."

"How did you end up here, if you don't mind my asking?"

"I thought I was the only one who graduated from journalism school last year." She smiled. "I was wrong."

I pushed the camera all the way to the back.

Thud.

"Careful with that," she said. "If I break it, I have to pay for it."

I patted the camera, very, very gently.

"No broken bones," I said. Time to change the subject, hold onto the moment as long as I could. "Uh . . . Ms. Finch, uhh . . . Amanda, Where did you go to college?"

She got in the van, closed the door, arranged the various electronic devices as best she could.

"Cornell. The one in New York, not the one in Iowa. I'm here under an assumed name so my friends won't find out."

"I won't tell your friends, if you won't tell mine," I said. "I went to Brown Undergrad. What's the color of shit? Brown, Brown, Brown."

"That's a tough school to get into."

"Not if you get your grades up at the University of Maryland for a coupla semesters, then transfer."

"Law school?"

"American University, in Washington." I replied.

"Washington's cool. I could have gone to Georgetown for Law but got a masters in journalism instead. At Northwestern."

I didn't mention my lengthy and unfortunate stint on the Georgetown waitlist nor my time on Northwestern's. I wasn't the smartest person in the room for a change.

I changed the subject. "Anyway, Aguilar is a mecca for young professionals like ourselves."

"A mecca?"

"A place in the middle of the desert without any night life."

She laughed, a quiet gentle laugh. God, we were actually having a real conversation in the back of a messy van in the middle of nowhere.

"How long have you been here?" she asked.

"A few days now. You know, if you only had a month to live you should live it here because it seems like forever."

"Look on the bright side. You're a lawyer, I'm doing this for minimum wage."

"You live on that?"

"My parents love me," she said.

"I can see why."

Indeed I could. Wow—I come all the way to Aguilar, for God's sake, and find the perfect woman: beautiful, cynical, vulnerable, witty, charming, amazing legs. And best of all, we are probably the only two people in this town who could get the cartoons in the *New Yorker Magazine*. She had in her hand a camera that could convey pictures of me all the way to the big city or halfway around the world via satellite. It was too perfect. There had to be a boyfriend.

She put her hand on my shoulder. Her eyes met mine. Her lips whispered softly in my ear. I slowly, inexorably, involuntarily, embarrassingly grew aroused . . . She reached for the van door with her other hand.

"Now that we've gotten to know each other. . . ." Her voice was low and breathy. ". . . could you tell me a little about this Pete Baca fellow? Doesn't he run things around here—"

That night, home and very much alone, I couldn't stop thinking about her. I was so deep in thought that I didn't turn on the TV until six-twenty-seven. Too late . . . The station now showed the high school sports up in Albuquerque.

I took stock of my life here: a television, bare walls, and those six damn chairs. I turned the lights out and turned on the TV. In the shallow darkness I could at least pretend that I was in one of the many familiar but anonymous dorms and apartments I'd lived in during college.

I took a whiff of my dirty clothes. Big time television reporters like guys with clean underwear, right? It was laundry time. . . .

About halfway through the rinse cycle, an Anglo kid stumbled in and almost tripped over the bench. He had long puffy blond hair, a cap with a marijuana leaf on it and a black T-shirt that said METALLICA-AND JUSTICE FOR ALL.

Hmmm . . . long blond hair . . . just like one of the suspects. I couldn't help but imagine my left temple getting rammed against the sharp metal corners of the dryer. I was smarter than Victor. Would I bleed more?

Young Mr. Rocker Trash steadied himself against a vending machine, then stared at me with those glazed eyes as if he really wanted to say something but was scared, even petrified. Even more scared of me than I was of him. Something wasn't right.

"What's up?" I asked.

He looked up at me. "Not much, man. What's up with you?"

"I just moved in."

"Yeah, I know. Just a few apartments down from us." He began to laugh, one of those stoned laughs where something mundane was extremely amusing. Maybe it was the washer on rinse cycle.

I dumped my wet underwear into the dryer. "I'm Dan Shepard."

That must have been good news because he smiled. "I'm Joey Lilly. You need any, uh, fabric softener?"

"Sure. Are you *the* Joey Lilly?"

"I guess so."

The Joey Lilly lived in the same building as me? So much for midnight meetings in the barrio. The barrio was right here. "Dora's your sister, right?"

"Yeah."

"Good. I'm supposed to talk to both of you."

"She's, uh, out of town until Halloween."

He had lost his train of thought again, his attention caught by the fabric softener sheets orbiting in the machine. This was going to be harder than I thought.

"Can you tell me about Jesus?"

He started to say something, then stopped when he heard footsteps outside. His back stiffened up and his hands began to shake. "I'm supposed to meet with you tomorrow, anyway," he said. "Let me talk to you then. I gotta get out of here, like right now!"

Chapter 8

The Devil You Know

October 18

JOEY ARRIVED AN HOUR LATE the next morning. No surprise there. Today's T-shirt was Guns 'n Roses. His hair was down, with his unshaved face there was something biblical about him, as if one of the apostles dealt a little reefer on the side.

"Cool band," I said as he sat down. "'Welcome to the Jungle' was one of my favorite songs growing up."

He gave me a sheepish look. "Dude, I'm not even into that classic rock shit from the sixties any more. It's just a T-shirt, I think I swiped it from the 99-cent store."

Fresh out of school, I was already over the hill, the icons of youth in the bargain bin. Joey was just as nervous as he'd been in the laundromat last night.

"If I talk to you now, it's like a secret, no?" he said.

Anglo or Latino, apparently living in Aguilar had an adverse effect on everyone's grammar. Must be something in the water, no?

"Sure. Anything you say to me, no matter what it is, is attorney-client privileged. Don't worry about it."

He nodded but looked as if he had forgotten what he wanted to tell me.

"I need to know something about Jesus," I said finally.

"Like what?"

"Did he and Victor know each other?"

"Yeah. They were like related for a while. They lived together."

"Related?"

"His mom was married to Victor's dad or something like that."

Everyone in a small town is related, I should know that. "So they were pretty close?"

He laughed. "They like hated each other. Always fighting and shit. Victor used to go out with Anna Maria. And Jesus used to say he was going to like 'totally fucking kill' him someday."

There went my "oops-it-was-an-accident" defense. For my first case, my client has to mouth off to everybody in town he's going to "totally fucking kill" the victim.

"I thought Jesus wanted you to come talk to me," I said. "What is this you're telling me?"

"Maybe he didn't all know what I was going to tell you."

I sighed. "So what happened that night?"

"Like I told the cops, I wasn't there. Neither was Jesus. I could be like your alibi or something."

Yeah right, I said to myself. With friends like these. . . .

"I'll think about it." I said.

He looked a little disappointed that I didn't jump on his offer. I was about to ask him if he wasn't there, how did he know that Jesus wasn't either? But I didn't see the point. Joey seemed almost too eager to help and that made me nervous. But I had to ask something. . . .

"If you weren't there, why did they question you?"

"I'm one of the, uh, usual suspects." He laughed. "Old Aguilar joke. They like to pop me every time something big goes down. But all they ever pinned on me was some petty shit."

"Why go after petty shit when—" I stopped, not sure if I was asking why he always got busted or why he was always getting off.

He shook his long blond hair, opened his arms to display various demonic tattoos. "Just look at me," he said, as if answering both questions. "Talk to Dora. She can 'splain it better."

"And Jesus?"

"He's one of the usual suspects, too."

He began to laugh at some private joke. I looked at his eyes. Was he still high or was he just stupid? It was useless to ask him any more questions about the crime. As much as guys like Joey resented being one of the "usuals," there usually was a good reason.

"They don't got me on any serious shit yet, do they?" he asked. "I get all confused about what they're chargin' me with. I mean, all the shit runs together after a while."

I glanced down at his file. "Just inhalants. They're not charging you with anything else right now, far as I know. It says here you were sniffing paint while doing a community service project."

"Talk about petty shit. That can't be against the law, is it?"

I wasn't one hundred percent sure, so I grabbed Volume 6 of the bulky orange *New Mexico Statute Annotated* and looked up the statute cited in the police report. I read him NMSA 30-29-2A (1978): "No person shall intentionally smell, sniff, or inhale fumes or vapors from a glue or aerosol spray product for the purpose of causing a condition or inducing symptoms of intoxication, elation, euphoria, dizziness, excitement, irrational behavior, exhilaration, stupefaction or dulling of the senses, or for the purpose of in any manner changing distorting or disturbing the audio, visual or mental processes."

He laughed. "Cool. . . ."

"I don't get it. How do you sniff paint?"

"You, like, spray it into a paper bag and then you put your whole face in the bag and inhale. It's a pretty good buzz or euphor-whatever you just said. But I quit."

"So, what do you want to do with the case?"

"Whatever you recommend dude." he said. "I trust you."

Somebody had finally given me a vote of confidence. "So what are you on probation for, uhh, dude?"

"Last time it was glue. I've had some shoplifting and shit. Like I said, they've never really had shit on me."

"So what happened this time?"

"Probation and parole kinda messed up." He laughed again. "They wanted me to paint over the graffiti at the senior center—with spray paint! I lasted about ten minutes on the job before huffing away and they busted me. Pretty funny, huh? But like I said, I quit, for reals this time."

I looked at him. He maintained eye contact for at least a few seconds this time, maybe he did want to quit for reals.

"So, neighbor, you got a chick?" he asked after a moment.

I shrugged.

"Dude, you should meet my sister when she gets back in town. She's twenty-one. You know, old like you. She'll be back for the Halloween party."

"I'll think about it," I said. "Stay in touch."

He turned to go, then stopped. "Thanks for listening, bro."

"Well . . . hey, glad to help."

"Yeah, and now that my sister's not living at home any more, there's no one. . . ."

"You ever need to talk about anything, just drop by . . . to the office."

"Cool," he said. "I'm there, dude. We can hang out. . . ."

I sniffed his breath, looked into his eyes one last time. No, he wasn't stoned, this was the way he really was. He shook my hand warmly as he left as if he now had made a new "bestest" friend in the whole world to hang out with. I smiled.

My smile quickly faded as Pete rushed into my office once Joey closed the door behind him. "Come with me to the hospital, and bring your shit with you."

Along the way, Pete mentioned something about "getting a girl knocked up," but I couldn't tell if he was joking or not. We waited in the hallway of the dingy brick building on Oil Avenue. The hospital was the regional center so it was a little bigger than I expected. More modern too, only felt ten years out of date. I recognized several faces from court that morning, anxiously awaiting news of loved ones. Pete joked with a few of the other people in the hallway about how if he'd "only had the three quarters for the vending machine," he wouldn't be in this predicament . . .

Yet his eyes were not on the maternity ward, but down the hallway toward another door. Finally, some orderlies wheeled out a body, face covered. I could hear the sound of a woman's crying in a distant room.

An orderly nodded at Pete. "Victor," he said, softly.

"Thanks for the call," Pete replied, looked over at me. "The guy your little Jesus kicked is now a stiff."

I shivered in my chair as a sharp burst of cold passed through me. The orderly wheeled the body away. What the hell was I supposed to do anyway? As the door closed behind the gurney, I pictured Victor in his white football uniform, good ol' number 42, the broken glass in the parking lot, the bloodstain on the curb. Hasta la vista and all that.

I looked over at Pete, who measured my reaction. That's what this was all about. I had to tough this one out. "What does it mean?" I asked after a moment, trying to hold my composure.

Before he could answer, Jovanka emerged from the room. She still looked sharp in her Fighting 14th blazer, but her make-up smudged slightly as if from tears. She hugged a blond haired woman in a black polyester outfit one more time, than walked over to me, handed me some papers.

"Sign these." Her accent was vaguely Eastern European, Not German, not Russian, but something from that neck of the woods. She directed me to the last page of several. I signed something that read "receipt of service."

Without another word, she walked out with the blond woman. "I know what you must be feeling right now," she said to her on the way out.

I looked down at the first page. It was an amendment to the original petition. Jesus now faced an open count of murder. She must have filled out the papers before coming to the hospital, the date of death had been blank. A blue pen now scribbled in today's date.

I felt numb as I turned to Pete.

I opened the Villalobos files, mushed the new papers inside and handed the whole thing to him.

He made no effort to take the file from me—everything fell on the floor, the new papers spilled everywhere . . .

"Aren't you going to—"

"You better talk to him before the initial appearance on the new charges."

"I'm doing a murder case?"

"Remember what I told you—he's your client for life—yours or his."

There were three boxes filled with new papers waiting for us by the time we got back. Damn that was quick.

"When is this hearing?" I asked Pete.

"As soon as you read the papers and talk to him." He opened my file and pointed to a paper. "It's called the 'perp walk' down here."

I had heard the term "perp walk" from a million cop and lawyer shows so I nodded, pretending to know what the hell I was talking about. I had to look up "open count" before I talked with Jesus. It could mean anything from involuntary manslaughter to the death penalty. I had never completely worked out the difference between voluntary manslaughter, involuntary manslaughter, and second-degree murder. For first-degree murder, didn't there have to be a motive? Or was it premeditation, or was it both?

Did Jesus have a motive? Well, he only hated the guy and threatened to kill him, according to Joey. Jesus was still under eighteen, so he was considered a juvenile. Right? Worst case scenario was four months at a boys' school. Right?

Wrong.

I turned my attention to a white sheet of paper with the title, "Notice of Intent to Transfer." I looked it up in the statutes. There would be a hearing in which it would be determined whether there was probable cause and whether Jesus was amenable to treatment. If transferred, and then convicted, Jesus faced adult time in an adult facility.

I called out to Pete on the way out. "What do I say at initial appearance?"

"At initial appearance, you pretty much are required by law and office policy to waive a reading and enter a denial." he yelled back. He handed me an index card with those exact words written down. "Think you can handle that?"

I ran over to see Jesus in jail. Inside, Gardea, Veronica, and another guard hovered over some inmates on a bench waiting to be booked. Veronica kept calm as she asked these men to recite their charges. Was one of the inmates her companion at the bookstore? It was hard to tell, now that he wore orange instead of black.

She smiled when she saw me, told me that the Court would let us take as much time as we needed. "But don't overdo it," she said. "It's the busy season."

Gardea left, and quickly brought Jesus down. I noticed that the waiting inmates looked over at Jesus with respect, if not awe. Killers were like rock stars.

Jesus nodded to them like he just won the gold medal in speed skating and this was his victory lap. So this was the Jesus Villalobos perp walk. Even Veronica stared, impressed.

We went into the room and shut the door. I looked at Jesus and tried in vain to see what was behind the glasses. Was the empty tattooed tear filled in now?

He slumped a little in his chair after the door shut, like he had just walked off stage. I didn't even offer my hand, leaned back, avoided eye contact. Maybe I was star struck by his newfound celebrity as well. There were many times in my life that I would have loved the ability to fatally kick someone in the head, even give them a good hard shove to the solar plexus.

Real violence did have cachet. I could hardly impress the vatos locos on the kitchen crew with tales of my brutal "Memorandum in Support of Plaintiff's Motion for Production of Documents and Things Pursuant to Rule 34 of the Federal Rules of Civil Procedure."

"You know that Victor died?" I asked. "We have initial appearance in a few minutes on the new charges. You're being charged as an adult."

"Whatever."

Whatever? That's all he had to say?

His nonchalance angered me a little. "This is not like pissing off your teacher here. This is serious shit. You have to talk to me if you want me to help you. I hear you hated him and wanted him dead."

"Lot of people wanted him dead."

"That may be so, but you're the one who's been charged."

"I don't want to talk about it now."

"I'm trying to save your ass, goddamit! Why won't you help me?"

"Because you have no fucking clue what's going on here."

God, I wanted to slug him. Not just him, this whole damn town with its inside jokes, its "usual" suspects. Just one shot at Merril, Clint, Pete—one sharp jab per smug face. I uncurled my fists and folded my hands together on the table as if in prayer.

"Jesus, I'm a lawyer, not a detective. I don't need clues, I need information so I can defend you. Now, tell me what's going on."

"It's so fucked up. . . ." He shook his head. The victory lap was over now, reality started to bite. "I don't even know any more."

I stood up. "Right now the judge will read your new charges. I have to 'waive reading and enter a denial.' I'd like to know what I'm waiving. I'd like to know what I'm denying."

Before he could say anything, Veronica opened the door.

"Ready? It's go time." She winked over at Jesus again. Or was it at me? I couldn't tell. Maybe I now shined in Jesus's reflected glory.

"No," I replied. "But let's get it over with."

Chapter 9

Perp Walks

I HAD TO LET GARDEA take Jesus to Magistrate Court over through the back way. Gardea made sure that the cuffs weren't too tight for his buddy. I hoped my jailers would be that cool when I got sent up someday.

I hurried over through the main entrance to the Magistrate Court, which was across the parking lot. The territorial-style building was adobe with brown tiled roofs and arabesque openings. The courtroom was very small, musty, and dark.

Lamb entered, gaveled the court to order. He made eye-contact with me. I was supposed to say something. When I didn't, he began to talk very, very slowly. "Mr. Villalobos," he said, "the first count you are being charged with is—"

Pete, who stood along the sides, glanced at me and whispered "now."

"Your honor," I interrupted. "We waive a reading and enter a denial on all of the charges."

Lamb nodded, relieved that he did not have to go through the entire litany line by line by line. After making a few more rote comments, he ordered Gardea to take Jesus back to the detention center.

I looked around for a moment. I had actually done something right for a change.

Merril came over to me, he'd entered after the hearing had ended. "It'll take a couple of days before Jovanka and I can get a plea offer to you. In cases like this we have to check with the folks upstairs. And by the way, some more charges might be coming down on your boy Joey Lilly. You might have a conflict coming on."

A "conflict coming on." I didn't like the sound of that.

Amanda came over to me. Cameras weren't allowed in Magistrate

Court, so she was armed only with a notepad.

Pete checked her out, as if frisking her with his eyes, than gave me a look. "He has no comment," he said to her.

That night, as if on cue, right at six-twenty-two, the News 14 theme music came on and Amanda materialized in my living room. There was a graphic of a gavel coming down over a caption reading "arraignment." She then voiced over tape of students at Aguilar High. Since she was the only reporter, she also interviewed each and every student herself, her pink outfit a sharp clash with the dusty parking lot.

"We'll miss Victor. We all loved him." This from a pimply-faced girl with braces. "It's definitely going to affect our season. He was our best hope for State," a football player said.

The camera now focused on Merril, who stood outside the high school, flag flying at half mast in the background. Amanda's microphone wavered near his lips.

Back in the studio, Amanda took one last deep breath and came to her conclusion. "Jesus Villalobos now faces an open count of murder," she said. "We'll be following this story in the weeks to come."

I had never been followed before. Cool. . . .

Chapter 10

Alternative Sentence

STILL NO PLEA OFFER FROM Jovanka and Merril, so I had some time to concentrate on the rest of my life. Early Thursday morning, I called Amanda. "Dan Shepard. Remember me?"

"How could I forget?"

"I'm representing a defendant on alleged open count of murderer now." I'm bragging about this?

"Good for you."

"Want to have lunch?"

"I'd love to, but it's got to be right at noon. I've only got an hour, max."

"That's terrific, see you at twelve sharp."

At eleven o'clock Anna Maria showed up wearing jeans and a black T-shirt, her hair pulled back and less make-up, as if she had just got out of bed after a night of tossing and turning. Something was on her mind. She carried a long-stemmed white rose in her hand.

I shook her hand delicately and she squeezed my fingers. "Please give this to Jesus."

"Sure."

"Now they're going to kill my baby."

"Are you pregnant?"

"No, nothing like that. Jesus. . . ." Her eyes flared. "He's mine! He belongs to me. Now they have him locked up, maybe forever. He told me about the new charges."

She broke down completely and I gave her a tissue. I've always been a sucker for tears.

"You really love him, don't you?"

"He's everything to me. He's the first boy who really listens to me. Will I get to see him before they kill him?" She was serious.

"Hey, it's not that bad yet." Or was it? "I'll try to get him out," I said after a moment, "but it's real hard to get furloughs which are trips outside the jail."

I glanced at the inscription on her black shirt, it had a picture of the Virgin Mary crying with an inscription in Olde English reading "In loving memory. . . ." regarding a family member, a cousin I think.

"You mean I might not ever see him again?" she asked me before I could finish reading the memory.

"That's a possibility, I guess, but I honestly hope it's a remote possibility." I handed her another tissue.

"Are you going to see him today?"

"Possibly. What do you need?"

"I wanted to ask you this the first day at the restaurant, but I didn't have the nerve."

"What?"

"Could you do me a favor? It would mean everything to me."

"Well, of course, it depends."

"I've been thinking about this for weeks now, ever since Jesus got locked up, and I've finally made up my mind."

"About what?" I looked in her piercing brown eyes.

"Will you tell him that I want to marry him?"

"What?"

"Tell him that, oh, please. I want to make it official, forever."

"You want to marry him even if he's going away for the rest of his life?"

"I want to do it now, before it's too late. I love him. Will you help me?"

I shrugged. "Sure. I'd be . . . ah . . . honored to propose to Jesus on your behalf."

I meant it. Maybe Jesus would open up if he thought he had something to live for. And what a terrific topic for my lunch date with Amanda. Then again, what the hell? She was a nice young lady. If this was what she wanted. . . .

When I arrived at the jail, Veronica smiled when she saw the rose. She frowned when I explained it wasn't for her. In the interview room, Clint sat inside with Jesus, an opened bible between them. I didn't know whether that was good or bad. .

"Who's the flower for?" Clint asked.

"Jesus."

Clint took it, looked it over, then gave it to Jesus. He gave me a most peculiar look.

"It's not from me," I said.

"I don't care. You're going to meet with him in the visitor's room. We have enough jailhouse romances as it is."

He walked away, laughing. Another great story for the community calendar. When was I going to learn?

The visitor's room held two cubicles on each side of the glass partition. Clint put Jesus on one side and me in the other. A blond-haired prisoner in the other cubicle kept his hands against the glass, across from his significant other, an obese woman in a pink tank top. She squashed the vast expanse of her tank top against the glass, just like that scene in *Midnight Express*. The back of her shirt said "I'm not fat, I'm just fluffy." Fluffy mouthed, "I miss you, I miss you. . . ."

Jesus rapped on the glass with the fist holding the flower. "What's with this shit, ese?" he said into the phone. "You like me now?"

I didn't know how to respond. I changed the subject. "No word from the prosecutors."

He frowned.

"But I've got some good news—Anna Maria—I talked to her in my office a minute ago. She wants to marry you."

"Cool. Could you, like, get me a furlough for that?" Not the most romantic response.

"Furloughs are tough," I said. "Especially when you're facing a murder rap. Don't hold your breath."

"Well, what else did she say?"

"She said she still loved you."

He bit his lip to suppress a smile of satisfaction. "Orale, ese," he said. "Orale."

"Look, Jesus, I have a lunch date, and—"

"One thing I gotta ask you, man, you being my lawyer and all."

"So ask."

"If I marry her, do I still got to go up to the prison?"

I sighed. "Marriage isn't usually thought of as an alternative sentence."

"But when I get out, I can live with her, no?"

"You'll be over eighteen when you get out, no matter what. You can do whatever you want."

At the other booth, Fluffy kissed the glass partition, Blondie touched his hand to the lipstick stain. I shook my head.

"Did she say if she would wait for me?"

"Yeah, she said she'd wait forever. There were tears in her eyes."

"She really said that?" He was ecstatic. "Even after all this shit? Did she say anything else?"

"No that's it," I said. "So what do you want to do?"

No hesitation at all. "Tell her yes. Definitely. I'll marry her whenever we can set it up. I was going to ask her anyway."

"I'll tell her. Congratulations and all that."

He was too choked up to respond.

"You really love her don't you?" I asked.

He wiped his eyes, laughed after a moment. "You act all surprised. Just 'cause I'm here, don't mean I can't love."

I looked down at my watch. Just past noon. "I really have to go."

"Hey, you can be our flower girl," he said, holding up the flower. He was smiling.

He was laughing with me, not at me. Good. I smiled back.

Fluffy lit a cigarette and exhaled with a satisfied grin. I didn't even want to think about her and Blondie without a pane of glass between them.

Anna Maria was still in my office, pacing anxiously. I could see why she stayed so thin. Anxious myself, I glanced over at the clock—it was already past the magic hour and this engagement of theirs stood in the way of my own chance at romance.

"Congratulations." I took her hand. "Once we can get everything straightened out, you guys can get married. It could take a while, though."

She hugged me, crying.

"Then that's how long I'll wait. No matter what happens."

I looked out the window and saw Amanda, camera and tripod in hand, get into the News 14 van and rush away at breakneck speed.

Anna Maria would wait forever for Jesus but Amanda was already gone. Five minutes was too much for her. . . . So much for lunch.

• • • •

I looked out the window to the parking lot. Joey sat smoking something, eying the tumbleweeds dancing in a swirling breeze. Joey's head bobbed up and down as weed after weed flew over and under the cars. It took so little to entertain him.

He waved at me through the window, motioned to me as if he wanted me to come out and watch the weeds for awhile. Instead, I closed the blinds, caught the evening's rerun of *Friends*.

The roar of motorbike approached. I glanced outside the window—it was Aryan Eddie, the kid who had mad-dogged me at the mall. He went to Joey's door. They talked for a few moments, glancing in my direction more than once, then Eddie rode away into the night.

Joey turned his attention back to the dancing weeds. A big one flew into a car, then came out the other side as if it had magically passed through solid matter. Cool . . .

Chapter 11

A Cut Deeper

THE WHOLE PROPOSAL THING WITH Jesus weighed on my mind the next morning at work. How could such a romantic be so violent? I looked over my own framed family photograph that I still hadn't bothered to hang up yet. It sat in a pile with my unframed diplomas. In the photo, we all looked so happy at my law school graduation. What the hell happened to us?

That gave me an idea for Jesus's case—it was time to return to the womb. I found the work number for Jesus' mother from the file and dialed it.

"Aguilar Hair Care."

"Senora Villalobos, please."

"Speaking. Who is this?"

"Dan Shepard, Jesus' attorney. I need to see you."

"You can come by the shop up until seven. It's right behind Rosalita's, in the alley. You need a full cut or just a trim?"

Had she said that for the benefit of whoever was close to the phone? Better not tell her I needed to talk to her about her son.

"Just a trim. Six-thirty all right?"

I still had to handle one case that day, the sentencing in District Court of a forty-year-old burglar named Sammy Quintana who had failed his urine test after two years of a perfect parole record. Sammy, had nearly managed to clean up his life. At least until he got caught with his pants down, so to speak.

He wore the blue ACDC jumpsuit of a short-timer. His original conviction had been in Crater County. Quintana stiffened the minute he laid eyes on the DA, who had come up from Crater for the hearing.

"What's the matter?" I asked.

"That DA, I know him. We grew up together. Before I was on probation I sold him a couple of bags down in Crater."

"Don't worry," I said. "I don't think he's going to bring that up today before the judge."

Sure enough, the hearing went off without a hitch after I cited the seminal case of State v. Halsey, 884 P.2d 1, which held that merely testing positive for cocaine while on probation was not grounds for a new felony conviction and the enforcement of infamous "bitch." I pronounced the magic words "consumption does not equal possession" and Quintana got credit for time served.

"You were right, man. Thanks a lot." Quintana smiled and shook my hand. "If there's anything I can do for you, let me know."

"Sure." What could he possibly do? Wait a minute . . . everybody in this town knew everybody else. "Do you know Jesus Villalobos?"

"Of course. It's Aguilar, everyone knows everyone. You're his lawyer right?"

"So far. You know anything about what happened between him and Victor?"

"I heard some of those movie people might be involved. You should check it out. They got this big party coming up at the Tumbleweeds."

The movie folks. This was bigger than I suspected. "Thanks. How about Joey Lilly?"

"Just a fucked up kid."

"Is he a killer?"

"Could be, but I've always thought he was just a wannabe. He's like a stoned puppy dog that'll follow you around all day."

"Do you know his sister Dora?"

He smiled. "Nobody really knows Dora."

I shook his hand. "Good luck on the outside."

He smiled at me once again, positively beaming as Clint unclicked his handcuffs. "I owe you one."

He slapped me on the back with his free hand as Clint moved to undo the other. The unclicking of handcuffs—music to my ears.

Aguilar cared for its hair in a small suite in a crumbling strip mall way out on Santa Fe street. A woman with a terrible orange dye job headed out as I walked in. Inside the streaking mirrored walls of the "salon," Senora Villalobos nodded to her boss, an elderly woman. The older woman left, locking the door on her way out, and putting up the "closed sign."

Senora Villalobos took me to the reclining chair in front of a sink. Before I could do more than say hello, my hair was soaking wet and she lathered it with a vengeance.

"Chuwy talked about you when I saw him the last time," she said as she started rinsing. I could see a tear tattooed under each eye.

"Chuwy?"

"That's what I call my little Jesus."

I squeezed my eyes shut tight. "What did he say?"

She led me over to the barber's chair, grabbed a pair of shears and spun the chair around slowly until I was facing the mirror. She was so short I could barely see her head.

"Wait a second, I've got to get something," she said.

An image of Sweeney Todd's straight-edged razor flashed through my brain. Who knew what Jesus had told her about me? She didn't seem all that friendly, and we were in the back of the store. No one could see us.

She came back with a step-stool. "You're so tall, I need to step up to reach you." She got a firm grip on my shoulder with one hand and held high a whirring electric razor in the other." How much you want off the back?"

"Cut it pretty short. It's getting messy."

She brought the razor closer. "You know, I keep telling my Chuwy to get his hair cut, but he keeps it long. I got nothing against long hair, but he's too pretty. He looks like a girl, no?"

"I wouldn't say that. He's got a strong face, and long hair's pretty common on guys around here."

She relaxed her grip on my shoulder. "When you came in, you know who you reminded me of?"

"Who?"

"Clark Kent. You know, from Superman. You wear those same kind of glasses."

"Yeah, that's what Jesus said."

"He says he likes you all right."

"That's nice to hear," I said, profoundly relieved.

She pulled the hair on top straight up and began to snip, causing a small hair shower down the front of my face. "Because you listen to him."

"He's a good kid. He just seems to have taken . . . uh . . . a wrong turn or two."

"Yeah, mi hijo's a real good boy. Always minds me at home. Always looking out for me."

"How many kids in the family?"

"It's just him now. The other two were taken from me. I know. Some say the tear is for killing someone, but a friend of mine told me that when someone is taken from you, you can wear the tear. So that's why I did it. What do you think?"

As someone who had never killed anybody or had anyone close die from violence, I couldn't think of anything to say.

"These days," she said, "having the tear means you got five bucks to give to the tattoo guy."

Snip. Snip. Snip. She cut quickly—too quickly—time to get down to business.

"He lives at home, right?" I asked nervously about breaking the silence. "I mean, he did before he got picked up?"

She sighed. I had struck a chord somehow. "After his real father died and I was alone again, I had trouble working and keeping track of the boys. Now that the other two are gone, it's just me and him. We do okay."

"Could you testify about Jesus turning himself around and all?"

"Yeah, sure. Mi hijo's doing real good. Or was." Which sounded like it was as good as it was going to get on that subject.

She said nothing for a while and kept cutting. Then she grabbed my hair so roughly it actually hurt. She picked up a little tuft of hair she had left uncut in the back. She held up a mirror. "You like?"

"Fine." I now had a rat tail for the first time in my life. She began working on the sides. "How was he related to Victor?" I asked.

"He wasn't. I lived with Victor's father for a while. Ted Slade. We all lived together for like a year, until Ted went back to his wife. Long story. That was when Jesus was thirteen. Ted beat me. Jesus, too."

"And Victor?"

She shook her head. "Spoiled him rotten. That's why he was so bad. . . ." She walked toward the broom closet in the back and returned with a long pair of scissors that she carried casually, like a small sword.

Slowly but firmly, she brought the scissors forward. I wished I hadn't opened up painful memories for her. She stood in front of me, staring.

"I don't know what you heard about my boy. He don't have no

halo and, yes, he hated Victor ever since they were brothers for a year. But mi hijo, he's no killer."

She backed off a little. There were so many things I wanted to find out, but she set the scissors on the counter, began sweeping up the hair on the floor. I looked at myself in the mirror—I'd had worse haircuts, but not many. I looked like a marine after a hazing.

I shrugged, reached for my wallet.

I stopped—how much to tip? It was a lousy haircut after all, but her son was facing some serious time. That was worth 30 percent tip at least.

She grabbed my hand before I pulled it out my wallet. "It's on the house," she said with her first smile of the evening. "This is Aguilar, we take care of people here."

As I turned to leave, she touched my shoulder. "Just save my Chuwy."

Chapter 12

Getting Bitched

AN ENVELOPE WAITED FOR ME in my office the next morning—inside was a standardized plea-offer form—"eighteen years, adult" scribbled in red ink on the blank space.

Eighteen years—Jesus wasn't even eighteen years old yet.

There was a handwritten Post-It note from Jovanka Smith: "Copier down. More discovery available soon."

I crumpled the note. Shit. The most important case of the year and they can't give me the information because the copier is low on toner. Coincidence?

The expiration date on the plea offer for Jesus was Monday, November 8, at 11:00 a.m. Two weeks from now.

Clint greeted me when I signed in to speak with Jesus. "You're going to have to meet in the kitchen."

"How come?"

"We're shorthanded right now, so we got to keep him in there where we can watch him."

Clint escorted me to the kitchen. I almost gagged. The heat from the ovens enveloped my face. A grease trap had overflowed and Jesus was down on his knees scrubbing the tiles. Scrubbing residents covered the entire floor, guards with surgical masks over their faces hovered over them. The glamour of being a killer was long gone. Jail was just jail now.

"Four on one, five on one." Clint said the magic words and the doors opened between the kitchen and the corridor. As we got to the small space between the doors we waited, then Clint said the words again and the doors slammed shut. I could still smell the grease from when Jesus had shaken my hand.

"Eighteen years is what they're offering."

"Eighteen years as an adult? That's longer than I'd been alive, bro."

"I know. Eighteen years in the joint. Out in nine, maybe—right now, its sounds like a good deal. We don't have to go through a trial. Get you on your way quickly."

"I don't want to get bitched up there," he whispered.

I tried to be matter-of-fact. "There is no habitual offender enhancement for juveniles."

"That's not what 'getting bitched' means once you're in the joint."

He didn't have to spell it out. Maybe it was the fumes, the onions, and/or the heat, but there were real tears in his eyes that flowed over his tattooed ones.

I was surprised—there was moisture in my eye as well. A tear? I quickly wiped it off, before he could see it. Must be the onions in today's stew. . . .

"You really think I should plead?" he asked.

"You could be looking at even more time when . . . uh . . . if we lose," I said.

"Five on one, four on one," Gardea said, the doors slammed open.

"Excuse me, we're not done here," I said.

"The grease trap on the other side is gushing," Gardea said. "Someone's got to clean it and it ain't gonna be me."

I stood up instinctively.

"Not you," Gardea said, laughing. "Him! Sorry, Jesus."

As he walked back to the other grease trap, Jesus regained his composure and shifted into his tough perp walk. "Don't worry, bro. I got it all under control."

Gardea smiled as I wiped my brow. "Mr. Shepard, if you can't handle the heat. . . ."

Anna Maria excused herself, the minute Pete and I walked into Rosalita's on Tuesday, as if she couldn't bear to face us for the next eighteen years. Another waitress had to serve us.

"Look what you've done," Pete said. "Now I'll never get my menudo."

We spent the rest of the meal in silence.

"You gonna plead Jesus?" Pete finally asked.

"I don't know if I should go to trial on something like this."

Pete was non-committal. "Let's just see what happens. These things have a way of working out."

He kept a poker face and said nothing more. Then he slipped twenty-three dollars under his plate for a four-dollar meal.

It was windy on the walk back to the office. "Are you going to the dance at the jail Saturday night?" he asked.

"Dance?"

"Every Halloween we have a dance for the kids at the jail, to boost morale. It's called the "Hope for Tomorrow" Dance. You know, we get kids from all over the state in there after some of the other districts closed their facilities, so it's a pretty big deal. The long-timers tend to behave themselves because they don't want to miss it."

I looked at the big ugly depressing building known as the jail down the street in the distance. I could see his point. "It works?"

"Fuckin' A it does—kids on the outside try to get picked up so they can attend, too. They also ship some girls down from the Girls' School up in Albuquerque. The ones on good behavior, that is."

"So why should I go?"

"Traditionally the baby lawyer in the public defender's office attends. In case one of them thinks about starting something, they see you and remember who defends them."

I took another look at the jail, smiled. "Should I bring a date?"

"Unless you're into jail bait that's already in jail."

"Do I have to wear a costume?"

"It's crazy enough without them. So you'll be there? You can call your little reporter chica."

"I'll try."

I called Amanda at the station several times, but the news van was out all day. I turned on the evening news hoping for a glimpse of her and got the Albuquerque sportscast. But they had a cutaway to Amanda's interview with Coach Ernie Aragon of the Aguilar Eagles, discussing the upcoming big game against top-ranked Eldorado after coming back from tragedy.

I dialed Amanda's phone number to leave a call-me message.

"Hello?" she said.

"Wait a minute, you're on television. Right now."

"Haven't you heard of videotape?" she said, giggling. "Didn't the fact that my interview took place in daytime give it away?"

"I was looking at you, not the sky. You looked great."

"It was a hard-hitting interview, let me tell you. Coach Aragon said the two keys to the game were offense and defense."

"Hey, I had to sit through interviews with Joe Gibbs of the Redskins growing up. I don't think there is such a thing as a good sports interview."

"So what's up?" she asked.

"Still working on the Villalobos case."

"Any progress?"

"Hard to say. I've always had this feeling I'd make a better comedian."

"I always wanted to be an actress."

"What stopped you?"

"I grew up."

"I haven't yet."

On the screen her image was replaced by the bombastic sportscaster up in Albuquerque, now interviewing the coach of Eldorado and showing clips of their big game against Sandia.

"Hold on a second," she said and clicked off to answer another call. In less than a second, she was back. "I'll just call him later."

"Who was it?"

"This guy I went out with out in L.A. He does the sports for one of the locals out there."

"Are you still. . . ? Hold on. Let me turn off the TV." I did, my heart pounding.

"Not really. It wasn't working out. Funny how different people seem once you get some distance from them."

"How's that?"

Her voice bristled. "All he ever did was bitch about his career. As far as he was concerned, I was nothing more than a shoulder and a cunt."

I was shocked. I didn't expect that kind of language from such a pretty mouth. But I sensed an opening. She was naked in her confession, vulnerable, as though asking me to come in and rescue her. For a minute I heard Jesus' voice: "Go for it, ese." Well, here was my chance.

"Amanda, I've been invited to a Halloween dance. Would you like to go with me?"

"Where?"

"At the jail, of all places. The dance is sponsored by the county, to keep the juvenile inmates' spirits up. I'm like a chaperone."

"I heard about that dance—I don't know—I'm usually pretty tired after work. . . ."

"I'd commit a crime just so you'd come dance with me in the jail, if that's what it takes."

"A felony?"

"Only a misdemeanor. I don't know you well enough."

"I'm worth a felony at least," she said.

"I don't know if I'd kill for you. Embezzle, maybe. That's a fourth-degree felony."

"Anything under two-hundred-fifty dollars is a suspended sentence. I'll only dance with you if you're willing to risk some jail time."

"I'll grab three hundred dollars from petty cash tomorrow. Besides, sounds like a good human interest story to me . . . 'hope for tomorrow'and all that."

That was the clincher. "What should I wear?"

"Regular clothes, I guess. It should be pretty casual. It's not like I need to impress my clients."

"I can wear my new perfume—Incarceration—for the woman who can't be caged."

The next day, I was able to get Anna Maria and Jesus' guest list, but I had to wait for a background check on Amanda. Pete went before the judge on his motion to compel a confidential informant. Pete could be a prick, but he was a terrific lawyer. Amanda filmed from the back of the courtroom. When the red light went off, she waved to me. I signaled for her to meet me outside, but by the time I got there Pete had already cornered her with yet another tale of legal triumph. The camera was off and her notepad was down.

"What I'm wearing here is called a brushpopper shirt," he said, touching her shoulder. "You know how they got their name?"

"No." She ran her fingers over the rough fabric. "It's nice, though."

"Well, in the old days, cowboys rode through pretty rough brush chasing after stray cattle. So when they were done, they'd just pop the brush right off."

She smiled. "That's a great story."

"You know what they call him when one of them cowboys was chasing after sheep?"

"What?"

"Extremely horny."

She laughed, completely unaware that I stood nearby.

Pete kept the patter going. "After I quit playing football, I gained a lot of weight. A guy came up to me once and said, 'You're so fat that when you look down you can't even see your dick. Why don't you diet?' I told him even if I dye it blue, I still won't be able to see it."

"You're real funny, Pete," I heard her say as I started back toward the office. "Did you ever do stand-up?"

"About five years ago I was supposed to go on *The Tonight Show* and get discovered and shit, but I had to do jury selection in a criminal sexual penetration case. . . ."

Chapter 13

Trick or Trick

October 31

THERE WAS A KNOCK ON my door, that morning before the dawn. It was a little early for trick or treat. I got on a towel and opened the door to reveal Joey.

"I'm outta here man," he said. "Too much freaky shit about to go down."

"Uh . . . what about court?"

"I'll be back in time, don't worry."

He looked at me in the eye, he was able to maintain a steady gaze at me. "Is something wrong?"

He broke off his gaze, looked down at his feet, "I can't tell you man."

"Then why are you here?"

"Could you like lend me like twenty bucks? Like right now. . . ."

He shivered in the early morning cold, more from fear than fahrenheit.

I politely told him that it probably wasn't a good idea to lend money to a client. He shook his head, disappointed. "A client? Is that what I am to you, man?"

I didn't answer. He turned and headed back out to the parking lot, then went back into his home. He had a grim expression as he closed the door, as if returning to prison.

I pulled up in front of Amanda's that night right at seven, wearing my new bolo tie purchased at Wally's Western Wear on Oil Avenue. The bolo clip was shaped like a little silver rattlesnake. Its turquoise eyes set off my blue Ralph Lauren Oxford shirt rather nicely.

Amanda wore a short red cocktail dress that showed off her long legs, a connect-the-dots series of freckles below her collarbone, and the dying remnants of a California tan on her bare arms. A dream dress for a quiet cocktail party, but way too much skin for the captive audience that awaited us.

We began with dinner at the Peking West, which was in the same shopping center as Aguilar Hair Care. The host, who was not Chinese, led us past the usual faux Oriental decor with fans and etchings, but we stopped to stare at the beat-up saddle hanging over the entrance to the kitchen.

Our waitress was a pale heavyset Anglo woman with black hair who kept smiling at me and patting my shoulder. "You represent my son, Joseph," she said.

"I do?"

"Joey Lilly."

I didn't want to recount our morning conversation. "Uh how is he?" I asked trying to sound as innocent as possible.

"I'm worried about him," she said and left, as though she needed a moment alone. Why did it keep surprising me that these mothers actually cared about their kids?

She came back with the water. "You going to the party at the jail tonight?" she asked.

"Yes."

"Maybe you'll meet my daughter. Dora said she was gonna stop by. She just got back in town. "

She looked at Amanda, as if checking her out. "You're a pretty girl, but you should see my Dora."

Amanda frowned. "What's the special tonight?"

Was that a slightly aggrieved tone of voice? A touch of jealousy?

"Honey, I'd recommend the chicken fried steak, Texas style, with green chile on the side. You'll like it a lot."

"Chicken fried steak in a Chinese restaurant?"

"Trust me, honey. It's the best thing on the menu."

"Don't you have any vegetarian plates?"

"No."

Amanda stuck with hot and sour soup and some rice. I went for the Moo Goo Gai Pan.

"I hate when these people check me out trying to see if I'm prettier in person."

"You are pretty in person. You look great on camera too."

"Come on, tell me the truth." she said. "How do I look on camera?"

"Well," I said, risking honesty, "you don't always hold the mike straight."

"That's because it's pretty heavy and I pulled a muscle in my forearm doing tae-bo before I got here. Does it still show?"

"No, not at all. You're very poised on camera. You must know that."

"Well, I don't. They told me they wanted someone prettier when I interviewed here."

"They actually said that?"

"The station manager is an old cowboy. He runs beauty pageants on the side."

"If it wasn't such an insult to your intelligence," I said, "you could be in beauty pageants."

"Management considers investigative reporting way down the list from baton twirling. The last girl, Mary Pat, was Miss New Mexico."

"You could be Miss New Mexico," I said. "I'd vote for you."

Our little patter was interrupted when the waitress returned. "How much do I owe you?" I asked.

She smiled. "It's on the house."

As the waitress left, Amanda looked at her, then smiled at me. "You seem to be quite the big man on campus tonight, getting a free meal and all."

"I know the right people."

"Apparently," she grinned.

We drove the seven blocks down Oil Avenue and parked in the jail's main lot. A bus marked NEW MEXICO GIRLS SCHOOL was already there, a contingent of husky female guards escorting a party of girls in long purple polyester dresses.

"I wonder who does their hair," Amanda said.

Each coiffure was teased (or was it tortured?) until the front stood four or five inches straight up over the forehead. Many of them had roses or teddy bears tattooed on their bare shoulders.

Veronica checked IDs at the door. She smiled, didn't ask to see mine.

"Are you with the girls' school group?" she asked Amanda with just a tinge of ice. "You're not on the list."

"She's with me, Veronica."

The guards gave Amanda a dirty look as we walked past the metal detector with her camera case. They looked inside for contraband.

They found a few packs of gum and a pair of pantyhose.

"Always nice to have a spare pair handy," I said.

"I use it to polish the lens," she said, stuffing it back in.

The multipurpose room was about the size of a racquetball court, its unpainted cinderblock walls decorated with skeletons and pumpkins. The residents wore brown khaki one-piece jumpsuits, not unlike Halloween costumes. The local DJ, "Kid Coyote" who tried to look like a mix between gangster rapper and country crooner, manned the turntables.

Jesus chatted with Anna Maria, radiant in a red cocktail dress. The neck was a little lower than Amanda's, the material probably did not occur in nature, but otherwise the two dresses were identical.

"Someone's wearing my outfit," Amanda said. "Would I look better with my hair straight up?"

"I don't know. Taller, maybe."

"I'm going to the ladies room. Send in a search party if I'm not back in five minutes."

On the other side of the room, Aryan Eddie chatted up a redhead from the girls' school, his hands still in the pockets of baggy pants. An oversized sweater drooped over his pants. Eddie wore the light green of a short timer. A "weekend warrior" they called it. I wondered what he did to get picked up for the weekend. By the looks of it, he wasn't doing so hot with the redhead. She walked away, talked to one of the residents.

As Amanda headed for the bathroom, Eddie moved to intercept her. He stood a few feet in front of the door and stared at her. He started talking trash to her, something like, "Hey, Donna, you wanna?" He kept it up. "I'll fuck you on camera, bitch. Right now, right here."

Amanda looked around for someone to shut him up.

"Turn around, bitch. I got a use for you," Eddie snarled. "No one's gonna stop me." He moved even closer toward her.

Amanda crossed her arms defensively over her chest. The guards stood back as if they were scared of Eddie. They were going to let this all play out.

Before I could think of what to do, Jesus walked confidently over to the bathroom door and held it open for her. "Eddie, why don't you shut the fuck up," he said. "There's a lady present."

The two mad-dogged each other.

Clint and the other guards quickly formed a defensive perimeter around Amanda, Jesus, and Eddie. They didn't care if Jesus and Eddie killed each other so long as no one else got hurt.

"Eddie," Jesus said, his voice strong as iron. "I said 'why don't you get the fuck out of here like right now and let the lady do her business?'" Jesus got closer to him.

Eddie said nothing, returned Jesus's stare for only a moment, then backed away. He took a final glance at Jesus. Again, Jesus did not flinch. Eddie shrugged his shoulders, left the multi-purpose room like a dog with his tail between his legs.

A female guard came over to Amanda and escorted her into the bathroom. Amanda nodded to Jesus, who held the door open like a perfect gentleman.

I swallowed the Doritos that had been in my mouth for the last minute. They were still crunchy; not a drop of moisture in my entire body.

Jesus stood by the door until Eddie clicked safely past the final metal doors to the corridor beyond. He then rejoined Anna Maria. Seated, quietly holding hands, they were the picture of an old married couple from a Norman Rockwell painting.

"Thanks a lot for saving Amanda, Jesus" I said, walking over to him. "That took guts."

"No problemo," he said. "It was nada."

"I owe you one." I said.

"I know."

He didn't have to say what I had to do in return.

Before I could regain my equilibrium and return to Amanda—an Anglo woman in a shiny turquoise dress breezed through the metal detector and headed in our direction. She was about six feet tall in heels, almost six-five with her hair. In her left ear, a gold skull earring dangled from a silver chain. A tattoo of a giant vine seemed to wrap around her entire body before flowering into a rose petal right over her ample bosom. The rose matched the dress.

Everyone looked at her—the residents, guards, even all the girls. Three tough-looking residents scuttled out of her way as she advanced. I moved away from Jesus. She had to be heading for him right?

Wrong. Like a cruise missile, she changed direction, headed toward me.

Out of all the people in the whole room, why was she coming toward me? She took my hand and whispered in my ear, "I need you."

The woman literally took my breath away. Quickly, I came to my senses. "I'm here with somebody, sorry—"

"You could do better, ese, much better." Though she was Anglo, she had adopted the Hispanic inflections of the valley. "What are you in for, anyway?"

"I'm a lawyer. I'm here as a kind of chaperon."

"Oh. I thought you were a killer or something cool like that." She smiled. She knew who I was.

"Sorry to disappoint you."

She folded her arms. "So you're Joey and Jesus's lawyer, no?"

I nodded. "Who. . . ." But I already knew the answer.

"Well, I'm Dora and my brother told me to talk to you. Got a minute?"

Her deep green eyes seemed to hold all the answers to Aguilar's mysteries. She put her hand on my forearm as if she wanted to yank it out of its socket.

By that time, a still shaken Amanda emerged from the bathroom. She was not happy, stared at me with as much anger as my mom on that fateful day so long ago. No need to make an impossible situation even worse. "No, sorry. Dora—I've got to go."

I shook Dora's hand as if it was radioactive, went over to Amanda. She leaned as far away from me as she could.

"Thanks for nothing," she said.

"I'm sorry."

I glanced back at Dora one last time . . . whatever she wanted to tell me would have to wait.

"I've got to do the weather tomorrow morning over in Crater first thing in the morning," Amanda said, breaking my concentration. "I can get one of the guards to take me home." Her voice sounded like ice. "That is if you're too busy. . . ."

"No, I'll take you," I said. "I've got to make things up to you."

"You got a long way to go."

In the passenger seat, she sat as far away from as she could, stared out the window.

"What about lunch next week?" I said, trying against all odds to sound upbeat.

She scrunched even further against the side door. "You just don't get it, do you?"

Chapter 14

November Pain

ON MONDAY'S DOCKET CALL, MY only sentencing was a seventy-year-old man with a walker and an oxygen tank. He had fifteen prior DWIs and advanced cirrhosis of the liver.

"Your Honor, my client is seventy years old with chronic medical problems including, but not limited to, late-stage alcoholism. I don't personally think he'd survive a week, much less a year, in prison. Do you really think prison would have any lasting effect on his behavior? I've arranged for him to stay for a year at the New Mexico Rehab Center over in Roswell."

"Your Honor," Merril said, "the State is willing to drop all charges on this defendant if Mr. Shepard will provide us with just one document from the Rehab Center. A one-page document signed by a doctor and we'll totally drop all pending charges against his client."

"And what document would that be, Mr. Merril?" the judge asked.

"A death certificate, Your Honor."

The judge didn't laugh. My client got the full eighteen months in the pen. Clint picked him up and half-carried him into custody.

There was a "breaking story" up in Albuquerque, yet another car chase. Amanda didn't appear on screen until six-twenty-six. Talking quickly, appearing slightly worse for wear, she discussed *Snakeskin Cowboys* and how the party would be the "hottest ticket in town" in her thirty seconds of airtime.

"Coming up, a quick look at today's sports," Amanda said. "Stay with us. There's a lot more to come."

No, she didn't look prettier in person.

The next day, after eight hours of frustration over Jesus' case and procedural paperwork, I called it a day. I tried to reach the mysterious

Dora at Joey's place, but no one picked up the line. I almost called Amanda about the movie party but decided against it. As a local celebrity, she was my one real hope of getting in but her "you just don't get it" had sounded about as promising as Jesus's "go to Wal-Mart and get a clue."

I checked the clock. I couldn't leave without accomplishing something. If my side wouldn't help me, maybe the other side would.

I called the DA's office and actually got through to Jovanka Smith.

"Ms. Smith, I was wondering when I could expect the rest of the discovery."

"Sorry, but the copier is still down," she said. Her voice was harsh, with an accent I couldn't place over the lousy phone connection. "You have no idea how jammed up everything is here."

"Then could I make an appointment to talk with some of the witnesses?"

"We'll see."

Once I got home and changed into my sweats, I felt much better. The sun set out on the mesa, casting the white cone of Sierra Milagro with a pinkish glow in the desert air. A cool crisp breeze from the east helped propel me along the wide-open spaces of the Acequia road. You didn't get sunsets like this back on K street.

It had rained a little that morning, so the Acequia actually had flowing water for a change. Between the jogging and the sound of the current, I began to relax.

I had almost reached the spot where I found the beheaded dog when I heard the pop-pop-pop of semi-automatic gunfire off in the distance. About a hundred yards ahead of me I made out some boys standing by a pick-up truck, shooting some old cans. No reason to be alarmed, but I was pretty far down the Acequia road, and very much alone. I turned around, headed home.

I heard a couple more gunshots, the sound of cans being hit, then silence. A few steps later, I heard the sound of the truck climbing over the embankment, coming up behind me.

I looked over the shoulder. The truck increased its speed. I breathed in some dust and began to cough.

The truck now kept pace with me—ten short yards back. I heard the boys in the truck laughing, then someone held a large dark object from the passenger side window. I'd always wondered why the passenger seat was always called the shotgun seat. Now I knew.

I picked up the pace. So did the truck. Soon, only inches behind me, I could make out only a few words over the noise of the engine. I heard "Jesus" and "lawyer," followed by more vicious laughter. If I stayed on the road, I'd get shot or run over. My only alternatives were climbing over the embankment or jumping into the acequia. After an anxious moment, I dived down, tripped, and landed face-first in the water.

One of the boys yelled, "For Victor!"

The water was only two inches deep and I tasted mud. My glasses were still muddy when I began to rise out of the water. The truck halted about twenty yards in front of me. My eyesight without my glasses was blurry, but I made out two figures in the back of the pickup, both with bandannas over their faces and L.A. Kings hats on their heads. Stenciled in on the truck's rear window was some writing that looked like "Oolloriusliee."

One of the bandanna boys picked up his gun, cocked it, then fired into the air. Instinctively I winced and dropped my head back into the water. Nothing happened for a long moment.

The truck began to drive off. One of the figures waved good-bye to me, contemptuously. He had some kind of dark tattoo on the palm of his hand.

I waited in the water, shaking, until I could see that they had turned back onto the main road and had driven off toward the city. In the distance, a cop car turned off on Oil Avenue but it didn't follow the speeding truck.

I searched for my glasses in the dirt. Shit. Lost a lens. I wiped the dirt off my face ran back home, still shivering.

What did we have here? Aggravated assault, easily; attempted murder, maybe. This would be enough to get them to the boys' school, maybe even prison, whoever they were.

Dora came out of her apartment as soon as I made it to the parking lot. She wore a silk bathrobe with a Japanese print—She'd been home all along. Why hadn't she picked up the phone when I called?

"Are you alright?" she asked, handed a towel for me.

"These assholes tried to—" I mumbled. "I'm going to call the police—"

"I already did," she said.

I looked at her expectantly. "And?"

She echoed Pete's famous words. "As long as you're alive, they don't care. This shit happens in Aguilar, every hour on the hour. You got any ID on them?"

I thought about how Pete had ripped apart the officer's eyewitness account, I would face the same fate before any good defense attorney.

"I wouldn't want to go to court with it if that's what you mean."

"Anything can happen in court," she said with a smile. "But you probably already know that."

She headed back to her apartment. "Don't worry. I'll make sure they don't come back here again." I believed her. Even in her Japanese bathrobe and without heels she was still a formidable presence.

I stared at her as she walked away. "Didn't you have something to tell me?"

"Not now," she smiled, shutting her door behind her. "Not now."

I heard some moaning through the cinderblock walls. If Pete had claimed to be loud, he had nothing on Dora.

Chapter 15

Hollywood on the Pecos

November 6

THE ACHES FROM MY LITTLE face-plant in Acequia increased my determination to crash the *Snakeskin Cowboy* party that night. It takes more than mud to run Dan Shepard out of town. I wasn't on many guestlists, but when I was a law clerk I had crashed many a cocktail party on K street. I even used the old stand-by of walking in backwards pretending I was leaving. Somebody had mentioned that the movie people might be involved in Jesus's case. Even more incentive.

I decided to dress in black to look like an up and coming screenwriter. Creator of *The Invasion of the Saber Yuccas* and all that. The only thing missing was my literary looking glasses which wouldn't be ready until Monday. There was no instant eye care in Aguilar. I would be doing this blind.

When I opened the rough wooden door at the Tumbleweeds, I saw darkness. The bouncer, a large man with a shaved head, double-breasted glen-plaid suit and a bow tie, shined a light in my eyes, blinding me even worse.

"Name?"

"Dan Shepard."

"Not on the list. This party is invitation only."

"Is Amanda Finch here yet?"

"Not here yet. Sorry."

One last shot. . . . "How bout Dora Lilly?"

"She didn't put you on her list. . . ."

This was not a man I could small-talk with, nor was he likely to be impressed by my Eastern identity as Shepard and Shepard's lost sheep.

As I turned to go, a middle-aged Latino man came over to us. "Raphael, it's cool. He's with me."

Raphael gave me one more dirty look but let me in. I followed my new host over to the bar.

"Don't you remember me?" the man asked, letting me get a good look at him.

He did look familiar. "I know I know you," I said. "What have you been in?"

"Aguilar County Detention Center for the last week," he said. "I'm Sammy Quintana. You represented me on my parole violation, remember? 'Consumption isn't possession' is what you said."

"What are you doing here?"

He grinned. "Tumbleweeds busboy, at your service. Remember when I said I owed you one? Let me get you a drink."

I had a drink with Sammy and checked out the scene. All the real frustrated screenwriter-types had gone Western for the evening. Kid Coyote, the ubiquitous DJ, wore all black except for a rattlesnake bolo of his own, as he manned the turntables.

There was an open mike on the stage. For a moment I flashed back to my stand-up days, I looked around and it was a pretty hip crowd. In the darkness, I could barely make out a large woman with dark hair sitting at a table eating chips and salsa. I knew that face from syndicated reruns of my youth. The one and only Roseanne, in the flesh.

She waved at me and motioned me to her table. "Hi, Mr. Shepard."

No way could Roseanne possibly know me. I'd only watched reruns maybe a half a dozen times. "I still don't know where Joey is," she said after a moment. "I'm hoping he shows up tonight."

Joey? How would she know him?

"My son, Joey," she said. "You represented him on sniffing paint. Don't you remember me? Norma Jean Lilly. You know, from the Peking West. We're here doing the catering. I'm on a break."

Of course. "I don't get it," I said. "Why would Joey come here?"

"He knows some of the people."

I excused myself and went over to the food, unwisely passing up the chicken fried steak for the famous Aguilar egg rolls. Fried grease on the outside, God knows what on the inside. In an attempt to locate Joey I schmoozed a cinematographer, a gaffer and a best boy, whatever the hell that meant. I couldn't fake being Mr. Hollywood for much longer, so I gave up, dashed off to the men's room to ponder my next role.

I heard footsteps, then a voice said, "It's over. Your luck has pretty much run out."

It took only a moment to identify the voice: Officer Thompson's.

"Can I take a shit at least?" The other voice sounded drugged out. Joey?

"Go ahead. I'll wait outside."

I heard the door slam. Not knowing what else to do, I flushed. "Joey, is that you?" I opened the door. Waiting outside was a scroungy-looking kid in sunglasses, wobbling on his feet a bit. It sure looked like Joey to my blurry eyes.

He laughed. "You think I was Joey Comanche?"

I didn't reply.

"You know the singer for 'Severe Tire Damage?' People get us confused sometimes."

"No, but you do look familiar." He obviously expected to be recognized so I tried a guess. "You're in the movie, right?"

"Duh. . . ." he said. "Sky Roberts, maybe you've heard of me." He stretched out an unsteady hand in a leather motorcycle glove. "*The* Sky Roberts. *Mother in Law*? *Resident Alien*? You do get cable out here?"

I nodded vaguely as I shook his hand. My eyes struggled to focus in the light—on the second glance he didn't really look like Joey at all.

"Who are you?" he asked. "Don't tell me you got a great script for me to read."

I did have a twenty-five word or less pitch for *Invasion of the Saber Yuccas*, but quickly thought better of it. "I'm with the public defender's office."

"I played a lawyer once." He struggled with his memory. "No it was a pre-law student in a horror flick. Same thing I guess."

I didn't argue.

"Well looks like I need a lawyer now." He looked me over, shook his head. "A real lawyer."

I started to say something, but he'd turned his back on me.

"You're not even supposed to be here," he said disdainfully, walked out.

Hooray for Hollywood, I guess. I was glad he was gone, his holier-than-thou attitude made me homesick for my little criminals. Murderers returned my phone calls at least. I washed my hands vigorously and walked outside into the party. The mating game of agents, actors and the ambitious locals with "great ideas," intensified now that Kid Coyote was on break. That microphone up on stage sure looked inviting. . . .

"If I had one day to live, I'd spend it in Aguilar," I mouthed to myself. "Because it's so boring here, it would seem like *forever. . . .*"

Yet my eyes turned away from the stage to a twinkling figure of light outside the side window. It almost looked like an angel in the rise and fall of the headlights. An angel? In Aguilar? Suddenly a firm hand came on my shoulder. "You're not even supposed to be here." It was Raphael, the bouncer.

I took one last look around at the Hollywood shuffle, then glanced out the window at the woman in white. But then the truck passed by and she had disappeared. . . .

"You're right," I said, "I'm not supposed to be here."

I headed out the side exit. As the door slammed behind me, another truck rolled by turning the nighttime into day. In the light I could make out Anna Maria sitting on the hood of a pick-up truck.

"Baby lawyer," she shouted. "What's happening?"

I hurried over to her in the sudden darkness. "Not much, how about you?"

"My brother, Enrique, made me come here," she spat out his name with surprising venom. "He works for a liquor distributor. But I didn't even want to be there, by myself. Not without Jesus. I'm waiting for Enrique to finish his delivery so I can go home."

The music started again, loud country music. "That party sucked anyways," she said after a moment. "There was nobody there."

I smiled, about to protest that Sky Roberts and the rest of his bunch were hardly nobodies, but then stopped. "I know what you mean."

As if on cue a limousine pulled up to the front door. The chauffeur opened the back door and this time there was absolutely no mistaking who got out. It was Jack Nicholson, dressed in black, a starlet at his side. And getting out on the other side was Pete Baca. How the hell did Pete know Jack Nicholson? Could all his bullshit actually be true?

Now the chauffeur held the door open for a young woman in a red cocktail dress. Amanda? It couldn't be. But then Pete distinctly said, "Amanda, my darling, may I take you to the ball?"

Pete took her arm and tucked it in his. Amanda gave him her sunniest smile and the two of them followed Jack Nicholson into the Tumbleweeds Club. I wanted to vomit, but nothing would come.

By the time I got home my stomach was hurting worse from hunger pangs than gas pangs. I called Pedro's Pizza but they told me that they weren't delivering pizzas. Somebody had mugged their only driver and they still couldn't hire a replacement.

Chapter 16

Taking a Few Meetings

November 8

AT LEAST MY GLASSES WERE ready. I could see clearly again. Somehow that didn't cheer me up.

There were several messages on my desk. Jovanka wanted to know about the plea. Could I come over to her office and talk to her before docket call at eleven? Dora was in jail. She'd gotten a DWI on the ride home from the party. Would I please come see her? It was an emergency. Amanda was at the TV station. Could I call her there? I tried Amanda first of course, but the line was busy.

I dressed down that day in my oldest suit, wore a funky black and blue tie in honor of the scar. "Quit dressing like a little preppy," Pete had advised me. "Our clients don't want to see no East Coast wimp defending them. They want somebody they can believe in."

I stopped by Pete's office before heading over to the DA's. "What do you think? I bought this suit at a vintage store in Georgetown for a Roaring Twenties party."

"Nuke the tie," he said. "It's got too much of a pattern and shit. People here don't like ties with patterns and shit." He opened up a desk drawer, took out his brown clip-on tie, helped me clip it on, and studied my new look. "Bad news for you about your pants, bro," he said. "You been eating too many chips. Your zipper won't stay up."

I tired in vain to adjust it for a moment. "Fuck it. No one'll notice."

"People might think you're actually getting laid or something."

"I doubt that."

Pete smiled. "By the way, Amanda says hi."

The DA's office was in a two-story brown stucco building without any windows. There were aggressively long logs, vigas, sticking out of the top, almost like a fortress against marauding Apaches. Other than the vigas, the structure was utterly featureless.

The office was on the second floor, above the sheriff's. After crossing between the saber yuccas by the door, someone buzzed me in and I walked up a flight of stairs with round surveillance mirrors in the corners. A grim woman met me at the top, escorted me to an unmarked room at the end of a hallway. She knocked and announced me. "It's the baby lawyer over at the public defender's here to see you."

Jovanka Smith opened the door and motioned me into her office. Brightly lit by a skylight, plants everywhere, including some freshly cut flowers lying in a vase on her desk. Behind her, a Georgia O'Keeffe painting of a cow skull and a white and yellow flower mysteriously floating over some desert hills. On the wall to her left was practically a shrine—letters and photos from victims and their families. This wasn't just a job for her.

On her desk, a picture of her and her own family—only three of them, her, her husband the late judge and a beautiful blond daughter. I took a second look at the beautiful blond daughter, then realized that she was a he, a young boy of about twelve. Jovanka didn't seem the type to let a boy grow hair that long. She had the picture turned away from the desk, facing a wall. There was something familiar about the face.

She gave me a sharp glance, then motioned me into one of her comfortable chairs. I sat, hiding my embarrassing zipper with my briefcase.

She didn't smile. "Here's the other stuff we've got so far. Sorry about the copier."

"I have a terrible time with copiers myself."

"It's hard to get a repair guy this week. We busted the usual guy for a DWI last week. They have to send one down from Albuquerque when something happens down here."

"Couldn't you have given him a furlough?"

"Very funny."

"What about the person who mugged the pizza guy over the weekend? Did you ever catch him?"

She frowned. "We're taking care of that. That's not going to go through your office."

She sat down on the edge of her desk a few feet away from me, waited while I scanned the meticulously organized notebook of police records, forensic records, ballistic records, medical records. I still wasn't sure what a lot of them meant.

"Tea?" she asked.

I nodded. She poured me a cup of Darjeeling into an intricately carved piece of Jemez pottery. I took a sip. Too hot.

She opened another big black notebook labeled "Witnesses," handed it to me as if passing a treasured family photo album.

"What I've just given you is Officer Diamond's statement saying that he positively identified Jesus as a perpetrator. There's also a statement from the other officers, the ambulance driver, and a couple of eyewitnesses that put your boy on the scene with motive and opportunity. . . ."

She had considerately tabbed all the statements, put in a few post-its for the relevant quotes. "I'd say it's open and shut." she said. "More materials keep coming in because we're still investigating, but from what I've heard from the cops, the additional information will make things even worse for your client."

"What exactly are you charging him with?" I asked.

"We've kept it as an open count of murder, but we'll amend soon enough. Do you know what 'open count' of murder means?"

When I shook my head, she stood up, as though lecturing a fifth grader. "It means we can charge him with anything from manslaughter to first degree murder." She sighed. "I suppose we could violate his probation, too, since we arrested him at his girlfriend's house in violation of the conditions of his probation."

"You mean he's not even allowed to get laid?"

She couldn't help but smile. "No sex on probation if you're on house arrest. Unless you're married."

Ouch. I resisted the obvious one-liner responses. "Are you going for the death penalty?"

"You're lucky. He was seventeen when it happened." She laughed for a second. "But usually a life sentence for a kid his age is a one-way ticket."

That was amusing to her somehow.

"But it's all just an accident, damn it! All you've got is him kicking Victor—"

"Come on now. There's more to it than that." She grabbed the notebook from my lap, flipped through the pages. "We've got all kinds of witnesses that say Jesus has always hated poor innocent Victor since Victor . . . uh . . . had a relationship with his girlfriend. Jesus was the one who planned the whole thing. Then there's the drugs and some other items still under investigation."

"Other items?"

"Ongoing investigation. You'll know when we know. But your boy is looking at serious time. That's all you need concern yourself with at this point."

"Don't you still have to convict him first?"

"Dan, please don't insult my intelligence." She smiled warmly, as if trying to be helpful. "I'm giving you a chance to save his life here because I don't want to waste the taxpayer's money on a full-blown trial. And I think I have a duty as an officer of the court to tell you that I don't think you have what it takes to save your client's life."

That was a new one on me. "You have to know our decision today?"

"I told you I need to know by docket call at eleven. You still have some time to talk to him."

I walked to the door, then turned to face her. "Why do you hate Jesus so much?"

"You ever lose anyone in your family?"

"No."

"I moved out here for my husband, a local boy. I met him when he was over in Europe in the military. He was a DA here. Then a judge. He got killed by a bunch of punks just like Jesus, during a break-in. They never caught those kids. . . ."

She didn't say anything further. I didn't want her to finish her sentence.

"If there's one thing I hate," she said at last. "It's kids who kill. After that, I went to law school so I could come back here to try to bring justice to this part of my adopted country."

"Have you succeeded?" I asked.

"Not yet."

• • • •

"One on one, and two on one. . . ."

Clint greeted me inside the jail. "Yvonne's already bringing Dora down," he said before I could ask for Jesus. "You're really lucky you caught me in a good mood today. I'm letting you use the meeting rooms again."

Thank God for small favors. Yvonne came down the stairs with

Dora. Even in her jail uniform, Dora still had an aura. The orange khaki jumpsuit was unbuttoned as far as it would go without her breasts falling out. She had the bottom of the jumpsuit hiked up to her knees. I don't know how she did it, but the rose tattoo now matched the orange outfit.

I held my notebook tightly over my crotch as we walked into the interview room and sat down. Dora started talking before I even said hello. "This is a bullshit charge! I wasn't even fucking driving! It was some asshole from the party. He made me switch seats because he said he didn't have a license."

I wasn't officially her lawyer and I wanted nothing to do with her case anyway. "So why did you call me?"

"Sky Roberts is in here now."

"So?"

"He was there that night. He was the one who threw Victor down."

So that was the reason for his arrest. "Why would he do that?"

"The usual, drug deal gone bad. Guess he wants to be a cholo or something. He's got all kinds of money and he still pretends to be one of us."

"I confused him with your brother Joey that night at the Tumbleweeds."

"My brother wouldn't hurt a fly." She smiled. "The fly could probably kick his ass."

"So about Sky—"

The mention of his name set off something in her mind. "And you know the best part? He's a shitty lay. Got a real small dick."

More information than I needed, especially with a broken zipper. "Why are you telling me this?"

She leaned over, that orange rose almost in my face. I could smell an intoxicating mixture of lingering perfume and a sweaty jail. It was difficult, but I leaned back, politely focused on the crack in the wall.

"I heard about your run-in with him. He's talking about how his bodyguard kicked your ass."

There wasn't a real response to that. "That's what bodyguards do for a living."

"So what do you do for a living?"

"Lawyer, I hope," I said. "I'm not your lawyer as far as I know."

"Oh I know that," she smiled. "I'll get somebody good, don't worry about me."

"So why do you want to see me if I'm not even your lawyer?"

"You're Jesus's lawyer, no?"

I nodded.

"So Jesus's lawyer, are you going to plead him?"

"That's really not your business. Anyways it's up to him."

She double-checked that the door was closed. "Don't plead him."

"Why not?"

"Jesus didn't kill him."

I jerked back in my chair and almost hit my head against the wall. "What?"

"He didn't kill Victor."

"How'd you know he didn't kill Victor?"

"I was there. I know he left with Joey."

Joey was certainly no alibi witness, but with his sister backing up his story. . . .

"So who killed Victor?"

There were those crooked teeth again. "I don't know if I can tell you yet. Any of it."

"Why not?"

"Shit, maybe I killed him." She smiled. . . .

I tried to look into those steely eyes, but I couldn't maintain my gaze. My eyes drifted down to her long, lean calves poking out of the bottom of her jumpsuit. A fatal kick to the left temple was certainly within their power. She laughed after a second, as if she'd been playing me. "Then again, maybe not. I don't know if you can handle it, ese. We'll let you know when we're ready."

Without another word, she walked out the door. I would have followed her but I suddenly remembered about my fly. Before I could get myself zipped up she had the female guard escort her up the stairs. She yelled something over her shoulder about "calling me" but I couldn't make it out. It reminded me of Mae West saying, "Why don't you come up and see me sometime," but I'm sure Mae never said it on her way up to the fourth floor of the women's jail.

• • • •

"Jesus," I said before he had even sat down. "We have to decide in the next few minutes whether to accept the DA's offer of eighteen years as an adult for murder."

"Still eighteen years? Suppose I get married?"

"We're not going through that again. Eighteen years, Department of Corrections. I guess that means out in nine—if you're convicted you get life. Life means life. Take it or leave it."

He chewed his lip, then shrugged.

"Dora just told me that you didn't do it," I said.

He played with his glasses for a moment. Admitting he wasn't really a killer was almost embarrassing for him, like me telling my parents I didn't get into Georgetown after all.

"She's right," he said at last. "I didn't kill nobody."

"You were with Joey all night, weren't you?"

"Yes, I was with Joey when it all went down. We were screwing around in the mesa looking for snakes."

"So why have you been fucking with me?"

"There's a whole lotta shit going on here." He didn't elaborate.

I waited for a beat. Still nothing. What the hell did I have to do to get these people to trust me?

"Even if you didn't do it," I said at last, grasping at straws. "They might still get you as an accessory. But I don't know anything because you haven't told me shit."

"I don't have to tell you shit. That's the rules. Besides I don't want to plead. I need some time to work this all out. Let's take it to trial."

"Are you sure? This isn't like choosing between red and green chile on your burrito."

He drew me closer. "I'll tell you why, man. Why I really want to go through with this. Since I got in here I'm changing my life around." He lowered his voice. "I started reading the Bible. I believe it, man."

I looked at him. He sounded sincere enough.

"A few nights ago, you know what happened? I had a vision. Like when you're on peyote and shit, except like I was totally straight. You know, one of those times when you see and hear things."

"And?"

"I don't really want to go into it, man, 'cause it was kind of personal and shit. But I know you're going to win this case and get me off. I just know it." He smiled again. "You still have no fucking clue what's going on here, but you're my lawyer. You work for me, not the other way around. If I say you gotta take it to trial because I had a vision—then you got to take it to trial. Comprende? My mind is made up."

He stood up. "Remember what happened to your little girl at the dance. Ese, you owe me one."

He sure had me there. For the second time that day, someone was out the door before I could come up with some kind of response.

I sat alone for a minute in the waiting room. I closed my eyes, tried to pray, tried to see the vision that Jesus had seen. Please lord, help me win this case. Give me strength. Give me something.

No answer.

I tried again, but remembered Shakespeare. "My words above, my thoughts remain below, words without thoughts never to heaven go," or some shit like that.

In the waiting area, Clint pressed the elevator button as Jesus stood impassively. I nodded at him one more time. Jesus called out with a big grin, "Hey, by the way, pendejo, your fly's open."

Chapter 17

Deep Dockets

THE COURTROOM GALLERY BRIMMED WITH defendants out on bond and their families.

I had two quick sentencings scheduled. One a nineteen-year-old parole violator, wore a shirt reading:

UNDERACHIEVER AND PROUD OF IT

Amanda stood in the back talking to Pete. Her camera was off but she took notes while touching him on the arm. I turned away when she looked up.

The prosecutors sat erect at the table, wearing their Fighting 14th outfits. Jovanka leaned over toward me. "Well?"

"I think we're taking it to trial."

"You think? Have you talked with your client about this?"

"It was his idea."

"You're fucking taking it to trial?" Pete, who had finished chatting up Amanda, now stood right behind me. "Are you smoking the Acequia Madre loco weed?"

"He says he didn't do it. He wants a trial."

"He says he didn't do it," Pete mimicked. "Yeah, right. I heard that before. I could win his trial; I don't know if you're ready yet."

"Do I have a choice?"

"If your client says he wants a trial, then that's what he gets."

I had never seen that look on Pete before. Genuine surprise, as if the computer had just checkmated him in four moves. He shook his head. "I didn't think you'd have the balls to actually go through with it. I'll have to call the main office to get rid of all my shit, so I can hold your dick for you. A juvie case, shit. . . ."

My cheeks reddened, as if I'd been slapped. "Have I done something wrong?"

"You're letting your client run the show too much. Plus you're letting Jovanka take advantage of your not knowing what the fuck is going on."

"So what do I do?"

"Just get it set up for trial and we'll see what happens."

I turned and walked past Amanda without acknowledging her. For a moment I desperately wanted to tell her what Jesus had told me. I knew something important. She'd have to talk to me now. But I remembered Jesus and the Canons of Professional Responsibility. I remained silent.

I tapped Jesus on the shoulder. "I might not be your lawyer anymore after today."

He shook his head. "You don't understand, bro. You got to be my lawyer." He leaned close enough to whisper in my ear. "You were in my vision, too."

He handed me a piece of notebook paper with a drawing scribbled on it—it was of Clark Kent opening up his button-down shirt, to reveal the blue tights and the top of an "S." I crumpled the drawing into my pocket when everyone rose for Judge Perez's entrance.

My two simple sentencings were over quickly and I sat back down in the jury box next to Jesus. I looked down on the docket list and turned page after page until we'd get to Jesus.

Next came the famous/infamous Sky Roberts, who stood by a tanned lawyer named Rose, in an olive suit and a tie that looked hand-drawn by Picasso himself. The lawyer looked even more uneasy than Sky.

"Are you a member of the New Mexico bar, Mr. Rose?" the judge asked.

"No your honor, but I've got my own practice in Beverly Hills, California on Wilshire. I'm in the process of getting admitted pro hac vice—"

The judge banged down his gavel. He twiddled with the end of his mustache, almost like an old time melodrama villain.

"Beverly Hills?" He said after a moment. "Things here are more like the Beverly Hillbillies. So I take your answer as a 'no.' Pete, I want you to come up here and show Mr. Rose how us hillbillies do an arraignment."

Pete clipped on his own tie and joined them at the podium. He put his hand on Rose's shoulder, indicating who the boss was. "In order to avoid any potential conflicts," he began. "I'm only standing in for the purposes of arraignment. We waive the reading of the information and plead not guilty and ask that, since Mr. Sky Roberts has no prior criminal record before this court, he be released on his own recognizance."

"Your Honor, I oppose that," Merril said. "Just because he's some kind of movie star doesn't give him any special standing here. In addition to this charge, our investigation in the Victor Slade murder indicates that Mr. Roberts may be connected with other criminal activities related to that case."

Judge Perez was not happy. "Are you pressing charges or tossing out allegations?"

"We're not prepared to do so at this time, but we will be pressing charges soon."

"Is this all based on information from the same mysterious informant?" the judge asked.

"Your Honor," Pete said before Merril could respond, "I don't care if they charge Mr. Roberts with conspiracy in the Kennedy assassination. In fact, Mr. Merril did exactly that to a drunk driving defendant a year ago. But until they've something stronger than allegations, my client—excuse me—Mr. Rose's client, should be free to go."

"Your Honor!" Merril grabbed his podium as if he were about to throw it at the judge. "That's totally—"

Judge Perez lifted his gavel, banged both counsels into silence. "Counsel, I have made my decision. Defendant is free to go, but must remain within the jurisdiction and is under work release. I'll send you a trial setting soon."

Rose looked at the judge. "Could my client be free to return home to Los Angeles? I will personally vouch—"

There was something about Rose that irritated the judge. "I don't know you sir. I don't care if you're the best damn entertainment lawyer on Wilshire, wherever that is. Things operate, shall we say, a little differently down here. Mr. Roberts, if you or your lawyer mess up while on you're out own recognizance here in the confines of beautiful Aguilar County, I'll have you sharing a small cell with someone with a chronic snoring and flatulence problem. Some of the people you meet in that facility might also have some more interesting . . . ah . . . appetites that I don't think a nice little surfer boy would cotton to. Am I understood?"

Sky nodded.

"The tape recorder can't see you nod, boy. I asked you if I am understood.'"

"Yes, sir," Sky said, wringing his hands. "But—"

The judge cut him off. "You folks best remember one thing when you deal with me: There's no such thing as a Mexican Santa Claus."

Clint took the handcuffs off, and Pete shook Sky's hand. Amanda rushed over to them.

"No comment," Rose said.

As Amanda turned the camera off, Sky turned to Rose. "You don't know shit about court here in the boonies. Tell the studio I want the guy in the clip-on tie."

Pete laughed. "Just doing my job." He took off his tie, stuffed it in his pocket.

Seeing that there was nothing exciting to emerge from Rose's mouth, Amanda turned the camera back to the front of the court.

Jesus came a few cases later. When his name was called, I felt all eyes on my back, including the camera's. My bowels tightened.

"Do you want to waive reading of the criminal information?" the judge asked.

I froze.

"He waives it, Your Honor!" Pete shouted from the back of the room.

"How do you plead, then?"

"Not guilty, Your Honor," I said with pride, hoping that Amanda had failed to record the first part.

"Counsel," the judge played with his gavel. "I'll have my secretary send you the gift certificate."

"Gift certificate?"

"For young lawyers like yourself who are taking their first case to trial, I send a gift certificate from Aguilar Bookstore in the mall. There's always a copy of a book there, *The Student's Guide to Trial Practice*. I wrote it twenty years ago. It's written for high school students, but I strongly suggest you read it before you come into my courtroom again. I expect you to pay for it yourself, now son because—"

"There's no Mexican Santa Claus," I interrupted, much to his dismay. "I heard you the last time, your Honor."

I sat down as they took Jesus back into jail.

"By the way," the judge said, "you should have asked that your client be released while waiting for trial. Not that he had a chance of getting out while I'm his judge."

Amanda had all of this on tape and it would be broadcast all over New Mexico. Just what I needed.

Amanda glanced my way as I passed. "No comment," I said.

Part II

Chapter 18

Hot Tamales

November 9

THE NEXT MORNING ON MY way to work I passed Jovanka and Merril talking outside the fortress. I waved. They waved back, even smiled warmly at me. Maybe there was something to this small town charm after all.

Pete wasn't inside, but he'd left a xerox copy of an old "Motion for Competency/Amenability" with a post-it telling me to make one for Jesus. There were several pages of case law and cites, but all I had to do was go into the computer, hit "search and replace" a few times and voila I had done my first bit of legal research and writing since K Street.

So far so good. . . .

Once I sat down at my desk, it was time to get organized. I'd do what worked in law school, at least at first. I made an outline that reduced everything to a single page, then memorized the page. I remembered being really organized for one class, memorizing the first letter of every line in the outline, then turning the letters into a word. Unfortunately the word was "vigsapuhfdb."

The professor gave only one letter when grading my exam: "C." Still, it was a noble start. I put a Roman numeral "I" and wrote COMPETENCY/AMENABILITY HEARING. Feeling motivated, I called Dr. Marianne Romero, the psychologist on retainer to the Department, to testify about Jesus's "mental state" at the competency/amenability hearing. This vision thing of his was creepy; I didn't want to get blindsided by some psychological revelation. I kidded myself that anyone who wanted me to be his lawyer in a case like this had to be crazy.

I would try anything if it would work. Dr. Romero told me she'd set up an appointment with Jesus.

"How long will the testing take?" I asked her.

"We administer a battery of tests over several days." She replied with just the hint of a high class Castellan accent.

"Is there anything I should say to him beforehand?"

"As a matter of fact," she said, "I know Jovanka Smith and how she treats these tests. If she thinks you're coaching him on how to answer, she'll kill you at a hearing."

"So what should I do?"

"Once I start testing, avoid him until I've finished. No contact. Trust me on this."

I hung up. That did it for Roman Numeral I.

I put down a "II' and wrote MURDER TRIAL. Under II, I wrote:

A. Find out from Jesus what's really going on (after Dr. Romero has finished testing).
B. Talk to Anna Maria.
C. Talk to this Guillermo guy from the party.
D. Talk to Sky Roberts.
E. Find out about the mysterious shooter of Diamond.
F. Find out why Jovanka is playing games with me.
G. Find Joey. He knows something.
H. Get Dora to trust me. She knows something about Roberts and Joey.
I. Talk to the judge and try to get in his good graces.
J. Talk to all the experts, i.e., the coroners and the ballistics people. (None of that stuff makes sense to me). Hell, I'm on a roll, might as well shoot for bigger game.
K. Get Amanda to fall madly in love with me.
L. Get a life.

I looked it over again. It might as well read VIGSAPUHFDB.

Before I could make my first call, the temp secretary knocked on the door and announced I had a visitor. I was surprised to see Jesus's mother, Senora Villalobos, with a crockpot and a tin filled with little foil-wrapped packages.

"Daniel, I want to thank you for all you've done for my Jesus." She handed me one of the foil packages. "It's a tamale."

Before I could respond, Pete had entered the building as if he had smelt the tamale all the way from the depths of the jail. Senora Villalobos quickly put a tamale in his hand.

"We're not allowed to take money or gifts from our clients," Pete said, "but there's a tamale-exception to the anti-donation clause."

He wolfed down one and then another. "Guess there's no more evidence, anyway."

I sniffed before taking a bite, Senora Villalobos laughed at me. "Don't eat the corn husk, mi hijo." She opened the crockpot and began dishing out something else.

"What's that?"

"Menudo. It's got tripe and pig's feet. You'll love it."

I sighed and began to eat the menudo. The slippery feel of the tripe against the back of my throat was mildly off-putting, but it I quickly learned to love it by the second slurp.

"Good menudo, no?" She asked, filling my cup with some more. "Keep eating, mi hijo. There's plenty more."

She stirred the pot as Pete came back to thirds, or was it fourths. "Senor Bac, my boy Jesus wants to keep Daniel as his lawyer. He don't want no one else."

Pete turned, put his hand on her shoulder. "We'll do what we can. You get that competency motion done, Dan?"

I nodded.

She removed his hand, thrust another tamale into it starting talking. "My Chuwy had a powerful dream and I believe in dreams like that. Jesus' dream was that he was falling into the fires of hell. Just before the flames were to burn him up, Daniel flew out of the sky like an angel scooped him up and flew him back to safety."

"Super," I said, shuffling uncomfortably.

"He's definitely his lawyer through the next hearing," Pete said. "After that, I'll see what I can do."

She looked choked up. "Daniel cares, none of you lawyers ever cared about my Jesus before."

"Hey, I was the one that got him off a battery a couple of years ago," Pete said.

"Yeah, but you just pled him the next time around."

"That's cuz he was guilty."

"But he said he was innocent!"

"He was lying."

"No. Mi hijo always tells the truth. You people just don't know when to believe him."

• • • •

Later, I talked to Jesus and told him that he would be meeting with Dr. Romero soon and that I wouldn't be able to visit with him for awhile.

"I'll miss you," he said with half a smirk.

"Yeah, right. What about—"

"My mom's the only one who can see me . . . they don't let my Anna Maria in until we tie the knot for reals."

"Well, cooperate with Dr. Romero when she starts her testing."

"What should I tell her?"

"Tell her the truth."

Chapter 19

Socks Appeal

THE NEXT MORNING, NOVEMBER 11, I received word that Jesus's competency hearing was set for December 22 before someone named Judge Henry in someplace called "T or C." Apparently Judge Perez was taking a vacation or perhaps he didn't want to sit through another one of my hearings if he could help it.

I found Pete at the jail flirting with Veronica over her opened copy of *The Decline and Fall of the Roman Empire*.

"Want to see my purple heart?" he asked. "I'll show you my scar."

She laughed. After a moment he came over and joined me, exaggerating his limp, probably for her benefit.

"War injury?" I asked.

"I was a pilot for a while in the reserves. Seems like they called my unit up whenever heavy shit was going down."

"Are you still in?"

"Stupid question," he said, swinging his pony tail.

"What's a 'T or C?'" I asked Pete, grabbing his pony tail to get his attention.

"A town named after the old television show from the fifties, *Truth or Consequences*," he said, mildly irritated. "Really. The network had some contest or something and gave out a prize for the first town that changed their name. Look at a map if you don't believe me. It's right on the Rio, about an hour north of Cruces."

He leaned back toward Veronica. "One time one of those traveling preachers came by the courthouse. He kept yelling, 'All of you sinners will have to face truth or consequences.' Finally I yelled at him, 'Ese, it's three hours down the road that way.'"

I laughed politely. "Anything else I got to worry about?"

He pointed to Veronica's jail log. "Guillermo got busted and he's got a preliminary hearing in a coupla days."

"What did he get busted on?"

"Does it matter?" He smiled. "He's got the twenty-five year bitch coming on, no matter what. I passed it off to one of the conflict attorneys. They do the hearings on public defender clients when there are conflicts. Most of them are great. But I found one who shouldn't give you any trouble."

He gave Veronica a friendly punch on the shoulder, "Thanks for the heads up on Guillermo." She gave the pony tail a friendly tug.

"Can I see him?" I said, anxious to get this over with.

"He's got to get through his prelim first," said Pete, laughing. "And you guys say that nothing ever happens in small towns."

Guillermo's prelim came quickly. Too quickly. On my way over to the hearing, I walked out into a parking lot filled with police cars, lights flashing. Two knots of people faced each other, talking some serious trash. A fleshy woman pushed a skinny man to the ground. He bounced right up and stabbed her arm with a small knife. She pulled the knife out easily, swung it right back at him. Others joined the fight.

I tried to sneak over to the Magistrate Court, keeping as far away from the fists, bodies, bottles at the other side of the parking lot.

A body thudded to the pavement right in front of me. The body twitched for a moment. He was still alive, right?

Some screams and more breaking glass, then smoke.

Amanda stood outside our office, her camera running. This was the closest thing to combat journalism that she'd ever get, and she handled it like a pro. A bottle almost hit her. She dropped her camera, lost her balance.

I hurried over to Amanda who sprawled in a pile with her equipment on the pavement. I gave her my hand, made sure she was all right.

Before she could respond, Pete hurried outside, helped her put her camera back together. He glared at everyone who came close to her. His glare worked better than a forcefield, the fighting shifted to another part of the lot. After mumbling a "thanks" to both of us, she clicked on her red camera light.

The cops finally took control of the situation. Sheriff's deputies, city cops, and the black-uniformed state police swarmed the parking lots. They took the fleshy woman and the skinny man with the knife into custody, along with half the other people in town.

A short, heavy-set man with a cane began rushing around, handing out his card to those being arrested. He put one into my hand as I got up from the pavement. BONILLA BAIL BONDS, it read.

"Call me if you need help," he said, then went back to the people being taken to jail, making sure they all had his card. Who said crime didn't pay?

Magistrate Court was an old decaying building across Oil Avenue—a crumbling brick facade barely supported the red tile roof. Once this had been the county historical museum. The courtroom wall still had a magnificent mural depicting the founding of the West, with cowboys, Native Americans, farmers, ranchers and oil people all holding hands.

Thankfully, Gardea frisked every one going inside. He smiled at me, waved me through. I didn't know whether to take that as a complement.

The courtroom was already filled to capacity. On one side were men from Guillermo's family, all of them wearing black T-shirts and jeans. Some had smuggled in lunch and snuck a few bites. Guillermo was able to get more family to his prelim than most bar mitzvahs. And the food was probably better, too.

The other side of the aisle accommodated Victor's family and friends, all dressed in white. I recognized the blond woman from the hospital, and a few others. I was happy that Aryan Eddie was nowhere to be seen.

Walking down the aisle between the two factions, everyone there stared at me, looking at my feet. I remembered my Santa Fe-style green chile socks my mother had bought me as a going away present. Green chiles and red paisleys on a sky blue background. Fashion faux pas.

I sat down, watched Amanda make her way into the courtroom. Her conservative outfit was now straightened. Her camera had been checked at the door; it was not allowed in Magistrate Court. She glumly walked down the aisle to the only seat left, the one next to me.

The Magistrate called the court to order. He was a cowboy, a big man named Winston who looked like he had indeed stepped right off a cigarette billboard and put on a robe. A cop up to the time he ran for office, he'd won on the platform that Magistrate Court wasn't a court of "guilt or innocence, it was a court for justice," whatever that meant. The fourteenth district had abandoned grand juries because of the expense, viewing preliminary hearings as the fastest, cheapest way to get a defendant bound over for trial in district court.

After half an hour of anticipation . . . Guillermo entered the arena, escorted by Clint, Gardea and four other guards I'd never seen before. If Jesus was a rock star after his arrest, Guillermo was the Keith Richards of crime. In his fifties, with deep lines down his face and stringy salt and pepper hair, this was a man who had done everything and only been caught for some of it.

For the preliminary hearing Guillermo was clean-shaven and in civilian clothes, a black T-shirt and jeans, like the rest of his family. When Clint took off the handcuffs, Guillermo turned around and raised his fist at his supporters.

Pete had been right. Guillermo did indeed have his name tattooed on his right forearm. Not that anyone in the room could have forgotten his name.

I crossed my legs. Amanda looked at my socks and smiled. "I like the way you're just blending." She reached into her purse and pulled out a handkerchief with the same Chile and paisley pattern.

"You seem to be doing a better job of it than me," I said, coldly.

She didn't respond, stared up at the proceedings. We both looked at the conflict attorney, Woodford, an aging hippy, complete with gray pony tail.

"Your honor," Woodford began in a thick New York accent that hadn't been jettisoned after twenty years in the valley. He nervously glanced around the room at the volatile crowd. "We need to talk with you in chambers."

Court adjourned, security remained tight. I looked around, Amanda and I might have been the only people in the room without criminal records.

As we waited, Amanda nudged me, wrote down questions on her pad and showed them to me. She asked me about the judge, the officers, and the procedure. I wrote down my replies, reluctantly at first, but soon I started enjoying myself. She looked at me eagerly.

I decided to switch gears. I wrote down the oldest lawyer joke in the world, the one about sharks giving lawyers a wide berth because of "professional courtesy."

She snickered, even though she'd heard it before of course. A man next to her gave her a dirty look. She nodded politely to him, than smiled at me.

Screw physical appearance. The first thing I look for in a woman is a sense of humor, defined by the ability to laugh at my jokes.

After a nearly an hour, and a dozen more handwritten jokes passed back and forth, the parties returned. The magistrate announced that a plea agreement had been ironed out—Guillermo was bound over on trafficking only, all other counts were dismissed. Not that it mattered, he had so many "bitches," he would never get out after this one.

Guillermo took it all in stride as the magistrate recounted the terms of the agreement. It was just another plea to him in yet another courtroom.

"What does that mean for your client?" Amanda wrote to me, still conscious of the rough crowd surrounding us.

"I don't know."

I said nothing for a moment, stared at the cops as they dragged away Guillermo. Gardea was a little rough with him, murmuring came from the audience. The murmuring slowly rose up into cursing. . . .

Amanda and I held our breath. . . .

Clint followed behind the transport party, covered their back, his finger on his holster.

The crowd looked uneasy until the door slammed shut. . . .

Clint looked at everyone for a long, long beat. He held up his finger until a beep came on his walkie-talkie. He listened for another beat, then looked up at the crowd. "Y'all can go now."

Amanda and I finally exhaled . . . Guillermo had left the building.

Before I could say another word to Amanda, she was already up, interviewing Woodford outside in the foyer. On camera, he looked like a deer in the headlights.

She frowned and quickly cut short the interview. Pete wandered by and she asked him a few questions as a "criminal law expert."

He touched her on the elbow as she talked. She didn't pull away. I tried to wait for them, but it looked like the interview would take awhile . . .

That night on the news—footage of the riot. After some statements by the cops, Pete graced my screen for a full sixty seconds talking about the causes and the effects of crime in the valley. "This town is about to explode!" he said into the camera. Amanda nodded. Damn, Pete was good.

"We'll have part two of this exclusive interview tomorrow night." She said, signing off.

Chapter 20

How Low Can You Go?

THE NEXT MORNING I PACED around my office. Guillermo could talk to me now, right? His guilty plea waived his Fifth Amendment rights, right? Since he was probably looking at prison, I better find out what he knew about Jesus before he got sent up forever.

But talking to Guillermo? In person? I paced faster and faster, pulsating with nervous energy. Finally I took a deep breath, or two or three.

I certainly didn't want to do this alone, but Pete's door was shut tight. Sounds of movement came from inside. I knocked a few times before he finally opened the door.

Amanda was already inside, looking like she had hastily moved to the other chair the moment I knocked. Her pink outfit looked a little rumpled. She didn't say anything, just stared out the window.

"Yeah?" Pete asked, not happy.

I stared at him, stared at her as I tried to figure out the situation. No, it can't be! Not here! Not the two of them!

I needed to say something, but I didn't want to ask the obvious. Were you with her? In here? Instead I mumbled something like, "I need to know what Guillermo knows about Jesus." I tried to catch Amanda's eye over Pete's shoulder.

Amanda in his office? It was a body blow. I felt like throwing up. This hurt worse than the face-plant in the Acequia.

"So?"

"I uhhh . . . need to talk to Guillermo, before he goes to prison."

"You need me to hold your dick for you?"

"I need a translator."

He glanced down at my Italian shoes. "You got a pair of sneakers in the car?"

"I think so. Why?"

"You don't want to wear those shoes where we're going," he said. He looked back at Amanda, smiled. "Give me about twenty more minutes."

He slammed the door in my face.

I stumbled over to the jail in a daze. If I could lock myself in there for the rest of my life, shit I would do it in a heartbeat.

Veronica and Gardea were finished with the paperwork on another round of prisoners. Not an auspicious sign.

Because of the crowds, Clint made me wait in the jail interview room by myself until Pete arrived to take me down. I shut the door, hoped that it never opened again.

I took out my cell phone, dialed my mother's number.

It was scratchy. "Shepard and Shepard," the receptionist said.

"It's Dan . . . her son. Is my mom there?"

The static got stronger. I couldn't hear the receptionist's reply. Then the phone went dead. The walls were too thick. . . .

In rage, I threw the phone against the wall. It shattered on impact, shards of phone lined the edge of the wall.

The door clicked open. Clint entered, Pete right behind him.

"You alright, baby lawyer?" Clint said. "You having a breakdown or something?"

"Just take me down," I said, picking up the pieces of the phone, stuffing them into my pocket. Maybe I could still put them back together. "Let's get this over with."

"Hold on for a second," Clint said. "His lawyer is already down there—it's pretty full up."

Pretty full up, I didn't like the sound of that.

"How many inmates, ah, residents do you have down there right now?" I asked Clint.

"Three—Guillermo, you know. Kent, killed a little girl after he raped her, and Juan Tabo raped a whole bunch of people over in Mexico. They're all just dying to meet you. We always got room for one more."

Two deputies met us and we took the elevator down. As a strange sort of safety measure, there was nothing to mark each floor. Clint pressed a lever, and counted "one, one thousand; two, one thousand; three," until he abruptly stopped the elevator, then turned a special key. The elevator door creaked open to reveal. . . .

A basement, dimly lit and reeking of the usual jail smell, mixed in with human waste. Three small cells were clumped at the end of the hall. The left one held Kent, who sat upright in his bunk in the lotus position. Tabo paced in a tight circle on the left. The floor in front of his cell was damp, with scattered islands of unidentified debris.

"We had the trusties clean this floor this morning and it was spotless," Clint said. "Ol' Juan here gets a big thrill out of messing up the floor with whatever he can get his hands on."

Tabo glared at Clint through the iron bars, muttered a string of Spanish epithets.

Clint turned his back on him and escorted us to the next cell. Pete laughed as I stepped gingerly over some of Tabo's landscaping. "Bet you're glad you changed your shoes, no?"

At the end of the hall by Guillermo's cell was Woodford, Guillermo's conflict attorney. Up close, Woodford had the tired look of someone who had hung in for a few conflicts too many. Conflict attorneys only got about six hundred dollars a case, flat fee. With someone like Guillermo that usually amounted to about a dollar an hour.

I could see why Pete had selected him. Woodford didn't even want to go inside the cell with Guillermo. That was fine with all concerned.

"Up close and personal here," Pete said. "Clint, why don't you lock us in with him and wait over by the elevator. Baby lawyer here wants to get to know Guillermo a little better."

"Couldn't we just talk to him through the bars?" I asked.

Before Pete could reply, Clint opened the door. "It's up to you," Clint said.

"Call me if you need me—" Woodford said, remaining safely outside.

I stared at Guillermo. If his own lawyer didn't want to be there. . . . I took a deep breath, then another, then finally crossed into the cell. The door clanged shut behind me and the guards then retreated the long, damp forty feet to the elevator. For the first time in my life I looked out from the inside of a jail cell. I wondered if it would be the last.

Guillermo sat on his cot, looking slightly dazed, but otherwise relaxed. He fiddled absentmindedly with the tattoo on his arm as if it was still fresh. He really did look like one of the Rolling Stones after a particularly long show and even longer post-show party. He had no personal possessions but there was a stack of mail, (fan mail?) some opened, lying at his feet. One woman had even sent him a naked picture of herself. Not bad. . . .

He was glad to see Pete. The two of them went way back.

He ignored me for a moment, using a magic marker to draw a garden of flowers on the outside on a large white manila envelope. His flowers had green stems intricately wrapped around the mailing address. The blooms themselves were blood red and bloomed right below the return address that was in big block letters. GUILLERMO-Level D."

"That's beautiful," I said as he continued coloring in the blooms with a red marker.

He looked up at me strangely, as if he'd seen me before. "Mucho gracias," he said after a few seconds, then picked up another marker. If the same drawing had been on canvas, he could have sold it for some serious bucks to an art collector on either coast.

Pete introduced me to Guillermo in Spanish. Guillermo nodded, he knew the score. Woodford stared down the hallway toward the elevator.

"How does a guy who can do this wind up in here?" I asked.

Pete thought for a moment. "Let's just say he started small—a pretty girl who just happened to be fourteen."

He didn't have to fill in the details.

"It was fourth degree so he was only supposed to serve eighteen months. But he was inside during one of those riots. You heard about that one, where they played volleyball with people's heads and shit?"

I nodded politely. There had been several.

"Think about living through that shit." Pete looked at me. "He did what he had to do. There were a lot of rumors, that he did some major, major shit in there during the riots; but no one rats on anyone on the inside, so nothing happened to him. I heard he was involved with those mass graves in Juarez, some of that other shit in El Paso. The only reason he let himself get picked up again is cause he probably feels homesick for the joint."

I was so close to Guillermo I could hear his heartbeat. In his dark eyes, I saw my own reflection in the red exit light. This was someone who had been there. There was an aura about him. This was Jesus Villalobos if he didn't shape up and it was not a pretty picture.

Tabo wailed in the next cell over. Time to move things along. "What was he doing at the party?"

There was a brief exchange, then Guillermo laughed and said something else to Pete. "Like I said, he does what he had to do. Drug dealing, pimping, whatever."

"What happened on the night of the murder?"

"He says it started all right, then it got a little out of hand."

"People always get killed at parties he goes to?"

"No big thing to him."

Pete resumed with Guillermo in Spanish, then Guillermo recounted the story slowly, even laboriously. Pete asked him for some details and Guillermo kept pushing on. He must have said things Pete had never heard before, because Pete kept pressing him, acted surprised, almost shocked, by Guillermo's answers. After about five minutes, Pete looked over at me and shook his head. He looked nearly as dazed as Guillermo.

"What did he say?" I asked.

"He's changing his story every two minutes—there's a lot of . . . pressure on him. By the time the DA gets through with him, he'll be saying you were the murderer."

I looked around the cell with its exposed cinderblocks and damp floor. I was as far away from K Street as I had ever been, in a place that I had never imagined that I would ever, ever go. This was it, rock bottom! Literally. Yet instead of feeling trapped, I felt alive, filled with adrenaline. . . .

A strange electricity surged through my body, as if Guillermo's aura passed through me. My own petty problems seemed like such bullshit when I could hear the heartbeat of a Guillermo. I felt like I had bungee jumped into hell.

"Maybe I am the murderer," I said out loud, as if someone else had taken over my body. "Maybe I am."

Guillermo muttered something about me being "loco."

"I'm loco alright."

Pete stared at me as if he didn't know me anymore. Shit I didn't know me anymore. Suddenly the elevator clicked open. Clint strode purposely down the hallway, his footsteps echoing off the cinderblocks.

Woodford awoke with a start. "We're done here?"

He shook Guillermo's hand through the bars and reminded him about the prelim in creeky Brooklyn accented Spanish.

I stared at the old man. Woodford. He was nice enough, but his heart wasn't in it anymore. I don't know which scared me more—Guillermo or the prospect of ending up like Woodford.

"Visiting hours are over," Clint said, opening the bars. "It's a shift change. You know the rules; we have to go back up."

Another guard came in to make sure the prisoner stayed put. He needn't have bothered. Guillermo had gone back to coloring in the rose on the envelop, utterly oblivious to the opened door.

After carefully navigating the hallway by Tabo's cell, Clint led us into the unmarked elevator and manipulated the levers. We started to rise again. The bungee cord tugged me out of the depths and back into my old life.

"I don't understand how you guys defend garbage like that," Clint said over the din of the elevator. "All those guys should be taken behind a tree and . . . save us all the headache."

Woodford said nothing. As long as he got his six hundred bucks he didn't care one way or the other. But Pete took the bait. . . .

"I'm there to make sure that garbage like that get a fair fucking trial," Pete said. "They have the same fucking rights as anybody else. And if you've got a problem with equal justice under the law, you can take that silver star of yours and jam it all the way up your asshole."

Clint turned to him, "But—"

"You ever been up to a prison right after a riot?" asked Pete, still hot. "Ever walked through all the severed fucking heads and arms lying on the floor, floating in a pool of blood and piss? The day you see something like that, you'll know how I can defend someone who's innocent until proven guilty beyond a reasonable fucking doubt. Now shut the fuck up."

Clint stayed shut. When we mysteriously arrived at the proper floor, he manipulated the levers again and let us out. I reached into my pocket. The remnants of my broken phone were still there. I threw them in the dumpster outside the jail.

"Part II" of Amanda's exclusive interview with Pete ran that night. He repeated his speech about the riots and reasonable doubt, without the swear words this time. I was too drained to pay attention.

That night, half asleep, I pictured Amanda back in Pete's office. She interviewed him about something and he glowed in the reflection of a hundred bright lights. She nodded at him while he talked, enraptured by whatever brilliant observation he was making about the law.

The scene dissolved but the bright lights and cameras remained. Fade in to Pete in his chair, his pants around his ankles, Amanda on her knees. He turned to face the camera and shrugged his shoulders in triumph and rapture. After what felt like forever, a close-up of Amanda lifting up her head, smiling with Dora's canine grin.

Chapter 21

Getting Shrunk

THE NEXT MORNING, WHEN AMANDA'S interview with Pete—the criminal law expert—was rerun on the morning news, I still felt physically ill. This hurt way too much. What's this red pulsating thing in the trash? Oh, pardon me, it's my heart.

Going loco down in the dungeon down below was not a good sign. Heartbreak in combination with general feelings of inadequacy made me look up psychologists in the yellow pages. There were two listings. "Fundamentalist Family Therapy" and "Counseling Connection." I dialed the second one and made an appointment for that afternoon.

Counseling Connection was in the same strip shopping center as Peking West and Aguilar Hair Care. You could get your hair cut and head shrunk then have an eggroll for lunch. When I got to the reception area, a bulletproof glass partition separated the clients from the counselors. This was the only show in town for mental health—every felon in three counties had to pass through here. The waiting room contained half of last week's docket call, including good ol' Sammy Quintana, my former client.

Sammy smiled at me. "Condition of parole?"

I was about to say, "General feelings of inadequacy, unresolved oedipal anxiety, overall sexual frustration and ummm . . . felon envy." Instead I kept quiet, smiled back.

The door opened up. Aryan Eddie emerged with tears in his eyes. He must have been homesick for his weekends in jail. Therapy must have been especially heavy today. I didn't even want to imagine what he talked about. He walked by me, oblivious.

"I can see you now, Mr. Shepard," a woman's voice said. I recognized it as Dr. Marianne Romero, the forensic evaluator. She poked her head out the door. She was in her fifties, a short gray haircut on her head. “I’m the only one here these days.”

Upon hearing my name, Eddie perked up, turned around.

“I’m just checking to see when those reports on my client are ready,” I said nervously. “Nothing else. I can come back then.”

Chapter 22

Turkey Days

I SPENT THANKSGIVING IN AGUILAR because I didn't have enough annual leave days yet to warrant the day's journey up to Albuquerque so I could fly home to D.C. My parents were at home, entertaining my first cousin who was marrying a stockbroker, so they were full up anyway. My half-assed notion of going up to Albuquerque fizzled when I telephoned my old girlfriend Mary Alice and a recording indicated that her firm's phone system was not operational at this time.

I called Amanda, whose machine informed that she was in Santa Fe. Pete had told me he was in Santa Fe, too, visiting friends. Gosh, what a coincidence.

The Thanksgiving sky was dark. With all the leaves long gone, everything in town was the same shade of gray. By three in the afternoon, after hours of watching football and listening to the whizzing of the tumbleweeds in wind gusts, my apartment walls began closing in on me.

Or maybe it was my ever-expanding piles of dirty underwear that lined the walls. Time for laundry. As I put my clothes in the dryer, I spotted a mass of black hair on top of a black outfit out of the corner of my eye. Before I could do anything, a pair of powerful arms shot underneath my armpits and covered my eyes. The grip was solid; I couldn't break free.

"Guess who?" a voice said after a pause.

"I give up." It was more than just an answer to the question.

The hands let go slowly and I whirled around to see Dora. Her hair was dyed black now. She was dressed in tight jeans and a black sweater that covered most of her tattoos.

"Scared you, no?"

"I didn't know you were out."

"Charges dropped. Told you I'd get a good lawyer. Work's going great in El Paso, but I thought I'd come home for the holidays."

I pointed to her hair. "Traveling incognito?"

"No, I'm traveling in my Chevy." She laughed. "Old Aguilar joke. What are you doing for Thanksgiving?"

I sighed. "My laundry."

"Don't you got nowhere to go?"

"No, I don't."

"Well, shit, it's un-American to be by yourself on turkey day. My mom's having a little potluck and you're welcome to join us. You don't got to bring nothing."

I was uneasy. "I have to put my laundry away first."

"No problem. I'll give you a hand."

She followed me back to my apartment. She was amazed that I'd left my door open and couldn't resist looking inside at the scattered clothing and pizza boxes that decorated my chairs. I'd left the TV on, too.

"You really live like this, no?"

"Let's put it this way . . . I wasn't expecting company."

She sniffed, then wrinkled her nose. "Get some air freshener. It's on sale at Wal-Mart."

I followed her the forty steps to her mom's apartment.

"Just don't mention Jesus, okay? And don't ask me shit right now, because it's a holiday." She opened the door. "We got friends in all of the families here today, so don't say anything to fuck things up."

"What can I talk about?'

She sighed. "Football."

The apartment was identical to mine, though not the decor. Velvet pictures of Elvis and Jesus lined the walls, along with a big poster listing the Dallas Cowboys' football schedule. There was a gray vinyl couch with plain metal chairs scattered around for the overflow of guests.

A buffet was set on a metal table: turkey, Mexican food, potatoes, and two cakes shaped like football helmets, one gray with a blue star on it, the other gold with a furious eagle ready to pounce on a red frosted coyote that read "Go AHS, beat Roswell!"

Everyone was in a good mood. Joey shook my hand like we were long lost friends. I was surprised to see Jesus' mother, but before I could say anything she put a bowl of posole and a Coors Light in my hand. Dora's mother, the Roseanne lookalike, gave me some turkey. Sammy Quintana, the Tumbleweeds busboy, tapped another keg. He smiled at me but didn't mention the incident at Dr. Romero's. There were ten or so others I didn't recognize.

Anna Maria, wearing a white blouse and skirt, sat on the sofa with her brother, Enrique—a big cowboy who had worn the memorable "SHUT UP, BITCH" shirt at the mall. Enrique took most of the sofa, relegating her to the far corner. He wore another T-shirt of the same genre under his flannel shirt, but I couldn't make it out. She didn't look all that happy to be with him, twitched nervously on her cushion. How could a nice girl like Anna Maria be related to a jerk like that?

She saw an opening, escaped from Enrique to help Senora Villalobos in the kitchen.

"It's going to be all right, mi hija," I heard Senora Villalobos say. "It's in los brazos de Dios."

In the hands of God? I hoped so. Better His than mine.

The men settled in to watch the Cowboys on the Lilly family's ancient but immense television set. I put aside my fanatical Redskin loyalty and pretended to cheer for the Cowboys, though I passed up the sacramental piece of gray helmet cake and took mine from the one with an eagle on it. During half-time there was a promo for the local news, with old footage of Amanda interviewing Coach Aragon of the Aguilar Eagles.

"You know that Amanda, the newsgirl, don't you?" Senora Villalobos asked.

"Nobody really knows Amanda," I replied.

"What a fucking asshole!" Enrique said.

For a moment I thought he was talking about me, Amanda, or both. Thankfully, his eyes were glued to the screen, ranting at the image of Coach Aragon. "I can't believe they got blown out by fucking Eldorado. They haven't been shit since Jim Everett left all those years ago. Then fuckin' A, the Eagles lose to Alamogordo, Roswell, Crater, and some rich kids school called Albuquerque Academy."

"Losing to those smart kids from Albuquerque sucked the most, no?" Sammy said.

The men cursed in English and Spanish. I mumbled with empathy, certainly not bringing up that I too had gone to an elite private high school. The conversation shifted back into football. As far as these experts were concerned, Aragon had ruined the team.

"You heard that it took the Eagles ten hours to drive up to Albuquerque?" Sammy said. "They got stuck behind a trailer and Coach Aragon wouldn't pass."

Everyone laughed, apparently Aguilar football was five yards and a cloud of dust.

"Without Victor—" Enrique said, and abruptly there was silence.

Anna Maria rushed outside. Enrique was about to make a joke about it, but Dora cut him off. "Don't be starting shit, Enrique. This is a party."

He shut up. I was impressed. Who was she that even a tough guy like Enrique would back down?

Halftime entertainment was Joey, lip-synching and playing air-guitar to all the rock and rap since Buddy Holly and the day the music died. I turned down a chance to join him during his tribute to Guns n' Roses, politely excused myself to check on Anna Maria.

She paced outside, braving a cigarette on the patio in the windy night. She handed me one, but I politely declined. "You shouldn't smoke," I told her, giving her wrist a friendly grab. "It's bad for you."

"I know. I just started. With all the stuff that's been going on. . . ." She smiled in the moonlight. In white, she still looked like that angel I'd seen back in the Tumbleweeds parking lot. "Actually, it's just an excuse to get out of the room for a while."

"What happened?"

"It's Victor. I knew him . . . you know, before Jesus."

"You miss him?"

"I miss Jesus more," she said. "And he's not even dead."

"How did you know Victor?

"We used to go out," she said, not looking up. "But I wouldn't really call it going out."

"What would you call it?"

"Something else." She put out her cigarette by crushing it with her sharp heel.

Dora had warned me not to get into any heavy stuff at the party and though I still had questions, this just wasn't the time to ask them.

"If I'm going to help Jesus, I'm going to need to know a lot more than I do now."

She wasn't listening. "Whatever happens, you got to swear something to me," she said.

"What?"

"That you'll do whatever it takes—whatever it takes—to get my Jesus off." She took both of my hands, the way Senora Villalobos had taken hers earlier. Her shaking hands were wet with sweat. I could feel her pulse, felt as though I, too, was in the brazos de Dios.

"I swear." I said, without a moment's hesitation. Fuckin' A, I meant it too.

She smiled, took out another cigarette, then put it back. "Maybe you're right. I shouldn't smoke."

I went back inside and was met by a deafening roar. Joey had been shooed off the stage as the main even, the Cowboys had just taken the field.

Sammy and Mrs. Lilly plied me with food and drink until I was bloated, too exhausted to chew or sip. Conversation soon shifted from football to who was in the pen and when they were getting out. Apparently Dora's father was still in but would be up for parole soon.

I decided it was better to play it cool and didn't really say much to anyone, given the topic. Someone broke the mood with a joke, which started a round robin where each man tried to tell a funnier joke than the man before him. Eventually everyone looked expectantly at me.

"I had a kid in a custody battle once," I said, feeling the weight of all of their stares. "Judge asked him if he wanted to live with his mother. He said, 'No, no, she beats me, she beats me.' 'How about your dad?' said the judge. The kid goes, 'No, no, he beats me even worse.' 'So who do you want to live with?' asked the judge. 'I want to live with the Aguilar Eagles cuz they don't beat nobody.' "

Silence.

My god, I had just insulted their vanquished tradition, small-town football in the plains, in the middle of their biggest tragedy. I had read a book about the sanctity of high school football in Odessa, Texas, and remembered the death threats the author had received after its publication.

Then a light bulb went off in Sammy's head and he laughed, soon joined by Dora, then Anna Maria, and finally Enrique, almost in spite of himself. "Like I told you," he said. "It's cuz they don't fucking pass anymore."

Maybe it was the alcohol but I began to smile as I looked around the room. For the first time in a long while I felt relaxed. Mrs. Lilly brought me some more food. The metal chair actually felt comfortable, the pictures of Elvis and Jesus seemed a friendly velvet chapel.

• • • •

Before dawn the next morning there was a knock on the door. It was Joey. "I got a gig with some guys I know down at the border," he told me. "I need bus fare."

I gave him a good once-over with my eyes as if I was frisking him. It was too early for him to be scoring drugs. He did indeed have a guitar case strapped around his back.

What had Senora Villalobos said? "This was Aguilar, we take care of each other here."

I gave him the twenty bucks. "Your court isn't until January, make sure that you're back by. . . ."

But he was already gone into the windy parking lot.

Chapter 23

Who Was That Masked Man?

I SPENT THE REST OF the Thanksgiving holiday studying and renting movies. Cold and windy in late November, Aguilar was even starker and browner than before. By Sunday I wanted out of my house so badly—wanted to get back to the office, even get back to jail. I switched to watching the tumbleweeds race across the parking lot. I almost wished I had a digital video camera to capture a particularly large one that maneuvered through the lot, dodging cars like a slalom course. Maybe Joey was on to something.

Monday's docket included the sentencing of a man with four prior DWI convictions, now facing prison after his various stints in the relatively cushy Billy the Kid suite. He stood with his wife, yet another obese woman with blond hair.

As the judge began reading his name, my client interrupted. "Your Honor, two of them ain't mine," he said. "They was my brother Ted's. He's my twin and looks exactly like me."

"Your Honor, it's true," his wife said. "I can't tell him and Ted apart."

"Your Honor," Jovanka said, "we went through this the last time, seven years ago." She turned toward the woman. "Ma'am, you've never seen the two brothers together at the same time, have you?"

"No."

"Your Honor, we still contend that Mr. Jones has four priors. If he can bring a brother in willing to take the rap, we'll change our position."

The judge looked at me. "You got anything to say about this?"

"Your Honor," I said after a moment, grasping at straws. "I don't think they should be punished just because they're not a very close family."

Both Jovanka and the judge managed to restrain their smiles. The judge stared at my client for a long moment. "It's been nearly seven years since your last offense. For either of you. . . ."

My client nodded. That was a good thing to the judge, considering what he usually saw.

"I'll give you a year," he said. "I'll suspend six months however while you leave the county in search of your long lost brother. He'll have to serve the rest. You understand if I see either of you around here. . . ."

"Thank you," my client said as Gardea dragged him away with one arm, patting him on the back with the other. "From both of us."

The judge winked at me as he left the bench.

Back at the office I met my eleven o'clock appointment, one Heidi Hawk, caught sniffing starter fluid behind the gym. At fifteen, she was a junior varsity cheerleader at Aguilar High and, according to her mother, an honor student until this semester.

"Starter fluid?" I said.

"Sniffing paint was getting too messy," she explained. "It was ruining my makeup."

If Guillermo was a middle-aged Jesus, she was Jesus at fourteen. The thought of watching her career path follow theirs was disturbing.

"Heidi, I'll do whatever I can for you but I'll probably have to plead you, since you were caught with the stuff. You're a very pretty girl and your mom tells me you're very smart." I leaned across the desk. "I've got a boy in jail right now, just a few years older than you, and he might spend the rest of his life there. I'm not going to give you a sermon but stay away from that crap, will you?"

She nodded and they both left to go back to her cheerleader practice. On their way out I heard her mother say under her breath, "Her friend, Stephanie, she got charged with aggravated battery too. She hired a real lawyer and he told her they could win at trial."

I wanted to tell her that winning wasn't going to help her with her daughter's problem, but they were out the door before I could say anything.

I checked my "things to do list." It was time for Sky Roberts—after a few phone calls with Rose's office in L.A. It took awhile, L.A. had added a few area codes since the last time I'd been there. Was there a difference between 310 and 323? Back in 505, the one, the only area code for the entire state of New Mexico, I set it up that we'd all "do lunch" at the Oil Baron Club on top of the town's one skyscraper. The Oil Baron was the home of Aguilar's one big law firm (all of twelve attorneys) and also served as a bit of civilization here in the boonies.

• • • •

Eleven stories up, the Oil Baron Club had a magnificent view of Sierra Milagro and Pyramid Peak. Where walls intruded, Peter Hurd's majestic landscapes of sand and sky competed with the view.

I had broken out my best suit from back home, but it still smelled of the dirty socks that I often stuffed in the closet. And yet even though I scrubbed and scrubbed, I still felt like a slob. I knew I was missing something when I emerged out of the elevator and into the restaurant, but couldn't remember what it was.

I told the Maitre d' that I was with the Roberts' party, and he put me at a table right by the window. I looked around the restaurant—men wearing expensive gray jackets with rattlesnake boots devoured luncheon steaks with stylish women wearing business outfits with sensible shoes. Nearly all the patrons were Anglo. At least five of the men were dead ringers for the mythical J.R. Ewing of *Dallas*.

Three people sat at the next table, two well-dressed men and a woman, all about my age. The men talked about depositions and "motions to compel discovery"—must be lawyers who worked in the building. I'd seen the woman before at the mall, heading into the boutique.

The woman caught me staring, politely excused herself, and walked over to my table with a graceful stride of a runway model. She was tall and thin, with perfect posture, her light brown hair flowing down her back onto a dark blue dress.

"Are you here by yourself?" She had a soothing southern accent. "You're more than welcome to join us."

"I'm waiting for some people."

"You must be new in town. I pretty much know everybody in Aguilar but I don't recall seeing you up here before."

"I've only been here a few months. I don't get out much. I'm a public defender."

She frowned for a second. "So you have to defend these people even if they're guilty?"

"Yes, and they usually are."

"How do you do that? It must be real hard."

"Well, it's about equal justice," I said, echoing Pete's words. "It's making sure poor people get the same treatment under the law as rich people, no matter who their parents are." That came out sounding a little preachy, especially the part about parents.

She extended her hand. "My name is Deb LeFleur. My friends call me Deb-the-Deb because I was a debutante back in Houston. I'm working for my dad's oil company now, LeFleur Exploration. Welcome to Aguilar."

"I'm Dan Shepard. Nice to meet you."

She touched my shoulder, then gravitated over to Roberts and Rose, who now headed toward my table. They were joined by local counsel, a bland guy in a gray suit, whose name I didn't catch. He shuffled off to join Deb and her gang.

I looked at Rose. He vaguely resembled me, but had a better tan, a hundred dollar haircut, a thousand dollar suit and the best nose that money could buy. If I had guessed A instead of B on the LSAT, and hadn't overslept for that one communications class, I would have had his life. I doubted that his mother had ever fired him. . . .

After Deb politely shook Sky's hand, they joined me at my table.

"Great view," I said after they sat down.

"The food sucks," Sky said. "They can't do vegetarian for shit."

"Sky, this here is . . . " Rose said, forgetting my name.

"Dan Shepard . . . and we've met."

Sky barely acknowledged me.

"He's representing one of the other guys in your case," Rose said. "Jee-zus Villa. . . ."

"That's Hay-zeus," I interrupted.

"The little Mexican kid?" Sky asked.

"Yeah, him," I said. "A good kid if you get to know him."

"I guess I don't know him, then."

Sky Roberts was still an asshole, even on the eleventh floor. In the crisp daylight of the desert sun, he looked much older than his nineteen or so years. His nose was covered with heavy makeup, which puzzled me until I realized that his nose was pierced. His numb expression complemented a handsome face with a two-day beard. His long hair was in need of a wash, hard to tell what color it was beneath the grime. This was a movie star? Joey, the rock and roll paint sniffer, had more star quality.

Rose took out a tissue. "Allergies," he said between sniffles. "You guys got a major problem here compared to L.A."

"I don't know, " I replied. "I'd take pollen over pollution any day."

I waited until we ordered, steaks of course, except for Sky, then started with a safe question on a subject sure to interest him, himself. "How'd you get into acting?"

"My dad was in the business," he said. "He was a studio exec for Viacom."

"Did he set you up with your first part?"

"Yeah. It was on a TV show called *Mother-in-Law*. It ran on one of the cable networks for a few weeks. I guess I was about twelve."

"Sounds like fun."

"Well, I didn't like it that much. My dad made it clear it was either work on the show or straight to Sunset Hills . . . A place they send rich kids in L.A., if you really fuck up. My dad got me into show biz to keep me out of trouble."

Innovative rehabilitation. Instead of sending our poor kids to the Youth Development and Diagnostic Center for an evaluation, we could send them to Hollywood. Though to judge by Sky, show biz therapy hadn't worked.

We talked about his career for a little while, or I should say, Sky talked about himself and the famous people he knew and/or slept with. Both he and Pete had claimed the same Penthouse Pet. Rose claimed her twin sister.

"Sky," Rose said after we got our food, "why don't you tell uh . . . this attorney here . . . what happened that night."

I couldn't tell whether Rose's memory lapse regarding my name was an accident caused by the allergies, or just business as usual up there in the big leagues.

Sky took a big bite of his vegetarian burrito, then talked while chewing. "We hadn't started filming yet, so I was just hanging out, y'know, getting the lay of the land. I had to get out of L.A. as soon as I could. I was sick of all the tabloid shit."

"Did you know any one here?" I asked.

"I met this girl, six feet tall. Big hair, big tits."

"Dora?"

"Yeah, that was her name."

"She introduced you around?"

"Yeah. It was kind of weird, but sometimes no one knew who I was here. You guys don't get movies or cable in this shithole, do you?"

"Takes a while," I said. "We'll get *Citizen Kane* next week."

He drew a blank.

"It's an old movie," I said. "So what happened?"

"Well, Dora told me about this party, a real blow-out, sort of like a rave, at this guy's house up by the high school. Rito Juarez. It was that Guillermo guy's cousin."

"Who was there?"

"Everybody. I mean, everybody and their lawyer." He laughed. "You'd be real surprised at who you see at these parties. Anyways, Dora introduced me to Guillermo. He seemed real surprised she was back in town. She was already there, with this other girl, real cute, real thin."

"Dora's friend have big brown hair, big brown eyes, too much make-up, and sort of . . . uh . . . fragile?"

"Yeah. Real cute but she was just bawling and bawling. She went outside and puked. I don't remember her name."

"Anna Maria?"

"Maybe. I can't remember shit sometimes."

"So then what happened?"

"Then I got with Guillermo, inside the garage, and he sold me some shit. I did it up in the bathroom."

Rose gave me the "don't ask, don't tell" look. No real need for me to ask what the "shit" was.

I nodded, switched topics. "Did you see Jesus, the little Mexican kid?"

"Yeah, he met up with Dora's friend, the girl who was crying. He gave her a hug and I think she told him she was feeling sick or something and that Dora was going to give her a ride home when she felt better. I was just getting out of the bathroom, you know, sitting next to them. I was zoning out but I heard them."

"So what did he do next?"

"He left with Dora's brother. Joey, somethin' like that. Jesus said if he stayed he was going to fuckin' kill someone. That Victor guy."

I stiffened. "But he left before anything happened, didn't he?"

Sky looked back out the window and stared at the mountains for a second. You could almost see the wheels turning in his head as he tried to put things together.

"Yeah, he definitely left with that Joey guy. I'm pretty fucking positive about that. But afterwards, all the shit all kicked in and I don't remember so good."

I reached for my ice tea, made a silent toast. Ladies and gentlemen, we have officially achieved alibi. "What happened next?"

"I'm sitting on the couch, tripping. Then one of Guillermo's cousins or something came over and told me to come check out what was going on outside."

"What was happening?"

"This guy Victor, the guy who died, he was giving Guillermo shit about shorting him on a deal. They kind of drifted away from the house because the music was really loud outside. There was a bunch of people out there checking out what was going on."

"Did you know Victor?"

"Yeah. I had bought some shit from him and the fucker had shorted me, too."

"Then what happened?"

"Wait a minute." He thought for a moment. "Okay. Then they start pushing each other, people start yelling. He starts screaming shit at me."

"Who?"

"Victor. Said he was going to tell the papers that I was on drugs and stuff. I told him he'd better watch his own ass. Some of his friends started yelling, 'Don't take that shit from him!' Then he pulled a gun."

"Who?"

"Victor."

That was the first I'd heard about Victor's gun in a while. Judging by the reports, and the interrogation of Guillermo, no gun had ever been found, on Victor or anyone else. The cops never recovered the gun that was used to shoot Diamond.

"Then what happened?"

Sky looked over at Rose. Rose looked down at the table, as if to make sure I wasn't taping.

Shit . . . I knew I had forgotten something.

"Go ahead, Sky," Rose said after looking down at where the recorder should have been.

"Before he got the gun all the way out," Sky said, "I got real pissed off. I grabbed him and pushed him down. He was standing right by the curb and, boom! He hit his head against it."

"See it was an accident," Rose added. "He was protecting himself."

"I'm interested in what my client did or didn't do," I said. "Not what you did or didn't do Sky. Now you said somebody kicked him after that. Who?"

"I don't know," he said. "It was like a blur. Someone wearing some kind of school colors, like a jacket or a sweatshirt, but I didn't see the face."

"Was it Jesus?"

He thought again for a moment, looked over at Rose one more time. Again Rose nodded.

"Nah, I don't think it wasn't him," Sky said at last. "There was something about the face that didn't look quite right."

I stopped, gulped water triumphantly, as if guzzling victory champagne . . .

Sky kept going. "Then somebody yells that the cops are coming so everybody starts running in different directions. And then this kid with long blond hair grabs Victor's gun and starts firing, like a maniac. That's when the cop got shot."

For a second, a vision of Joey flashed through my head. Shit.

"Was it Joey, the kid who left with Jesus?"

"I'm not sure. It looked a lot like him. Maybe he came back and shit after he left. The kid had really wild tattoos and really long hair. But I don't know, it might have been someone else because I don't remember him coming back. Hard to tell us rocker trash apart, I guess."

I chugged some more tea, maybe that was why Joey had left. At least I had cleared Jesus, tape or no tape. "Thanks a lot, you've been really helpful." I turned to Rose. "If you want to interview Jesus, then we can compare notes on how we're going to handle the questioning during the trial. Make sure we protect Sky, since it's obvious Jesus wasn't even there."

Rose didn't say anything. He scrunched up that Beverly Hills nosejob nose, trying to survive one last allergy attack. It passed after a moment, but he still didn't respond.

"You are going to help me out on this one?" I said after a long beat.

Rose sighed. "I don't think you understand what's going on here, uh. . . ."

"Dan."

"Yes, Dan, of course. You see the studio wants this resolved quickly. We'll probably be pleading soon and hopefully Sky won't testify for anyone, one way or the other. The only reason I'm letting him talk to you at all, to put it quite bluntly is to. . . ."

He nodded at Merril and Jovanka who had just taken the table at the other side of Deb's. They nodded back at him, ignored me.

So that's what this was all about. Rose used our conversation to put the pressure on the DA to give him a better deal.

I was pissed. "So what you're saying is, I'm basically the Lone Ranger."

Sky stared.

"Old TV show," I noted for his benefit. "This isn't the last of this," I said, trying to sound as vaguely threatening as I could.

Rose looked at me one last time, sizing me up. "So Mr. uhh . . . Ranger, if that's the way you're gonna play it." He laughed, and said only half-jokingly, "You know the old saying we have in my neck of the woods, watch out or you'll never work in this town again."

I almost didn't hear him, I stared out at the majesty of the Aguilar valley sprawled out eleven stories down below. I turned, looked at him in his thousand dollar suit—this fucker couldn't even do an arraignment without Pete's help.

I forced a laugh. "I don't think you understand, Mr. Rose, we're in my neck of the woods, kemo sabe."

Chapter 24

Intelligence Tests

December 21

I SPENT THE REST OF December catching up on my other cases. I couldn't talk to Jesus, who filled in the blanks under the lengthy psychological testing of Dr. Romero. I did see him every once in a while doing maintenance work outside in the cold, clad only in his orange jumpsuit. One blustery December day, a sudden gust blew a plastic bag away from him. I hurried across the parking lot until I caught up with it. Then I carried it back, threw it in the dumpster by the jail.

People didn't use this particular dumpster that much, I still saw the remnants of my broken phone.

"Thanks," Jesus said, "I got some more shit around back that I missed." I smiled at him, as he emptied the rest of his load of trash in the dumpster, covering the phone once and for all.

• • • •

"I've had to retest him," Dr. Romero told me in her soft lilting voice over the phone. This was the kind of therapist I'd want. Not my old one, a strict Freudian who'd always talked about my "inner child" at a hundred fifty bucks an hour.

"It was hard for him to concentrate with all the distractions at the jail," Dr. Romero continued on, as if distractions at jail were an everyday occurrence. "Just stay away for a little longer."

"What do you think the tests are going to show?"

"The preliminary results are encouraging," she said. "But I never know with Jovanka Smith. I'll call you as soon as I get done."

On the Tuesday before the hearing, the temp secretary told me I had a person-to-person collect call from Mexico. The other party identified himself as "Axl Rose."

"Do you know who this is?" he asked in a voice that suggested he was once again experimenting with chemistry. "It's not really Axl Rose, man."

"Really? I'm disappointed, Joey. So where are you?"

"Across the border," he said. "I'm not saying which border, man. You got to figure it out."

"So how's it going?"

"I'm fine. Dora says hi."

"Where is she?"

"She's working at the Princess, in El Paso. Dude, you got to come see me over here."

"Why?"

"Because I can help you out."

"Joey, I'm actually starting to think that you can be helpful," I said. "Can't you tell me over the phone?"

"I'm scared, man. I gotta tell you in person."

"How can we talk in person if you won't tell me where you are?"

"Just go to the Princess. It's right off I-10, near downtown. Dora will bring you over to me."

"I don't know. I'm going to be in T or C tomorrow."

"Dude, that's only about an hour and a half away, if you're really jamming."

Christ, growing up in Maryland I was scared to drive across the border on the beltway into Virginia.

"I'll think about it," I said.

"You really got to see me. You know why?"

"Yeah?"

The phone went dead.

A second later the temp secretary buzzed me again. She wasn't very good. Hadn't Pete represented her on a solicitation charge? Was this part of her work release? "Another call for you. I couldn't make out the name."

I picked up the receiver. "So what's so goddamn important?" I yelled.

There was silence on the other end for a second. "Dan, it's Dr. Romero. Is there a problem?"

"Sorry. I got cut off. I thought you were someone else."

"Well, I've finished my report. Jesus is such a remarkable boy."

• • • •

In his office, Pete had sticks set up with string drawn between them. The string kept going until it terminated in a hole in the wall, a fresh bullet hole.

"I'm doing a toolmark test for my case down in Carlsbad," he said as if that explained everything.

I didn't want to know if he had recreated the crime, complete with bullet hole, in his office. "You ever been to Juarez?" I asked at last as I tried to follow the string.

"What do you think?"

"What's it like?"

"Well, at least once a year, little white boy like you gets killed and dumped in the Rio. You should go after you do that hearing in T or C."

"It's a long ways away."

He tapped the hole with a finger. "Well good luck in your hearing. Maybe you'll prove incompetency and the whole thing will go away."

"I doubt it. Why am I even doing this in the first place?"

Pete looked up at me. "I don't think you get it. You do these hearings in juvenile cases to set things up for the sentencings. The kid always sounds better before the trial. Afterwards they're usually freaking out and the probation officer creams them on the pre-sentence report."

"A pre-sentence report? Doesn't he have to be convicted first?"

"Duh . . ." He pulled the string taut. "I'll see you after you get back from wherever."

I waded through Jesus's psyche profiles the minute I got them, all one-hundred-fifty pages. Dr. Romero was right—he was a remarkable boy. In the file, a charcoal picture of Anna Maria that was a near-photographic likeness. The background was very dark except for a lightness over her head, almost a halo. There was a subtle glow to her skin and in her eyes. There was a handwritten note from Dr. Romero that I should ask her about the picture at the hearing.

I'm glad she included the picture; the rest of the file was psychobabble. Jesus had a severe "anger management" problem and some minor organic brain dysfunction from substance abuse in his past, but was otherwise well adjusted along the various axes. He was oriented to time and space and amenable to treatment. That was good, wasn't it?

I was shocked to find that his IQ was equal to mine. Overall, according to the tests he was better off psychologically than I was.

"You done good," I told him in the interview room. "Worse case scenario, even if we don't win . . . I suppose we can use Dr. Romero as a character witness."

"Cool," he said nonchalantly. His sanity and competency were never at issue with him.

"Joey called. He wants me to go to see him over in Mexico."

"Cross over the line and see him, bro. Joey will help you on the case."

"I don't know," I said. "Mexico, I've heard it's pretty scary over there."

"Scary? What's a matter, ese? Too many Mexicans over there?"

I looked over at the white cinder blocks. "I want to make sure I'm prepared for your hearing in T or C." I said, pointed to the inches of psychological reports. "This psychological stuff is pretty complicated," I said. "I probably need an extra night to practice."

He frowned. "Do what you gotta do, man."

Chapter 25

Truth or Consequences

December 22

I LEFT MY APARTMENT BEFORE dawn for the three-hour drive. The westbound convoy of pickups on Oil Avenue was slow, but I had the road to myself, once I passed the dried grass of the soccer fields and entered the llano's last gasp before the foothills began. This was outlaw country, where an infamous bank robber hid out in the ravines after ravaging Aguilar.

I wore jeans, a flannel shirt, and a beat-up pair of cowboy boots. My rat tail had grown long enough that I could tuck it under my collar.

"I'm a cowboy / on a steel horse I ride / I'm wanted dead or alive," I sang with Jon Bon Jovi on the hand-held radio and tape deck that now served as a car stereo. I turned the radio off as soon as Kid Coyote, the DJ, blathered on about yet another "blast from the past."

The hills got higher and the ravines deeper as I proceeded west. The sun rose over the hills and sagebrush gave way to scraggly juniper trees that clung to the hillsides. After scaling a steep ridge, I descended into a lush river valley with ranches and roadside stands bearing signs for "piñon brittle" and "red chile ristras."

I left Aguilar County and entered Buchanan County, where either Billy the Kid—or was it Butch Cassidy and Sundance—had robbed one of the banks.

After winding up through the tall pines of the valley for about an hour, I entered the Capitan Apache Reservation. With a bit of leaning, I glimpsed Sierra Milagro. Up this close, its white cone reminded me of Mt. Fuji or Kilimanjaro.

I turned off the radio and found a tape Pete had given me of a continuing legal education course he taught on "cross-examination."

"It's going to be a long drive," he had told me. "You might as well learn something. I practice my cross-examinations in the car sometimes. They always sound better on the open road."

I slotted in *The Secret Art of Cross Examination*, the judge's instructional tape. His voice followed a few strains of country and western instrumentals: "The secret to cross-examination is getting jurors to visualize the event, step by step. Perhaps the best way to learn how to cross-examine a real live person is by practicing on inanimate objects, since usually you know what to expect from them.

"For example, I had a DWI trial where I knew I would have to cross a police officer to show that my client's driving could be caused by something other than his being intoxicated. I got ready for that trial by cross-examining a Coke can. That's right, a Coke can. 'You're red. You're round. You have a top with a hole in it. When you open the top there's a fizz. You're a Coke can.'"

He tried his technique on a pencil. "You're about eight inches long."

I couldn't help but smile, but the tape kept going. . . . "You're yellow. You're made out of wood. You have lead on one end. You're a pencil."

Now for the cop in a DWI. "It was dark. It was wet. The brakes could have failed. My client's vehicle could have hit the car for reasons other than drinking and driving."

He offered more tips: "When you've got 'em on the run, get to a certain point and then sit down. Never ask the one question too many."

He stressed those words again "one question too many." He gave some more examples but I didn't hear them, thanks to a series of loud explosions in the distance. I must be getting close to the missile range.

I had now left the reservation and entered the White Sands region of the Tularosa Basin. The Trinity sight was somewhere in this basin, an area so barren that the first atom bomb had been exploded here because nobody would notice. There were rumors of mutated frogs and jackrabbits that lived near the blast sight.

There was a roadblock in the middle of the highway. A grim-faced MP signaled me to stop. "We got testing today," he said. "Only be a few minutes. Wait here until I give you the go-ahead."

No one else was behind me or in front of me, so we waited alone. In the interval, I played the tape again.

I lip-synched, "You're a Coke can," while the MP stared at me.

Another loud blast, then some shockwaves raced under the

ground. The MP didn't even flinch. He got a call on his radio, had a heated conversation for a few minutes, then waved me through. I glanced at my watch and cursed.

I couldn't see the road clearly through the white sand blowing at me. Occasionally, headlights came directly at me out of the dust, so I stayed to the far right of the road. When I began to climb out of the Tularosa Basin through San Roberto Pass, the wind abruptly stopped.

I took the turn-off for the road to T or C and checked my watch again. Shit . . . unless I violated the laws of physics I'd be late in front of a judge who didn't know me. To make matters worse, I still wore my grungy outlaw clothes. I'd have to change clothes in the car or risk contempt.

As I coasted down the other side of San Roberto Pass, I kept my left foot by the brake and my left hand on the steering wheel and pulled off my right boot, switched feet and pulled off the left. After stepping on the gas to pick up speed, I tugged off my jeans and heard a police siren. It was the military police. Breaking the laws of physics were now the least of my concerns—was it indecent exposure to drive in your underwear?

I pulled over, grabbed my suit pants, and struggled to pull them up before he got there. God was merciful: his car sped past me.

Back on the road, I put my shirt on and buttoned it with my left hand, one button at a time. By the time I hit the T or C exit, I was halfway presentable.

Downtown T or C reminded me of "Frontier Land" at Disney World, exactly what you'd imagine an old Western town to look like: Victorian houses, wood store fronts, adobe and white stuccoed Spanish haciendas. The land was rugged: steep buttes littered with cacti and saber yuccas. Other than the freeway, the truck stop, and the mobile home parks on the edge of town, little had changed in a hundred years. The only indication that television had even reached here was the name of the town itself.

The courthouse was much smaller than Aguilar County's, since Sierra County was about a third the size. It was built like a Spanish mission, with four tall cypress trees in front.

I smiled when I pulled in to the courthouse parking lot. I had made it to court with a full minute to spare. I ran into the building, tucking in my shirt and straightening my tie.

Court was practically empty. Perhaps time passed by at a slower rate here. The judge hadn't even arrived yet. A young woman in a gray business suit sat at the prosecutors table, talking with a cop. She saw me, got up from the bench, and started over. Oh my god! It was Mary Alice, my old girlfriend who had studied for the bar with me that fateful summer in Albuquerque. She still looked radiant. She had been a teen model in her previous life. That's when I noticed the engagement ring.

"What are you doing here?" I asked, keeping my eyes off the ring.

"My firm folded; it went bankrupt. Didn't you hear about it?'

"We're out in the boonies. We don't hear much of anything out there. So what's up?"

"I'm a DA out here now, believe it or not."

"You like it?"

"I've already worked it out with my fiance's firm up in Albuquerque. I do this for six months, get some trial experience, and then they hire me for more than my original salary. It's all worked out for the best."

I couldn't even gloat and certainly didn't want to ask about the new man in Albuquerque. This wasn't a step down for her, it was just a detour. She always managed to stay in control. I used to joke that she spent her entire life in the 88th percentile.

I paid for a coke from the machine. I wanted to have something to do with my hands while I talked with her. "So what's up with you today?"

"We scheduled Jovanka Smith's other hearing first. That's going to be in a few minutes, then your hearing will be right after that. Your client won't be here for a little while, anyway. They got held up by some blasting in White Sands."

"I got stuck in that, too, for a little while. But Jovanka is here already?"

"Yes. She's going to be doing her other hearing in a few minutes with Judge Edwards, who came down from Socorro."

"Her other hearing? Is that a public defender case?"

Mary Alice shook her head. "I guess you can wait inside and watch it. It's going to be an unpleasant business."

Jesus still hadn't shown up, so I waited with Mary Alice. I remembered our break up. I'd faxed her office a copy of an ABA best-in-the-nation award for my "Litigating for Godot" article, only to be told that I was immature and self-centered because I viewed accomplishments as a means of gaining her approval.

As the scenario of the doomed relationship with Mary Alice played out before my eyes, she excused herself and went to court. I took a few last gulps of my coke, then followed her in. The hearing had already begun.

It took me a second to figure out what was going on. The prosecutor, Mary Alice, sat on the right side, a cop at her table. Jovanka sat on the left, the one reserved for the defense, with the bland guy in the gray suit I'd seen at the Oil Baron. That guy sure got around. Next to her was a young man I could only see from the back.

Mary Alice was in the middle of a speech. "Your Honor, we've tried and tried with this boy, as you well know. I know that his mother has gone out of her way and done everything she could, but nothing seems to have worked so far. . . ."

His mother? Jovanka was here as the mother of a defendant? Before I could fully absorb that piece of news, Mary Alice continued. "Your Honor, the battery on the pizza delivery boy in Aguilar a few weeks ago was the last straw. It's obvious that the threat of the occasional weekend in jail is not enough. It pains me to say this, but Ms. Smith can no longer control her son. It's the State's position that he be sent up for full commitment to the New Mexico Boys' School or, alternatively, a suspended commitment while he is an in-patient at a residential treatment center for his substance abuse and other psychological problems."

Jovanka tried valiantly to fight back tears. When the boy turned his head to face her, I recognized him. Aryan Eddie was Jovanka's son??

"Anything else?" Judge Henry asked. Judge Henry was a distinguished looking African American with a Darth Vader baritone. "Ms. Smith?"

"No, Your Honor. We'll trust your judgment." Her voice sounded different—her Eastern European accent sounded stronger as if she couldn't contain it under such trying circumstances.

"Mr. Smith," the judge said sternly to the boy. No effect.

The judge lowered his voice, even further. "I mean Eddie. I don't know if you realize how much your mother has done for you. How she has always tried to do what's best for you, and you've repaid her with the kind of behavior that gets you brought up on charges again.

"Normally I would send someone with your history straight up to the Boys' School but I'm going to give you a break, son, and send you to a residential treatment center at the first available opportunity. I believe the Hogares program up in Albuquerque can take you after the first of the year. I will release you to the custody of your mother, once the State van transports you back to Aguilar."

"I could transport him," Jovanka said. "After all, I am going back there."

"This might not be appropriate," the judge said. "You need to keep your eyes on the road driving back. You can pick him up when you get back home. This could be your last holiday season together for a long time. I suggest you use it wisely. Court adjourned."

I took a good hard look at Eddie's face. A teen, he had that same look that the wizened Guillermo had had back in his cell—it didn't matter one way or the other. . . .

"Your Honor," Jovanka said, "I will be prepared to proceed on the other matter after a fifteen-minute recess."

"Fifteen minutes? Are you sure that's all the time you need?"

"I'll be fine, Your Honor. And thank you for asking. I think we all knew this day was coming."

The judge nodded, stood up. As he walked out of the room he turned to Eddie. "One good thing, son. You look much better with shorter hair."

I left the building, sat down under a cypress tree, and stared out at the majestic ridge called Elephant Butte. Jovanka walked over to me, smoking a cigarette. She barely glanced up as the Sierra County guards escorted Eddie over to sit in a holding cell.

"Are you alright?" I asked her.

"Not really," she said, puffing away on a pungent smoke as if she was back in a cafe in Belgrade or wherever she was from. "But that never slows me down."

"What happened with Eddie?"

"Nothing, everything. It's too late. . . ." There was a ring of Eastern Bloc fatalism in her voice.

"Is that why you're so tough on kids like Jesus?"

She put out her cigarette, crushed it under her feet. "To me, the greatest tragedy of all is a wasted life. If you were a mother, you'd know what I mean."

I didn't tell her about my own rocky relationship with my mother at that point. She didn't say anything more, and headed back into the building.

The State van pulled up in front of the courthouse. Clint brought

Jesus out and took him into the courtroom. I followed them in, the two joked like old friends.

"Orale vato. Que tal?" Jesus said when we sat down in the empty jury box.

"Okay, I guess. How about you?"

"Not too bad. So what's up today?"

"This is just a hearing on competency and amenability, not a trial. Do you understand what that means?"

"What's 'amenability' again?"

I had told him before, but "amenability" was a mysterious word—he may have been intelligent, but he still wanted to be reassured that he was not going to be injected with any needles at the end of the day.

"We put Dr. Romero on the stand and she testifies as to whether or not you're amenable to treatment. You two get along okay?"

"Yeah, fine. But it was a pain taking a bunch of those tests over and over again."

"Like I said, her report was pretty good. It did say you were 'amenable to treatment.' She likes you. A lot. . . ."

"Cool."

"What about Eddie? Why didn't you tell me he was Jovanka's son?"

"I thought you knew; everybody does. Didn't your office tell you that?"

No point in telling him things were a little sticky at the office these days. "Did Eddie have anything to do with this?" I asked.

"Yo no se, he might have. I don't know for sure but I've heard all kinds of stories one way or the other. Find out from Joey and Dora. They would know."

I didn't respond.

The gavel banged. Judge Henry looked in my direction, gave me a welcoming nod.

Jovanka was already seated at the other table. She held herself rigid, banishing all emotion from her body. Eddie's lawyer was long gone, at her side were two of Aguilar's finest.

Jesus borrowed a piece of paper and quickly sketched pictures of everything around him.

"Are you sure you're ready to begin?" the judge asked Jovanka.

"Your Honor," she said, "my personal problems should in no way interfere with the swift execution of justice. I'm ready to proceed immediately."

Even her accent was buried. This woman was one tough bitch.

There were no opening statements. "Mr. Shepard, you may begin."

I called Dr. Romero to the stand.

Dr Romero wore a conservative outfit, tall and imposing after years of listening to the woes of the murderers of the valley. I was glad I hadn't sought her out for therapy to hear me whine about not getting into Stanford. My own little muddles must seem like small potatoes compared to abuse and addiction she saw day after day after day. But there was a kindness in her brown eyes—she saw the best in even the hardest of cases. At least I hoped so.

After the preliminaries, I asked her some questions about Jesus and whether he was "amenable for treatment."

"Yes," she said. "He's had a very difficult life but I'm sure that he could be treated. He needs counseling. He's a very troubled boy which explains his problems with anger management."

After a few more questions about the details and the testing, I decided to be dramatic. "We agree that this child can be 'saved,' but I'm curious. Is he worth saving?"

Judge Henry's deep voice preempted Jovanka's objection. "Normally, I'd have doubts about the relevance of that question, but if I'm going to commit fifty thousand dollars a year for psychological treatment for the boy, I would like to know if the boy is, indeed, worth saving. Dr. Romero, you may answer the question."

"Yes, Your Honor. Jesus is very much worth saving. He is a very talented artist and scores well above average on all the intelligence tests. Your Honor, here are some of the sketches he has made."

"Mr. Shepard, do you intend to offer these into evidence?"

"I'm happy to, Your Honor."

He looked at the sketches. One was of a horse, another of Sierra Milagro, and yet another of a tree outside of the jail. Then there was that sketch of Anna Maria and the way the light caught the background and made it look like she had a halo.

The judge smiled at all of them. I sat down, feeling triumphant. I glanced back, Amanda was in the room as if she had appeared out of thin air . . . Today she was a vision in peach. The vision gave me a thumbs-up sign. The red light was on. . . .

"Nothing further, Your Honor."

"Ms. Smith?" queried the judge.

"Dr. Romero," said Jovanka. "You are aware that the defendant has not fully cooperated with the authorities on this matter?"

"Well, he never gave them a statement."

"Objection, Your Honor!" I jumped up. "My client has a Fifth Amendment right not to give a statement to the authorities."

"Your Honor, I am not asking or commenting on his Fifth Amendment rights. I am merely ascertaining the extent of Dr. Romero's knowledge of the defendant."

"Objection overruled. Continue, Mrs. Smith."

"And you are aware of his prior criminal history?"

"Objection, Your Honor. Juvenile adjudications. . . ."

"Your Honor, again, I am reviewing the extent of Dr. Romero's knowledge."

"Proceed."

"Yes, I am very well aware that he has a prior criminal history."

"Then you are no doubt aware that in all of those other incidents he has made a statement to the police?"

"Yes, that is true."

"So he no longer is cooperating with authority figures as much as he did in the past?"

"Well, I wouldn't say—"

"Yes or no—good communication is essential for treatment?"

"Of course."

I stood, ready for Jovanka to ask the next question, something along the lines of "So his not talking to the cops indicates that he will be difficult to treat." Such a question was objectionable and if said before a jury, could be grounds for a mistrial because you were commenting on a person using his Fifth Amendment right. I was ready.

But Jovanka apparently knew about the "one question too many," questioned Dr. Romero about Jesus' substance abuse problems, his problems with his teachers, his association with known delinquents. Every time I stood up to object, she quickly changed the subject.

Jovanka was good, but she hadn't really laid a glove on Dr. Romero. Slightly despondent, Jovanka began heading back to her chair. For a moment I hoped that the judge would throw out the whole case on the grounds that Jesus was "worth saving." It was all going to work out. . . .

Suddenly Jovanka changed her mind, and walked over to the collection of Jesus's artwork that sat on the table.

"Dr. Romero," she said. "You showed us all of those sketches by

Jesus. All of them were done while he was incarcerated, were they not?"

"Yes. I think they show true talent."

"I agree. All of them were done by memory, weren't they?"

"Yes. I don't think they allow the kids in the jail to go horseback riding, and here he has drawn a horse."

"Now, Dr. Romero, I know you're not an art critic but based on your personal experience as an educated woman who no doubt has purchased art in her lifetime, would you say his work is good enough to deserve being shown in an art gallery?"

"Yes. I'm very impressed with his work."

"Dr. Romero, during the course of your training and licensing you've no doubt been to the Maximum Security Facility in Santa Fe?"

"Yes. It's a requirement for all forensic psychologists in the state."

"And what type of offender is housed in that facility, Dr. Romero?"

"Those the Department of Corrections has deemed the most violent and least likely to be rehabilitated."

What was this all about?

"And what is in the entry foyer of the maximum security facility, Dr. Romero?"

Dr. Romero looked blank for a second or two, then smiled. "Oh, you mean the gallery . . . all the paintings by the inmate artists?" She was strangely excited and turned to Jesus. "You really must see it, Jesus. Those artists up there are so impressive. Their style is so much like yours. There was this one murderer who drew the most beautiful landscape, and this rapist—"

"Nothing further, Your Honor."

I slumped in my chair.

Judge Henry waited only a second. "In light of the evidence, I find that the child will be tried as an adult and will remain in custody rather than being transferred to any residential treatment facility. Judge Perez will set a hearing. Court is adjourned. And one more thing—"

We all looked up at him.

"Merry Christmas to all of you. God knows, you all deserve it."

I wanted to grab some lunch before I headed out. My stomach kept grumbling. Before I searched the phone book for the address of the town's McDonalds, Clint came over to me, put a hand on my shoulder.

"You might want to have lunch with us over in the jail before we head out," he said cryptically. "It would mean a lot."

Intrigued, I joined him and Jesus in the jail multi-purpose room, talked about everything but the case. Clint was actually friendly as he told a few war stories. I didn't even have to ask which service—he was "semper fi do or die" marine all the way. The green chile stew was the best I'd ever had—Hatch, New Mexico, the green chile capital of the entire world was just a few miles down the road. Jesus gave me a drawing of Superman dying standing next to a glowing rock.

"What's that?"

"Kryptonite," he said. "It's what kills Superman. Don't you know nothing?"

Before I could answer, Clint emerged from the kitchen, carrying a small brownie with a candle on it. Immediately all the residents in the multi-purpose room sang "Happy birthday, Jesus."

I joined in, somewhat sheepish. "If I had known, man" I told him.

Known? What do you get for the man who has nothing?

"Eighteen," he smirked as he blew out the candle. "Guess I'm legal now."

He smiled at me again. "Guess what I wished for—"

Amanda sat on a bench outside the courthouse. Thank God she wasn't smoking, smoking women seemed to be a bad omen. Instead, she smiled at me. "You're really getting pretty good at this. You heading back?"

"No," I said. "I've got to make a little trip."

"Call me if you make it back," she said. "I've got to talk to you."

"About us or about the case?"

"Both."

Jesus got in the van with Eddie to be transported. Clint had to separate them between the bulletproof glass.

"Where's Dora again?" I yelled.

"Princess Club," he shouted. "It's right off I-10." He looked over at Clint. "I won the bet."

Clint reluctantly nodded, handed Jesus his personal cellular phone, as if that was the prize. Jesus dialed, then said "He's coming," and hung up.

"She'll be waiting for you," he said with a cryptic smile. "Yo superman! Watch out for the Kryptonite when you get there."

The door slammed behind him.

Chapter 26

Donkey Show?

I CRANKED THE IGNITION, PEELED out of the dusty dirt parking lot of the courthouse then headed toward the entrance to I-25 south.

I drove down the barren stretches of I-25 at eighty, racing past the village of Hatch with its row after row of delicious green chile crops, then past something called Radium Springs. I slowed only slightly after the road merged into a little more crowded I-10 in Las Cruces.

Las Cruces was a blur, a nice medium-sized city set against the Organ Mountains, whose uneven, rocky peaks had looked like organ pipes to the conquistadors. The city even had a few straggly palm trees. A few months before, this would have looked like a dusty desert town, but now I it could see that it looked a lot like Rio de Janeiro.

I drove past a gigantic pecan grove and after a few more miles, crossed the Texas border, an ominous place marked "Exit 0." On the right loomed the foreboding white Spanish mission buildings of the La Tuna Federal Correctional Center. Jesus wouldn't be sentenced there since he'd only committed State offenses, but La Tuna, with its mass of barbed wire and high observation posts, gave me a knot in my gut.

Ironically, just a few hundred yards from La Tuna was "Wet and Wild Water World," a park filled with water slides, artificial wave machines and murals of cartoon characters. I'm sure some child of a felon told his mother after visiting La Tuna, "Mommy, after we're done visiting daddy, can we go on the water slides?"

About ten miles past La Tuna, I crossed the El Paso City Limits and I-10 became four lanes of heavy traffic. After I passed the "Sun Bowl," I could see the University of Texas, El Paso (UTEP) with its magnificent Mongolian architecture of arched roof and brown brick. On my right, over on the other side of the river, little white shanties perched on the steep, treeless hillsides, smoke billowing from the chimneys. Ciudad Juarez, Fronton Chihuahua, Mexico.

There was a billboard for the Princess Club—Jesus was right I couldn't miss it. The club was built like a barn the size of a football field. When I walked inside, the bouncer was a big cowboy. This wasn't an urban cowboy type place, this was the real thing. . . .

I wandered through the bar, and tried to do my best interpretation of the perp walk. It must have worked, nobody messed with me. One cute cowgirl even asked me to dance during the "Cotton Eyed Joe," but I demurred. I finally spied Dora serving a longneck bud to an obese cowboy. She was dressed as a cowgirl with very high hot pants, and very high heels. He gave her a quarter tip, then tried to pinch her butt as she turned. Wrong move. She grabbed the bottle, threatened to break it on top of his forehead.

"Don't think you're getting shit, ese," she said with a snarl toward the fat man. "Not on no twenty-five cent tip."

I was perhaps a bit disappointed that she was just an ordinary waitress—for some reason I had a vision of her as a dancer, or a spy, or perhaps both. . . .

She smiled when she saw me, as if she too was happy to have won a bet.

"Can you take me across—" I asked, as she gave me a hug.

"I thought you'd never ask."

We parked on the American side, a short ways down the interstate. "You don't want to drive across the border without no insurance," Dora said. "It's a pretty easy walk, but you better stay close if you've never been to the other side."

A man immediately got in my face and demanded money. Instinctively I brushed him away until I realized he was the parking attendant.

As we walked toward the bridge, cab drivers kept asking "Take you to the other side? You and your chica can see a donkey show."

"We gonna see a donkey show?" I asked Dora.

"Not even," she said. "Believe me, you don't even want to know."

We paid a quarter to get through a gate. The bridge arced over the Rio Grande for a hundred yards. Thousands of domestics and laborers were walking back with us. At the crest of the bridge were the flags of the two countries.

Mexico . . . I had a few politically correct thoughts about American imperialism, and then we began the descent. Other than helicopter skiing in Canada, this was my first trip to a foreign country. I thought about what Jesus had said about Kryptonite.

We officially crossed the line when we walked under a sign that read:

BIENAVIDOS A MEXICO

On the other end, we passed through a creaking iron turnstile. . . .

The main street in Ciudad Juarez was Avenida Juarez. We passed cut-rate liquor marts, jewelry stores, and dentists. There were cut-rate dentists on every block.

"I'm finally going to the dentist," she said. "I go to that one over there." She pointed to a small office building next to a gigantic liquor store. Her smile now contained braces. "I'm still sexy with metal in my mouth, no?"

"Si."

We continued down the street for a few blocks. It was brightly lit by dirty neon lights and crowded with Mexican nationals from all walks of life. Every few steps another taxi driver offered to take us to see a donkey show. Dora dragged me by the arm, as if leading a child. The disgruntled drivers shouted at me derisively in Spanish, questioning my manhood. It didn't seem like she was taking me on a direct route. She kept checking her watch. Almost as if she was killing time. . . .

We finally went down a side street to a place called the Sunset Club. The building was a crumbling adobe building that had been stuccoed white. The street was quiet except for some Tejano rock and roll coming out of the Sunset. Further down the street, I saw a Ciudad Juarez Policia standing next to his car, hand on his holster, confronting a group of American teenagers. One kid was yelling that his friend didn't mean to throw the bottle at the car. The policia said nothing.

"Fuck you," the kid said. "You're just a beaner cop."

The policia showed no expression, drew his gun, motioned the boy to assume the position against the squad car, then cuffed him and put him in the back seat.

The Americans argued all at once. "What the fuck are we going to do now?"

"We're never going to see him again."

"They're taking him to jail here. A fucking Mexican jail."

The policia didn't care. He drove away without a backward glance.

The friends chased after him, but the squad car quickly left them in the dust.

I started shaking. Here I was, a nice young man from Maryland, walking in a bad neighborhood in Mexico with a strange woman who had a criminal record, going to meet a drug dealer for information about a murder. At least when I'd met with Guillermo I was still in the United States. . . .

Dora grabbed my arm roughly and pulled me toward the bar. "Just don't do anything stupid. You'll be all right."

At the Sunset Club, the large bouncer, a reincarnation of Pancho Villa, waved us through without a word.

"You could back out now if you want," she said. "There's a cab over there."

She didn't wait for an answer, hurried inside.

I heard a noise from within. Was that a donkey braying? I took another deep breath, then followed her into the darkness. . . .

It took a few seconds for my eyes to adjust to the smoke. Yet once my eyes cleared I was surprised. The Sunset was just a college bar, an American college bar. There wasn't a donkey anywhere to be found, the closest thing to animals—red-headed frat boys with Lambda Chi sweatshirts under their UTEP and NMSU hats, drinking Coronas and Carta Blancas with their blond-haired dates. The bar was decorated with skiing posters and banners of local colleges.

In the corner of the bar, a grungy looking band warmed up. The guitarist, whose back was to us, had a gray hooded sweatshirt, the kind wrestlers wore to lose weight. I almost didn't give it a second thought until I saw the purple letters that read "VILLALOBOS."

My heart froze for a moment, then I took a good look at the guy's face—thank God it was Joey, not Jesus under the hood.

He took the hood off, motioned for us to join him at a table by the jukebox. He pointed toward a sign that advertised

CERVEZAS-DOMESTIC 50¢

Coors and Budweiser were listed under "imports" and sold for 75-cents.

"Don't worry," he said. "Ain't no drinking age down here." I reluctantly brought a round of Carta Blancas and brought them to the table.

"What did you have to tell me that was so important?"

"Right. We got cut off that one day," said Joey. "I had a lot more to tell you, but I don't trust the phones in this country. People will sell you out for a beer here, man."

He opened the Carta Blanca and took a chug. A young Anglo woman with a white Alpha Chi Omega sweatshirt asked us for an ashtray. I handed it over without comment. Dora pointed to the young woman's bare ankle, which was tattooed with AXO, her sorority symbol, and a small lyre underneath.

"Oooh, little Alpha Chi," Dora said. "She's such a little rebel."

"Well?" I asked Joey again after he took a big chug of his beer.

"Oh," he said. "You mean about the murder?"

"What the hell else did you think I wanted to talk about?"

"Oh . . . I was just going to tell you that my band is doing all right and we might get a record contract."

"Is that it?"

He looked over at Dora. "He's cool. I told you he'd come all the way over here."

She nodded. "We didn't think you had the balls. If you didn't come, we weren't going to tell you."

"Tell me what?"

"Who do you think kicked Victor?" She smiled, the lights danced on her braces.

"Who?"

Dora glanced behind me, as if nodding at someone. She looked at me. "This is privileged, right, baby lawyer?" she asked. "If we tell you, you can't say this to no one?"

"I don't know," I said after a moment. "I'm not really sure how this privilege thing works."

Dora smiled at me. "This is Mexico," she said after a moment. "Like what can you do to anyone down here. . . ."

I wasn't sure how to take that. "No bullshit . . . just tell me. Who killed Victor?"

"I did," said a soft voice over my shoulder.

I turned to see Anna Maria.

The beer dropped out of my hand and was soon all over my lap. It seeped through my jeans and into my underwear. I heard the Alpha Chi sorority girl giggle. I waited a second, cold and wet.

"Not even!!" I shouted. Not even? When did I start talking like that? "But wouldn't people tell you, uh . . . tell them apart?"

Joey put the hood back on and drew the draw strings, then turned around. "Not if she was wearing this."

I had jumped to a conclusion seeing the hooded sweatshirt, the witnesses and cops had also made the leap of faith, especially in the dark. In heels, Anna Maria was Jesus's height, with a sweater underneath, they'd have the same build. And the name on the back of the sweatshirt. . . .

"She was wearing this sweatshirt that night," Joey said. "A few days later she gave it to me to give to Jesus but I was all cold and shit, so I kept it."

"Did you know that?" I asked Dora.

She smiled, her braces flashing from a nearby light. "I know everything."

"Why didn't you tell anybody?" I asked her.

"I tried to tell the cops when they arrested me, but Thompson just pushed me down, called me a puta. They wouldn't listen to me. Kept saying how they were finally going to put Jesus away once and for all. They always thought my Jesus was there when Jovanka's husband got whacked. But he wasn't there at all."

So that explained why Jesus was one of the "usual suspects." I looked at her. "But why didn't you go to the police?"

"As they dragged Jesus out, he kept yelling at me 'not to tell nobody.' He'd go down for me. But the cops weren't even listening. They didn't care, cause they wanted him so bad."

"So why are you telling me now?"

"Jesus called me," she said. "He likes you now, because at least you're trying. He thought you should know."

He thought I should know. . . . "Uhh . . . thanks, I guess." I looked at the thin, nervous girl who had sat down next to me. This couldn't be a killer. "Why, Anna Maria? Did you kill Victor in cold blood?"

Anna Maria shook her head. "I got all freaked because Victor had a gun."

"They never found a gun on Victor, you know."

She was firm. "I know Victor had a gun." There was something in her brown eyes, a madness, a certainty. For some mysterious reason she knew that there was a gun alright.

"But why?"

That struck a nerve. She started crying. The worst I had ever seen. She covered her face in her eyes. I gave her tissues. Anna Maria was out of commission for a few minutes. I wanted to put my hand on her shoulder, but Dora gave me a dirty look.

"Don't you know when to quit?" She said.

One question too many, all right. When Joey went up for another beer. I thought about Jovanka for a moment, then followed him up to the bar. There was something else that bothered me.

"What about Eddie?" I asked. "Was he there?"

"He was by the time we got there," he said. "His mama don't have that much control over him so he goes to all the big parties."

I remembered something the judge had said to him about a hair cut. "Did Eddie used to have long hair?"

"Long as mine, dude," Joey said. "People used to confuse us and shit. Pretty funny now, no?"

"So after Victor went down, somebody with long hair took his gun. That was probably Eddie."

"I guess so, I have been telling everybody I wasn't there, but nobody believes me."

Joey walked away. "Hey man, I got to start playing again."

"Wait a minute," I said, loud enough for nearly the entire bar to hear. "You realize I'm going to have to subpoena you, all of you?"

"In Mexico?" said Dora, laughing. "For a bottle of tequila or a blow job, I can bribe a cop and get out of a subpoena. Good fucking luck on getting my ass back there. And I'm keeping my home girl back here too."

She put her arm on Anna Maria's shoulder, but it was still a firm arm nonetheless. Anna Maria started to squirm, but she knew she was no match for Dora. Once Dora was sure a message had been sent, she released Anna Maria. Anna Maria regained her composure, said nothing.

Dora looked at me. "You can have her back, when we're pretty sure that you've got enough to save her. Like get the gun."

She turned to Anna Maria. "Anna Maria, it's for your own good."

"But—" Anna Maria said. But she looked at six feet of Dora towering over her, then turned to me. "You won't let me down, let Jesus down, will you? You promised"

I touched her on the shoulder, looked her square in the eye. "I promised and I keep my promises." There was one thing I had to know." Are you going to stay here . . . with Dora?"

"Oh no," she said, shaking her head. "I got family down here. But they don't want me to testify neither."

Not a good sign. I had to salvage something from the night. I then looked at Joey "Hey man I came all the way here, I need someone to go back with me. You don't have to mention Anna Maria at all, I promise."

Joey thought for a second, smiled at me. "You did lend me that money, and you didn't even know me."

I smiled. "No problemo."

"I'm going to finish out my gig here tonight," he said, getting up. "But you got to buy me some stuff—"

"I can't buy you anything illegal back in the U.S."

"Don't worry, man. It's cool. I'll help you get Jesus innocent."

As he got up and went over to start playing with the band, Dora ordered two fifty-cent shots of tequila and gave one to me.

"To innocence," I said to her.

"To innocence," she agreed.

We did the lime and the salt thing and when we tossed them down, I almost choked on the harsh tequila. Dora motioned to a waitress, who brought her another shot.

"You know what," I said, slamming down another. "Mexico's not such a big deal, after all."

I spent the whole night at the Sunset Club which apparently never bothered to have a last call. After much prodding, and a few more Carta Blancas, I even joined Joey on stage for a spirited medley of *Welcome to the Jungle* and *Sweet Child O' Mine*.

For his encore, he invited Anna Maria up on stage to sing some old Spanish ballad. The shy girl protested of course, but Dora practically pushed her up on the stage. She downed a shot, then launched into a lilting soprano. Even the most stuck-up Anglo sorority girls soon cried in their beers.

I managed to get the number of an Alpha Chi who'd had a few Carta Blancas too many, telling her I was a big time lawyer "on the other side." She smiled at me, but she soon quickly grew transfixed with Joey as he seemed to channel Jimi Hendrix and Jim Morrison during his final encore. She crumpled up my number, left with him.

"Just be a few minutes, bro," he said. "Meet me outside."

Fifteen minutes later, he came back.

"Call me," the Alpha Chi said to him, as she got into a taxi. "I know you are gonna be a star."

Chapter 27

Alienated

I NEVER WENT TO SLEEP that night. I had about ten cups of coffee in a Denny's back on the American side. Joey pounded the coffee with me as well. In exchange for his testimony, I promised him I'd buy him a few electronic games at the new mall. He was amazed that we had similar taste—violent games with pretty girls on the cover. I don't think he'd ever met somebody with a credit card before. We didn't leave until late that afternoon.

We drove on a back road over the San Roberto mountains. Extremely animated, Joey kept telling me stories about Aguilar, people, pretty much everything except the case which was fine by me. He knew Sammy Quintana, Heidi Hawk, Oswald Thomas—everybody I knew in Aguilar.

Down in the desert valley, we passed mile after mile of sagebrush and arroyos. Joey's patter transported me back to a distorted version of my high school reunion at my prep school. Back home, my friends talked about who got into medical school and who was leaving Wall Street for an internet start-up. Here in the desert Joey told me about my new friends—unfortunately their fates were invariably prison or probation.

On the cut-off back to Aguilar near Roswell, Joey pointed out the road to the alien crash site, back in the forties.

There were all kinds of signs advertising various alien trinkets and what not. The lawyer in me wondered if the aliens got a cut of the proceeds.

"You believe in that uhhh . . . shit?" I asked him, driving past the turnoff.

"I don't know," he said, pondering his own existence. "Sometimes I wonder if y'know . . . I could be one."

I didn't laugh. He was serious.

"I mean, I don't really fit in sometimes. I always liked to think that somewhere. I could fit in. Who knows? Maybe there's a special planet for guys like us."

I looked around at the desert. The sun set behind a cloud to the west, the pinkish dirt did indeed resemble one of the less fashionable parts of Mars, or perhaps the homeworld of the Vulcans. There was nobody out here but us in any direction. "I know what you mean, man."

We didn't say anything more as we drove all the way into Aguilar. It got dark that time of year, so it felt like we were cruising through outer space in the pitch blackness of the desert. Every pair of headlights that rose and fell over the rolling hills could have been a shooting star or UFO.

When we arrived, we both went to the mail boxes at the same time. He got a party invitation. I didn't get shit.

His mother opened the door and gave him a great big hug.

Chapter 28

Holly Jolly Christmas

I TALKED WITH JESUS THE morning I got back in the interview room. I told him about the meeting, thanked him for confiding in me at last.

"I couldn't tell you before man," he said sheepishly. "The walls got ears. And you got a big mouth. I'm still trying to figure this whole thing out."

"So am I. But why make me go all the way to Mexico?"

"I used to wrestle, you know? My coach used to say something about going the distance. 'Don't trust people who can't go the distance.'"

"And if I didn't go the distance?"

"I would have got another lawyer."

"So what do you want to do? There's got to be a way to force Anna Maria back here."

"No one's forcing her to do shit," he said, adamantly. "I don't want her back here in the U.S.A., until I know you can save her."

"I'm working on it." I said. "You know, you could always take the stand. Testify that Anna Maria—"

"You want me to go up there and testify that my girlfriend's guilty?" He stared at me with that tattooed eye as if I had insulted his manhood. "Not even."

Still no Christmas cards in my mailbox on December 24th so I decided to work Christmas Eve and save the vacation days for later. My parents were in Costa Rica, for two whole weeks—there was nothing for me at home either.

Pete still had a few more witnesses on his trial down in Carlsbad during the days. The office was utterly empty. He'd even taken his stick and string with him.

For lunch, I went to Rosalita's, but it was empty without Anna Maria. On the way back to the office one day, a blue pickup pulled up in the alley right behind me. I recognized the driver, Enrique, Anna Maria's brother.

"Don't fuck with my sister," he said, following behind me. I hurried over to the office, then looked around.

As the truck drove away, I clearly saw the writing on the back. What had looked like "Oolloriusliee" back on the acequia trail, now read:

OUT FOR JUSTICE

• • • •

A good movie played that evening at the local theater. I had to get out of the house, even if I had no one to take. Anyway, it was dollar night.

Every juvenile delinquent in town was at the theater when I arrived, and every single one had a date. At the front of the line was Tommy, the drunk driver and paint sniffer, accompanied by a knockout blond in a tight black Garth Brooks T-shirt. Adam, the teenage burglar who worked at the video store, was right behind them. He was with Heidi Hawk, the cheerleader who took starter fluid, and Stephanie Yi, a young Asian woman whose good looks belied her conviction on an aggravated burglary.

I went to the back of the line and stood behind the one yuppiesque guy in the crowd. I stared at his date for a moment, then recognized her. It was Deb-the-Deb, from the Oil Baron Club. His name was Cliff Something-or-other, and he did oil and gas law for the big local firm, Gibson and Yale. Cliff was explaining the difference between "sweet Texas crude," the basis of the commodities market, and "sour" crude, which apparently had either too much or too little carbon dioxide. Deb, who learned about the biz from her father, listened in rapt attention.

"Before tonight," I piped in, "I'd have thought that sweet and sour gas is something you get at a Chinese restaurant."

After a few awkward seconds without anyone cracking a smile, Deb asked me about Sky's trial.

"I don't really know anything," I said. "I'm handling a codefendant. I don't know. The cops haven't released any information."

They started talking about a New Year's Eve party in the Oil

Baron's Club. I definitely wasn't going to be on the mailing list for that one.

Sandoval and Thompson came in right behind us, dressed like preppies in blue sweaters accompanied by their pretty young wives.

"Hey Shepard," said Thompson, "you must have gotten a lot of furloughs tonight. All your friends are here in line with you."

"Yeah, right."

"Don't ask me any questions about the movie tonight, okay, bro?" Sandoval said. "I liked that two-question cross-examination you did on me once, you know? I wish all the lawyers did those. Make my life a hell of a lot easier."

"Hey guys, remember: in the cases I handle, I've got a higher conviction rate than you do."

Why was no one laughing at my jokes tonight?

"So how come you're by yourself?" Thompson asked. "In a county with one of the highest teen pregnancy rates in America, you'd think a hot-shot trial lawyer could get a date to a movie."

"I don't date my clients," I said. "I have some ethical standards. I guess that's pretty rare for a defense attorney."

"Ethics are not just rare with defense attorneys," said Sandoval. Thompson frowned at his partner.

When the movie began seating and the line began surging into the theater, I spied Amanda. She sat with Pete who was still in his clip-on tie for trial, his mind still clearly plotting his closing. She didn't look happy. I scrunched behind one of the cops so she wouldn't see me and strained shamelessly to hear their raised voices. Both of them were clearly angry. I caught a couple of swear words but couldn't get the drift of the argument. At one point Amanda actually walked out of the line, but before I could get my hopes up, Pete somehow convinced her to return. They still hadn't seen me, but from my seat five rows back I could hear a little soft sobbing from Amanda a few times during quiet parts of the movie. Were they sobs for the on-screen drama or the off-screen whatever it was?

At the end of the movie, they walked out arm in arm. They waved when they saw me. I reluctantly waved back, headed for home.

When I got home, I left a message on Amanda's machine. "One of the side effects of becoming a public defender is that you start to actually give a shit about other people. Are you okay? Give me a call sometime."

The phone didn't ring Christmas day or the day after. The office was closed so I watched football then caught a Lobo basketball game on ESPN. On Monday, the 27th, I went to the office. I could always play computer games for entertainment.

On the desk was another plea offer. Twenty years this time. Twenty whole years. I had already cost Jesus another two years and the trial hadn't even started yet. Behind the offer was a copy of Eddie's statement. Jesus, Eddie said, had planned the whole thing with Sky Roberts. They had lured Victor out as part of a drug conspiracy. They also had a statement from one Paul Celestino, the guy who hung up on me my first week, with a direct quote of Jesus stating that he "would fucking kill Victor before the night was out."

The fact that there was planning and premeditation, that was "malice aforethought" or something bad like that, hurt our case. Every time I found out something good about Jesus, the State found something to make his situation worse. My star witness was in Mexico and my alibi witness was . . . Joey. I was in great shape? Yeah right. . . .

I called Jovanka. "So how come we're up to twenty years now?"

"Standard procedure. The harder I have to work, the more time your client has to do. By the way, what is your defense? If any."

"Uhh . . . alibi," I said. "But I can't really tell you exactly."

She didn't let me finish. "You realize of course that you have to file a "Notice of Intent to Claim Alibi" detailing everything that any alibi witness is going to say and I will get to depose those witnesses."

I didn't realize it of course. So Joey and I were going to be spending a lot of time together. But would he be a good enough witness?

"So what happens if I take it to trial and lose?" I asked after a moment of doubt.

"I'll ask for life."

"How long is life?"

"Life is life if you're bad. Jesus can get out in thirty years if he's good. But most kids don't make it that long in the joint, especially if they kill a football hero in a football town."

I hung up and went over to the jail to talk to Jesus.

When he walked into the interview room, he looked much older now, thinner and paler. Adulthood wasn't agreeing with him so far. But his eyes lit up when he saw me. And lit down when I gave him the bad news.

"So what do you want to do?" I asked. "All we got is Joey to back you up."

He shrugged, picked up the new plea offer. "The plea's for twenty years—that's ten years with good time, no?"

I stared at the tattoo of the Virgin on his arm. "That's if we plead. It's life if we take it to trial and lose, which is at least thirty years."

"Thirty years? Dude, I'm only eighteen."

For a second I thought he would cry. I sure would have. But he kept his hands firmly over his eyes as if he were pushing the tears back inside of them. Then he took a few deep breaths. I watched him calm himself, took a deep breath of my own.

"I'm scared," he said.

"So am I."

"Will you fight for me?"

I couldn't help going with the cliché. "I'll go the distance."

"Will you save my Anna Maria?"

"I'll try."

"Let's take this fucker to trial."

"You got it."

Amanda never called, but she did send over a tape of the hearing in T or C, that I missed while I was in Mexico. I was famous and didn't even know it. I had a strange sexual thrill when she said, "Jesus's attorney, Dan Shepard, provided spirited argument for his client."

Sky pled out the next afternoon—misdemeanor aggravated battery. Judge Perez had been on vacation so Rose did the plea before Judge Henry who had come over. Judge Henry must have been playing Santa Claus that day, he gave Sky the year, then suspended the entire sentence, ordered him not to leave the jurisdiction until the whole matter was resolved.

The national media buried the story, but Sky was happy to make the cover of one of the tabloids.

I bumped into Sky in the men's room outside the courtroom. He was so happy to be free of it all I don't think he remembered exactly how he knew me.

I certainly didn't want to remind him that I could be questioning him in a few weeks. I asked him how it was going.

"It's been great, man. My agent says her phones are ringing off the hook."

"What do you mean?"

"I might even get a series out of this. I mean, this shit is like a good career move."

Rose entered as we were both leaving. "I don't know why you're so stressed," he said, opening his zipper. "This criminal law thing isn't that hard if you have the right client."

I wanted to dunk his head into the urinal, but I restrained myself.

Dora and Anna Maria stayed out by the border as far as I knew, so Joey remained starved for companionship. Day after day, he came over to my office and played my knockoff of the Tomb Raider game. He showed me how to get past the tomb with all the snakes in it.

"It's not that big a deal man," he told me over and over again, until I finally navigated through it successfully by using a rock to kill the last snake.

I finally succeeded. He seemed as happy as me when the computer triumphantly announced "Welcome to the next level."

His mother had given him a new computer game for Christmas, and he vowed that he'd show me how to win at that one too. "I hope you're a better lawyer than you are a game player."

As the week went on, he kept inviting me to go to a local New Year's Eve party with him. The party would rock. That sorority girl would even be coming over from Cruces.

I politely told him that it was not a good idea for me to hang out and be a potential witness against any of my clients.

• • • •

New Year's Eve itself was windy and cold enough to be unpleasant, but not enough for snow. The sky was overcast, everything drained of color, like a black and white movie.

It was dark by the time I drove home down Oil Avenue. For once I appreciated all the neon of the few tacky tourist motels. Since I couldn't see the encroaching desert, I could pretend I was actually in civilization.

I stopped to rent a video. The store was empty. Everybody in town was out partying somewhere except me. An ancient *Playboy* "video calendar" was the only erotic video in town and I felt a little self-conscious about renting it from Adam, my former burglary client.

I don't know why I bothered with videos anyway. My Wal-Mart VCR had taken to distorting the top third of the screen from time to time and twice, as if on cue, during sex scenes. There was really nothing I could do about it. Yelling "lower!" at the actors didn't succeed in getting them to confine their antics to the untouched part of the set.

There wasn't much to choose from, so I went with urban angst: *Training Day* and *Colors* were about the most up-to date movies I could find. Walking into my building, I saw two figures walk out into the desert on the acequia road. It was too dark for me to make out who they were.

My spirits sank as I shut my door, locked myself in for the night. I turned on the tube. I turned on MTV for the year's Rap countdown, until the third one featuring a gangster surrounded by a harem of women pissed me off enough to switch channels. Every minute a local bulletin would traipse across the bottom of the screen: "Flash flood warning for Aguilar and Crater Counties. High-wind watch for Maljamar."

They weren't kidding. By six o'clock, a violent rainstorm made more noise than the TV commercials. The power went off at six-oh-five. I sat in the dark and listened to the rain, counting the beats between the thunder and the lightning.

After an hour the rain stopped and it was quiet. I heard the rushing torrent of water through the acequia. Finally the lights came back on and I started watching *Training Day*. It was weird, but at that moment I felt like Ethan Hawke's white cop after he'd been abandoned in the gang party.

Then I put on *Colors*, a flick I'd seen twice before about gangs in pre-riot Los Angeles. I loved the Rap song at the end of the movie, delivered by the legendary Ice-T: "Any problem I got, I just put my fist in."

One scene really got to me, a party at a gang members house. The party looked like fun: hot señoritas dancing in skimpy outfits, everybody hanging with their homeboys. Then suddenly, shots rang out from outside. The shootees drew their own guns, rushed to the windows to return fire. . . .

Since I couldn't think of anything else to do, I stopped the tape, grabbed some Vaseline and went into the bathroom. Happy fucking New Year.

I heard the Aguilar tradition gunshots in the air at midnight, but I didn't bother to get out of bed. I drifted into an uneasy sleep. I vaguely remember a dream about the gang party scene from *Colors*, except I was there—still in my underwear. Everybody was laughing, dancing. I even danced, with a sense of rhythm for the first time in my life. A vague approximation of Amanda, if Amanda had pledged the Crips instead of the Kappas, danced with me. Or was it Eva Mendez or Salma Hayek, one of them? Whoever she was, my name was tattooed in blue across her neck.

Some people left the party, but I couldn't place who they were. Suddenly, gunfire smashed through the windows of the house. Everybody ducked, then jumped up, grabbing weapons out of their clothing. They rushed to the door.

Someone was down. I looked down. It was Jesus, his white shirt was covered in blood. Anna Maria cradled him in her arms, the blood had covered her as well.

"Save me, ese," he uttered with his dying breath. "Save me."

• • • •

I woke up with the sun. I resented the fact that I didn't have a hangover. If I was this clearheaded, I might as well start the year off right and go for a run.

I wanted to avoid the acequia trail but in every direction I tried, loudly barking dogs lined the yards creating a noisy gauntlet. I certainly didn't want to wake anybody with a hangover who owned a shotgun so I passed the tumbleweed graveyard and started running along the quiet dirt of the trail.

The wind picked up behind me, pushed me forward. I soon ran faster than I had ever run before, breathing in the crisp air still damp from the last night's rain. Then suddenly the wind shifted—I sniffed the stench of the dead dog, only a thousand times worse. I looked down in the acequia—two bodies with bullet holes in their foreheads stared back at me.

Their bodies were sprawled as if they had been pushed around after death. It took me a second to recognize them now that rigor mortis had set in.

It was Joey and Eddie.

Chapter 29

Happy Fucking New Year Indeed

I MADE THE 911 CALL from my apartment, my hands shaking so badly I misdialed twice before getting it right.

"An officer will be there in a few minutes," Miss 911 replied. "Please wait for him in front."

Luckily, it was the friendly Sandoval rather than Thompson the asshole who arrived in the squad car a few minutes later.

"My head hurts," he said. "You party all night?"

"No. I didn't."

It took us longer to drive up over the mud, weeds, and rocks than it had taken me to run the distance.

"It could have been a satanic ritual killing," I said. "Both of those kids had ties. Or maybe it was just a gang thing."

He shook his head. "There are so many reasons to kill both of those kids, you don't even need to get to gangs or Satan."

"This is it." I said.

Sandoval stopped the car. I ran to the edge and looked over into the ditch. There was nothing there. Just some damp earth. Had they been moved. Mutilated? Was the killer still here? Were they ever there at all?

"Over here," Sandoval said, a few yards back by a bend in the ditch. "You must have gone a little too far."

He radioed for backup then gave me a ride back to my apartment. "Stay near a phone, okay?"

About an hour later I got a call to go back to the police station. I went to the interview room. Thompson and Sandoval waited for me, behind them sat a very testy Jovanka Smith.

The lights of the ceiling glared down at me. I had failed a lie detector test once when applying for a job at a bank and hated the prospect of being questioned.

"Do I need a lawyer?" I asked.

Thompson grinned. "Dumbfuck, you are a lawyer," he said.

"For the record, Dan," Sandoval said. "Will you please tell us what you found?"

"I woke up this morning and I took a run. After a couple of minutes I smelled something really bad and I looked over in the ditch and saw the bodies. I went back and called 911"

"You didn't touch anything?"

"No."

Jovanka stepped up close to my chair. "You didn't like Eddie, did you?"

Was she blaming me? "I didn't really know him. He wasn't an enemy but I certainly wouldn't call us 'friends.'"

"Did you ever have any prior dealings with him?"

"Yeah. He mad-dogged me in the mall. And one time him and Enrique Arias ran me off into the ditch."

"Enrique Arias," said Thompson. "You positive?"

"Yeah. I know it was his truck."

Thompson wrote down Enrique's name in his things-to-do file.

"So you didn't like either Eddie or Enrique?"

"Uh . . . no. Back East we tend not to like people who run us off the road. I guess it's a big city thing."

Jovanka kept up the pressure. "When was the last time you saw Joey Lilly alive?"

"A couple of days ago."

"What did you talk about?"

"How to kill the snakes in the last tomb in this computer game I've got."

"Sure you did," said Thompson. "What did you do last night? New Year's Eve."

"Nothing."

"No parties?"

"No. I stayed home."

"Were you alone?"

"Yes."

"Don't you have a life?"

"No, I don't."

"You read Eddie's statement saying it was your client that planned the whole thing?"

"Yeah."

"How did that make you feel?"

"Not good."

"Anything else?"

"I saw two figures go off from my apartment complex at about five, as I was coming in. I don't know who they were."

"Could it have been Joey and Eddie?"

"I guess so."

Thompson turned off the tape recorder and handed me a business card. "Here, take this. You might need it."

The card was for Bonilla Bail Bonds. I had become one of the usual suspects. I looked at Thompson, who couldn't keep himself from chuckling when he glanced in my direction.

I thought of a favorite Bob Dylan line: "When you got nothing, you got nothing to lose." Joey, this one's for you, ese.

I stood up and stared at the chuckling Thompson. "Yes, I hated Eddie. Yes, I have no friends in this shithole town who aren't criminals and can't get laid to save my life, so I don't have an alibi. Yes, I saw two figures leave my apartment complex. But I don't have a fucking gun. I have no fucking motive whatsoever, and I'm sure as fuck worse off with Joey dead. You can't fucking hold me and you fucking well know it. I'm leaving. Just round up some more of the usual suspects and call it a day."

I turned to Jovanka and lowered my voice. "I am sorry about your son. There were times when it looked like he was going to make it but he hung around with some rough people. But don't try to make up for his death by fucking with me."

Jovanka looked hurt. "Dan, you're overreacting."

"No. I haven't been reacting enough."

Sandoval smiled. "You're free to go now."

If I could only sound that tough in front of a jury.

Chapter 30

January Blahs

"POLICE ARE INVESTIGATING A SHOCKING double murder just outside of Aguilar," Amanda said from my TV screen at six-twenty-two that night. "The body of Edward Smith, the son of Deputy District Attorney Jovanka Smith, was found lying in a ditch outside town with a bullet in his forehead. With him was Joey Lilly, a suspect in the shooting of Officer Diamond. Satanic paraphernalia was found near the site. Although suicide has not been ruled out, police have not found a weapon at the scene of the crime. Anyone who has any information on this case should come forward and contact the Aguilar Police Department. The police are looking for Enrique Arias, a possible suspect in the case."

My mentioning Enrique had made him a "usual suspect." Oh well, fuck him. . . .

The scene shifted to a small adobe courthouse. "Jurors today reached a not guilty verdict in the murder trial of Dave Santisteven of Espanola. He was accused of killing five men in a shoot-out in Rio Arriba County, including former Aguilar resident, Sammy Quintana, the bartender at the Tumbleweeds Club here in Aguilar, who was in Espanola visiting friends."

I shuddered. The face on the screen was Sammy Quintana's. I remembered him from the bar. I felt a pang of guilt . . . if I hadn't got him out, he'd still be alive.

The camera now focused on a large man in a black cowboy hat captioned "RICKY CLARK, SANTISTEVEN'S ATTORNEY."

"This was not murder," said Clark. "This was the day that God abandoned Espanola."

"What's up with the weather?" said Amanda after the scene faded. "Details after the break."

I turned off the set and thought about Jesus. "It was not murder," I said to myself. "It was the day that God abandoned Aguilar."

On my desk the next morning was a message—Jesus wanted to see me. I headed right over to jail and saw the red-haired woman who'd carried a sign for Jimmy on the steps. Today's sign read:

I LOVE YOU, FRANKIE

"Could you say hi to Frankie if you see him?" she asked. Frankie was in on carjacking, I believe.

"Uh . . . sure. What happened to Jimmy?"

"Things didn't work once he got out. Hey, I saw you on TV coupla days ago! You looked good."

"Thanks a lot. Good luck with Frankie."

"Well, God bless you Mr. Shepard," she said. "Good luck."

Veronica sat at her desk as usual, turning the first page of her latest opus—*Crime and Punishment.*

"Raskolnikov was the killer," I told her, noticing the title. "It's a surprise."

"Don't spoil it."

After I buzzed through the gates. Gardea brought Jesus down. He smiled when he saw me and we shook hands in the local manner, which I had finally mastered.

"You heard about Joey and Eddie?" I asked.

"It's fucked up, man," he said. "I'm going to miss Joey."

"So will I," I said. "So will I."

"You going to the funeral? Go for me, okay?"

"Sure. But I don't get it. Why would Joey go off into the ditch with Eddie?"

"Joey was like that. He just wanted everybody to love him. You could say anything to him and he'd do it. Eddie probably just told him to go out and he went."

"So where does Enrique come in?"

"He doesn't." he said. He took a deep breath. "I'm gonna kill that fucker someday. He was the one who told Anna Maria not to complain about Victor. I hate him. I fucking mean it."

I laughed. "I hate Enrique too. I'll help you kill him. But if we do it right, you better not tell everyone and his brother this time."

He smiled, closed his eyes as if plotting the perfect murder.

"So if Enrique didn't do it," I said, breaking his reverie "Who killed them?"

"Think about it, bro. After Guillermo, who's the craziest fucker in this town?"

"I don't know. Eddie, I guess."

"You guess right, bro. I sat with him that day coming back from T or C. He had that look—the hasta-la-vista-life look."

"And what about Joey?"

"Eddie probably wanted to take Joey along for the ride. Him and Joey had been real close until all the shit went down and no one knew who to trust anymore."

I still wasn't satisfied. "If you're saying Eddie killed him, then killed himself, where is the gun?"

"Hey, you're the lawyer; I'm the criminal, no? You figure it out."

Chapter 31

Life's A Ditch

January 5 9

AMANDA WASN’T ON THE NEWS Thursday, Friday, or Saturday. The Albuquerque station didn’t even break for the local cutaway. Without Amanda, nothing worth reporting happened in Aguilar.

The messages I left on her machine grew progressively more desperate. “Call me when you get a chance,” on the first day. “Is something wrong? Please call me,” on the second. And on Saturday: “Whatever I’ve done, I’m sorry. Just call me, please. . . .”

On Saturday night, bored yet again, I watched network TV coverage of a terrorist raid in the Middle East, then a story about a group of hikers caught in an avalanche out by Sierra Milagro, New Mexico. The voice-over for the avalanche story sounded familiar. Sure enough, there she was, our own Amanda Finch, bundled up in a long black winter coat, interviewing the search crews. She’d made the big time at last.

There was a big turnout at the church that Sunday for Joey’s funeral service. He was more popular than he let on. His mother, the waitress who looked like Roseanne, was in the front with the rest of the family. A few teenagers were in the pews. Dora sat in a corner. Neither of them made eye contact with me, as if they blamed me somehow for Joey’s death.

I was surprised to see Amanda still wearing that long black coat, without her camera. I sat down next to her.

“Why are you here?” I asked.

“I always get real sad whenever a young kid gets killed.” She looked over at me. “And I figured you’d be here.”

“Where’s your camera?”

“Please, Dan. The station wanted coverage, but I have some scruples.”

"I just spoke to him a few days ago and he was really turning his life around. He was going to testify for Jesus." I expected her to ask me what about, but she didn't. She had scruples after all.

"I don't know if there's any attorney client privilege after death," I said, "but he was going to clear Jesus."

"What was he like?"

"I never thought I'd say this about a long-haired rocker trash, paint-sniffing Satanist, but Joey was a friend of mine."

"It's just sad, real sad."

"If I hadn't gone to see him to get him to come back, none of this would have happened."

"You're not blaming yourself, are you?"

"Some. By the way, I was real impressed with your coverage of those hikers up in the mountains. You're really getting good. I can remember when you had trouble just holding the mike steady."

She smiled. "At my first performance review they told me to really work on that. Hey, sorry I couldn't call you. I was practically camping out up there."

"No problem. I'm the asshole. I shouldn't have left so many messages on your machine."

Before we could say anything more, the service began. It was brief, there weren't that many good things for the priest to say except how tragic it was to lose a boy so young. He asked if anyone in the audience had anything to say. He looked around for a long time—Joey's friends weren't real big extemporaneous public speakers.

Joey's mother looked over at me. "Joey liked you, Daniel. You should say something."

Reluctantly I went up to the podium. I stared at Joey's friends. I expected a tough crowd, but shit, I knew half of them from court. They nodded at me with recognition. I wondered if any of them could say they felt the same . . . alienation that Joey had felt. I looked at them closely. In their T-shirts and tattoos, they looked pretty human to me.

"I got to know Joey pretty well," I began. "Not just as a . . .client, but as a person . . . as a friend. But I never got to tell him that. Joey taught me how to get past the snake room in this video game we used to play together. . . ."

They smiled.

"He was my neighbor," I said after another moment. "He taught me how to kill snakes."

I forced a smile. "Wherever he is . . . I hope he made it to the next level."

It wasn't onions this time. There really was a tear. I sat down. I certainly didn't want to say the one thing too many with a crowd like this.

Dora nodded to me. I had said something right. She left without saying another word to me. I still had a long way to go with her.

Amanda wanted to clear out after the service. "I don't think I want to stay to honor the skinhead from hell."

"Amanda, I'm sorry about what happened that time."

"It turned out all right. There were guards everywhere. I probably wasn't in any real danger."

I looked at her. "I'm still sorry."

Part of me wanted to leave with her but a part of me had a sick sense of curiosity. Like a horror movie, I wanted to make sure that he was really dead.

The chapel was cleared of all of Joey's mourners, except myself, when Eddie's much larger party streamed in. There were lawyers, cops, family members . . . but no teenagers, which didn't surprise me. He hadn't been exactly popular with his peers. The only person his age was that girl he'd been with at the party, the one from the girls' school. She was dressed in black.

There was another brief service, then Merril got up to say how sad it was that this poor young boy had never reached his potential and now would never get another chance. "We don't know how it happened," he said at the end, "but we're going to bring whoever did this to justice!"

Jovanka got up and said a few words about how we would all miss Eddie, but mainly she thanked all of us for coming and offering our support. As before, her accent, whatever it was, had thickened up, as though she was homesick for the simpler times of her youth.

It was an open casket. Eddie was dead alright.

"You here in your official capacity?" I asked Sandoval, who stood guard by the hearse outside the chapel in case anyone tried to steal the body.

"You better believe it. Never could stand that little sh—uh, kid, Eddie. I hate to speak ill of the dead but. . . ." He looked around to make sure that no one else was in earshot. "You'd be surprised at what people are saying about him now that he can't do anything to them. Very surprised."

"As a matter of fact," I said, "I probably know a lot more about Eddie than you think." We made eye contact for a moment. "Something I'd like to know, though, is whether he owned a gun?"

"Hell, I don't know. All I know is that Jovanka hated kids with guns, so I'm positive she'd never allow him to have one at the house. Her crusade was, 'If there's one thing I hate, it's kids who kill.'"

"What about outside his home? Anyone ever see him with one?"

"You might want to talk to George Cloud," Sandoval said. "He's an actor on the movie set. He might be able to tell you some things about the Late Great Eddie Smith."

"I take it you still haven't found the gun?"

"It could be anywhere. If they were shot, somebody must have thrown the gun away somewhere. Or Eddie killed Joey, or Joey killed Eddie, and then kids could have come around and stole the gun out of their hands. But as of now, we still haven't found it."

"Maybe you don't know where to look."

"Maybe we just aren't looking that hard."

I remembered Pete's words on my second day in Aguilar—time to take a little road trip to the scene of the crime. If the cops weren't going to look that hard for the missing gun, maybe I should. Enrique was an asshole, but he was just a usual suspect, and didn't have anything against Joey as far as I knew. If Eddie had killed Joey, as Jesus had suggested, the gun was probably still there. And it just might be the thing to bring back Anna Maria.

I called Amanda the next day. "I really think that you should come running with me out by the Acequia this afternoon."

"I don't know," she said. "It's freezing and the tumbleweeds are blowing like crazy."

"I've got a hunch. Trust me on this. You might want to take your camera. It might be worth your while."

"Don't you watch TV? I go on at six-twenty-two!"

"If we leave at four you'll be back by five and you might have something exciting to say at six-twenty-two."

We met in the parking lot of the Acequia Vista. For all her complaints about the cold and wind, she was dressed in tight black Spandex biking shorts and a thin windbreaker without a hood. Her pale legs still looked great, even with goose pimples. I was freezing in my ski-team sweats.

"I'll leave my camera in the truck, okay?"

"Sure."

We jogged slowly to the acequia trail and in a few minutes made it to the site. The acequia was now bone dry, the shallow indentations where the bodies had lain in the sand unmistakable. I looked at the two indentations and my mind flashed to Eddie returning the magazines he could have shoplifted, saw Joey making it to "Level Seven" on one of the computer games in my office.

"Welcome to the next level," I mumbled to myself.

"We didn't get any good video," she said. "The bodies were moved before we got here."

For a moment a tumbleweed came to rest, and then a gust of wind blew it down the acequia. Subsequent gusts carried it down along the ditch until it was out of sight before, presumably, coming to rest at the tumbleweed graveyard by the grating.

"Let's look around the ditch for a while," I said.

"What for?"

"We'll know it when you see it."

I crossed over the embankment to the target range, its terrain pock-marked with holes. In one pit, the decaying remains of a small animal; in another, a small pile of bones. There were some sharp rocks arranged in circles filled with dead embers, empty bottles of Jack Daniels, and empty aerosol paint cans. Every few feet, a pentagram was etched in the dirt.

"What do you see?" she asked from below.

"Come over here. You've got to check this out."

I watched her emerge from the ditch. The wind kicked up all kinds of dirt, swirled her chestnut highlights—she was now a Botticelli Venus rising from the dust.

"What is this place?" she asked.

"It's sort of a Mickey Mouse Club for the young Satanist."

"What would they do here?"

"Some target shooting in the day, a little animal sacrifice at night."

"People, too?"

"I don't know," I said. "I don't even want to think about that. Hopefully, they stuck with rabbits and lizards."

"What about cats? I lost my cat a few months ago."

"I really don't want to look for it right now."

She looked around and spotted some bones in a circle of rocks. "Me either. You think whoever did it hid the gun here?"

I pointed to an empty tool shed against the side of a ridge. "It was probably hid in this shed here before. I think Eddie kept his gun out here and came out to get it."

"How do you know?"

"I don't."

"You mean these kids would leave guns in that shed?"

"I don't think his mom would let him have one at home," I said. "Besides, would you come here if you didn't have to?"

"Do we have to be here now?"

I sighed. "Let's just look inside. There's probably nothing inside."

We walked over to the little shed. I opened the door. Suddenly something lunged out of the darkness, a rattlesnake. The rattlesnake had good taste—it coiled in front of Amanda instead of me.

"Dan! Do something!"

I remember what Joey had taught me in the computer game—I grabbed a sharp rock from the circle and hurled it on the snake, stunning it. I grabbed another, slammed it over the snake's head. I threw the dead snake off into the ditch.

"My hero."

"No problemo."

"Let's get out of here," she said.

We crossed back over the ditch to get to the road on the other side. As we crossed into the ditch, a weed jammed up against the embankment before being carried down the ditch by the next burst of wind.

"Maybe the snakes got the gun," Amanda said. "Or maybe it was the wind."

My eyes followed the weed as it tumbled along. I remembered that the shooting took place on New Year's Eve, the night the storm knocked out the power. If the gun was left in the ditch, maybe it had been carried off by the water flow from the storm. If that was true, the gun might be in the Gulf of Mexico by now. Or. . . .

"Come on! Follow me."

We ran back in the ditch until we came to the tumbleweed graveyard. All the weeds were piled up against the grating by the tunnel under Oil Avenue. I combed my fingers through a few weeds right by the grate until I felt something hard and metallic—a Tech-9.

"Is that it?" Amanda asked.

"I don't know yet. You probably want to hold off on the news until we know what to do with it."

"Is there someone I should call?"

"Could you go back to your truck and call Pete? It's only about four-thirty, so he should still be there. Tell him I'm over here with something real big but don't tell him I've told you anything."

"Sure," she said. "Once again, thanks for killing the snake. It pretty much makes up for. . . ."

She didn't have to finish the sentence. She put her hand on my arm. "By the way, I might want to interview you and your boy soon."

I smiled. "Who me?" And when did Jesus become "my boy?"

She ran back to the station's truck, started it up, and drove past me, waving. The truck had a bumper sticker whose first letter had peeled off: _ITCHES ARE DEADLY. Ditches? Bitches? Witches?

Since the office was only a few minutes away, Pete would show up soon. I stayed down in the ditch with the dead tumbleweeds in case someone came for the gun. After a few minutes I jumped around to keep warm, not easy with a full bladder. Finally tired of waiting, I peed against the side of the embankment when Pete finally showed.

"I've seen someone piss before," Pete said. "Is that why you called me all the way the fuck out here?"

I pulled up my sweat pants and pointed. "Look what's here. It's a gun."

"I can see that it's a gun," he said. "You know how many guns there are lying around in this town? Every asshole in Aguilar that ever robbed a 7-Eleven has probably thrown a gun into a ditch somewhere."

"Eddie and Joey were shot in the ditch a few hundred yards upstream," I said patiently. "On New Year's Eve. I was here New Year's Eve and there was a major, major rain storm. You know, when the power went off? The gun got washed away in the rain and ended up down here."

"So?"

"I've heard that Eddie was probably the guy who shot Diamond. And I think he shot Joey, too. Think about it. Where do you think Eddie got the gun? His mother wouldn't let him have a gun. He was high on some kind of nasty shit and he took the gun from Victor. Then he used that gun to shoot Joey. Then himself."

"So get some expert to say it's the same gun," he said. "Turn it into the police," said Pete. "Make sure you get a receipt. They'll send it to Lee Yazzie at the State Forensic Lab. Give him a call in a few weeks."

That night I knocked on Dora's door. There was moaning coming from inside, but I kept knocking.

Finally Dora opened the door, that Japanese robe rapped around her body. "This better be good, baby lawyer. I was about to see God that time."

"Tell Anna Maria she can come home now," I told her. "I found the gun."

"You've got to do better than that," she said, slamming the door again. The moaning started before I even made it to the door.

Chapter 32

Good News, Bad News

Late January

ONCE THE GUN WAS SAFELY(?) in police custody, Amanda broke the story over the air. The next day she reported that the gun "might have a connection not only to the deaths of Eddie Smith and Joey Lilly, but also to the shooting of Officer Diamond last fall."

The next morning I received a white carnation with a Thank-You note signed "Love, Amanda."

"Love, Amanda." Orale ese.

I called Lee Yazzie, the state forensics expert, and after a few days of phone tag, he got back to me. He generally testified as an expert witness for the state and didn't sound happy to talk with a defense attorney.

"Yazzie . . . that's an unusual name," I said.

"Not when you're a Navajo."

Thankfully, I had learned enough not to call him kemo sabe. "The gun I sent you, is it the same gun that killed Eddie?"

"It's the same type, same type of bullets. But it was a couple of weeks later so there weren't good fingerprints on it. We're still awaiting the tests and all that because there's kind of a backup after the holiday rush. Can't say for sure it is the exact one."

"Was it the gun used in the shooting of Officer Diamond?"

"Once again, same type of gun, same type of bullet. We did do the tests on that a few months ago and there was a pretty good match but I can't say anything else for sure."

"Can you say anything for sure?"

"Yeah. You better get someone who can make a positive ID on that gun. Don't count on me."

In my mailbox I found the official trial date for Jesus: Tuesday,

April 8. That didn't seem so far away anymore. That Monday, after docket call, I went to the jail to talk to him.

"Good news," I said. "We found the gun and the lab guy says it could be the one Eddie used to shoot Diamond. And if that's true, it could be the same gun that freaked out Anna Maria."

"So that means we can show self-defense for Anna Maria, no?"

"Maybe. Officer Sandoval told me to call this guy, George Cloud, who might be able to help us out on the ID of the gun. If we get that, we can pull it off. Win your case and walk Anna Maria at the same time."

"So, que paso with you?" he asked.

"Come again?"

"We're always talking about me in here. How things going with you, bro? Like how's your love life?"

"I don't know. Things are kind of . . . ambiguous."

"Ambiguous? That's too bad, isn't there like a shot for that?" He laughed at my expression. "Bro, I know what ambiguous means. You're like this big-time lawyer and shit. Chicks should be, like, throwing themselves at you."

"It's not that simple."

"I'm a poor little cholo with a record and I got laid all the time. That was before I knew the word, or met Anna Maria." He grinned. "So like I say, que paso with you?"

I thought about a summer I spent working answering phones as an intern in Washington, my face covered with pimples, my body flaccid from a diet of Big Macs and fries, bitching about grades and LSAT scores all the time. Women had indeed thrown themselves at me, but that was long ago, in a different place.

"It's complicated," I said. "You wouldn't understand."

Chapter 33

All's Fair in Law and War

February 5

THE AGUILAR COUNTY FAIR GENERALLY ran in October, this year it kicked off on the first Saturday in February to accommodate some famous traveling rodeo tour. The weather in February was quite pleasant, in the fifties and dry, the occasional tumbleweed blowing in the wind.

Everyone in town went to The Fair. Everyone. Residents from the jail besieged us with furlough requests—everybody had to visit a sick mother or grandmother. Even I had my part, helping Pete with the Aguilar County Bar Association's mock trial exhibition.

After I paid my dollar admission, I walked toward the rodeo grounds. Heidi the paint sniffer, Stephanie her co-defendant and Adam the burglar ate cotton candy, waiting in line to play Mortal Kombat at the arcade. I felt a little like Holden Caulfield, aspiring to be a catcher in the weeds, catching these poor kids about to go off the cliff, hopefully guiding them back to the innocence of youth. But it wasn't just criminals: Cliff and Deb-the-Deb kicked the tires on the brand new car that was the grand prize in a drawing. Sandoval and Thompson, complete with pretty wives, waited in line to buy hot dogs.

Thompson paid for his and brought them back to a table of kids. When we were alone, Sandoval asked me, "Talked to Cloud yet?"

"Not yet. I've been really busy."

"Real good idea for you folks to meet," he said.

I thanked him, then almost collided with a tall blond woman in a cowboy hat. "You're the bastard representing the kid who killed my son," she said.

I recognized her from the hospital. She was still wearing the same outfit. "Uh . . . yeah."

"Well, fuck you!"

"Ma'am, I'm . . . uh . . . real sorry about your boy. I really am."

"You lawyers, you're like the guys who rob 7-Elevens, using your law degree like a gun. Don't care what happens to the victims."

I stood my ground. Maybe I just wanted everyone in the world to like me. "Ma'am, Jesus's mother is worried about losing a son, just like you. I'm . . . uh . . . just making sure that Jesus gets a fair trial."

"A fair trial won't bring back my son." She abruptly turned her back on me.

Not much to say to that. I entered the Commercial Pavilion, a gigantic adobe structure stuccoed a light tan. The Commercial Pavilion was filled with booths from every business in town, from the western wear stores to pet shops. The TV station's booth was between a gun shop and a radio station. Amanda ignored the scary looking militia man to her left, chatted up the guy on her right—Kid Coyote, the famed local DJ, looking like the pimp in an old western bordello.

Great. Every time I drove to work in the morning and heard yet another "blast from the past," I'd think of him, and her. . . .

Someone came to get his autograph, he turned away from Amanda to greet his adoring public. "Lunch tomorrow," he said, as if she was caller number nine and had just won the free concerts tickets.

"Sure," she replied.

He turned on a switch and went back to his live broadcast "from the hottest place in Aguilar!"

I couldn't help but approach her as she sat alone at her booth. Today she was the epitome of Santa Fe style—blue peasant dress, concha belt, lots of turquoise. But she pulled it off beautifully.

"What's new in news?" I asked.

"You tell me."

"You said you wanted to talk to me."

"Did I?"

A little girl tugged on her sleeve and said, "Sign it to Cheryl Ann."

I decided to move on. I walked a ways down the concourse and felt a touch on my arm. It was Amanda.

"I'm sorry, I'm not myself lately. Things have been going to shit at the office."

"What's up?"

"The boss took me to the woodshed for not being deferential enough to Merril in an interview. They said I should've showed him more respect."

"You get in trouble for that?"

"Sometimes. This town hasn't totally accepted the fact that a woman can be smarter than the man she's interviewing."

"I see you got a new friend—Kid Coyote. What's the deal with you and Pete?"

"Kid Coyote is merely a fellow member of the media. And there is no deal with me and Pete anymore. I wanted to go native for a while."

"That's a politically incorrect way to put it."

"Oh, you know what I mean. I've always been attracted to the stuck-on-themselves macho-type. I like people who like themselves." She sighed. "You know, opposites attract."

"Well, did you guys have fun while it lasted?"

"Yeah, for a while. You called me too much, but he didn't call enough. And he was cheating on me. Well . . . cheating in his own way."

I couldn't imagine why anyone would cheat on her if she were around. "But you stuck with him."

"Like I said, it was fun for a while. And I've made some great connections."

"So what happened?"

"It was time to move on."

Somebody shouted in a whelp of joy. A man held up something he'd won in one of the carny games.

"You want to interview Jesus?" I said, raising my voice over the man's whelps.

"I thought you'd never ask."

"Would you still like me if I didn't let you interview him?"

"Of course."

Orale, ese. I touched her arm and she warmed to the touch, but then another little girl came up to her for an autograph so I headed over to the livestock pavilion where the mock trial was to be held. I glanced back over my shoulder. She kept looking at me even as Kid Coyote kept pestering her, trying to give her some free backstage passes.

In the livestock judging pavilion, tables lined the muddy floor, the smell of fresh manure filled the air. In the stands were twenty or so school kids who'd probably been roped in with talk of a "shoot-out," only to find people in suits talking about one rather than actually firing a few rounds.

Cliff was there with Deb-the-Deb, sitting up in the back row. I guessed he'd never seen a trial before, in his year or two of drafting oil and gas limited partnership agreements.

Since the prosecutors played the defense counsel, they dressed to fit their image of public defenders. Merril wore a brown wig with a pony tail. Jovanka Smith had on slacks and a tie-dyed shirt.

Pete handed me a little patch with some tape on the back. At first glance it looked like the patches the prosecutors wore but behind the eagle, a rat-like creature performed some kind of interspecies act. "Wear it with pride," he said.

Judge Perez played himself. He had a little name tag that read "Hanging Judge" with a noose around it.

The case, as provided by the National Institute of Trial Attorneys, arose in the mythical town of NITA City. I opened as I imagined a tough prosecutor would. The judge's book had said: "Tell a story. Don't get too argumentative. Don't use big words. When using units of distance or time, put them in terms that people can understand. And paint a picture."

"Ladies and Gentlemen," I began. "Our story begins with a dead body. . . ."

Within moments into my opening, the judge smiled. I was using the techniques in his book.

I called some witnesses played by local high school kids. Jerry Seinfeld had once said that objections were the adult's version of the child's "Fraid not." When they were overruled, the judge was saying, "Fraid so." And when they were sustained, the judge was saying, "Duh." Merril and Jovanka didn't get too many "duhs" against me. But when Merril delivered his closing argument, I saw how far I still had to go. He talked about "reasonable doubt" as if he actually believed in it.

"What is reasonable doubt?" he asked, facing the crowd up in the stands. "A reasonable doubt is like crossing Oil Avenue out there with one of your friends. Your friend says it's safe to cross the street because no cars are coming. Well, if you're like me, even if you've known your friend your whole life and know he has no reason to lie to you, maybe you hear a funny mechanical noise, the faint sound of a horn, whatever, but something causes you to turn and look both ways before crossing the street. Well, my friends, that slight hesitation, that slight wait to look over that causes us to pause in the graver affairs of life, is a reasonable doubt."

He talked for a few minutes more. After he sat down, Pete rose quickly for his rebuttal and transformed himself into an angry prosecutor.

"Well, I hope Mr. Merril isn't telling you nice people to go out to cross the street without looking both ways. It's a general rule of thumb, when a defense lawyer has the law on his side, he argues law. When he's got the facts on his side, he argues facts. And when he don't got nuthin', he talks about the old song and dance of crossing the street without looking both ways."

Pete then went into a ten-minute tirade about why we shouldn't be so soft on criminals.

After he was done, the audience was polled. Without hesitation, they voted to convict.

"Let's get a rope right now!" somebody yelled. "This is Aguilar."

After the audience filed out, Pete shook my hand as I got up to follow them. "Congratulations. This is the first time I ever saw you do a hearing without making a fool of yourself."

"Yeah, but you were the one who won it for us."

"That's what I do for a living. Sit down for a second."

I sat down. I could tell by the way he cleared his throat and gathered his thoughts that he was in his speech mode.

"Y'know, a long time back, I was playing poker with Willie Nelson and some other guys and one of those guys said, 'Pete, sing us that song you used to sing back when you played in that country band. Maybe Willie would want to hear it.' And I said, 'I think it would be against the law for a nobody like me to sing when Willie Nelson's in the room.'"

He paused for a moment, pained. "Well, someday I won't give opening arguments when you're in the room."

"You mean that?"

"Yeah. Someday you'll kick their ass so hard there'll be shit on your boots. "

"Thanks."

"But notice how I said 'someday.'" He shook his head. "You got to take it more seriously and not get so emotionally involved and shit. Jesus is your client, not your friend. You're not there to make sure he gets back together with his little lady love cuz you're not Dear Fucking Abby. And you still don't know shit about how to object or get something into evidence—all the boring stuff. But it's important.

"Just look around you. It's going to be all cowboys and old white women on the jury. You heard what that one guy said. 'This is Aguilar.'"

I looked around at some of the tough looking hombres walking around. They were no strangers to ropes. This was Aguilar alright.

Pete continued. "If you're not totally prepared, Jesus will spend the next few years of his life getting butt-fucked in the Santa Fe Penitentiary by guys like Guillermo. Even if you are totally prepared, he may still be spending the next few years up there. But at least he won't bar-bitch you for ineffective assistance of counsel."

"Thanks," I said. "But why are you such an asshole to me all the time?"

"Because you still haven't proved yourself to me yet. You got to show that you're tough enough to take it. And one more thing. There's something about you that really pisses me off."

"What?"

"I'm being as serious as a short dick here. You seem to think that being a Mexican is just about getting laid and beating the shit out of people, that's what we're all about."

"But that's all you talk about."

"You don't know me. You don't know shit. You don't understand nothing about pride in la raza, pride in yourself and your family, and sticking up for what you believe in."

I couldn't think of any response to that. What did I believe in?

"You don't got any of that shit. You're like Ernest and Julio Gallo, all you do is whine."

He got up. "But I got a feeling that you're starting to change." He hummed something that sounded like "mamas don't let your babies grow up to be cowboys" as he walked into the sunset.

Chapter 34

The First Villain to Die

February 9

AT WORK, I SAT AT my desk and stared at the walls. Pete was right. No more whining. Finally, I opened the file. When it came right down to it, all I really had in my life was this trial, so I might as well put everything I had into it.

I called the medical examiner and talked with his secretary. "He's in Texas, reviewing the autopsies that the coroner over there screwed up. He'll be back in a few weeks."

"So why'd they call him?"

Because he's always willing to travel. . . ."

For some reason, that didn't sound that promising.

• • • •

I finally called, and arranged to meet with George Cloud on the movie set. His agreeing to talk to me was a piece of luck, since he wasn't sure what the PD was.

"You in the police department?" he asked over the phone.

"No, ma'am. We're musicians."

"What?"

"It's a line from the movie *The Blues Brothers*," I said. "We get WGN from Chicago here on cable and it's on every night. I'm sorry. I couldn't resist."

He laughed. "I was in that movie, an extra in the country bar scene. You know, where we play both kinds of music. . . ."

"Country and western."

"Great scene, huh? Yeah, come on by tomorrow at lunch time."

I left at eleven-forty-five, only to find an accident on Oil Avenue, an overturned hazardous waste truck. Traffic was rerouted over some dirt agricultural roads. I stared at the back of a tractor for nearly an hour.

When I finally arrived at the set, a guard came out to meet me.

"Dan Shepard," I said. "George Cloud is expecting me."

"Don't I know you?" He asked.

I was about to say that maybe he knew me from TV, then I recognized Raphael, the same guard in a bowtie from the Tumbleweeds.

He paged Cloud, looked me over for about ten long seconds, then grudgingly waved me through into his world.

"Guess I'm supposed to be here," I couldn't help mumbling under my breath.

The set looked like Santa Fe Street in Aguilar a hundred years ago, right down to replicas of the town's Western store fronts. The road was dirt and a few horses were tied up to the facade of the Fortress. The high-tech camera equipment all over the place made me feel like I was in some kind of time warp.

Already filming when I got there, both Cloud and Roberts wore full period costumes. There was a draw: Roberts shot Cloud, then Cloud fell into the dust, his hat blowing away with a gust of wind from a fan.

They did the take over and over. Sky had to yell "line?!" about five times until he got it right. Once Sky's "line?!" situation was under control, the director made sure that Cloud would fall in just the right way, that the lighting was correct, and that the hat blew down the street just so. . . .

After an hour, the director finally yelled, "Take thirty."

Sky Roberts spotted me and came up to me while the other guy cleaned the blood off. I guess Sky was supposed to be the good guy in this scene, but somehow I just couldn't see him as a hero.

"Don't you hate it when those fuckers won't die right?" he said.

"What was wrong?"

"I don't know. I guess the lighting was kind of fucked. And the blood wasn't spurting the way it was supposed to."

"I hate when that happens," I said. "How's it going, other than that?"

"Considering that I've been whacking off for the last two weeks waiting to do this one stupid scene, it's been all right. I don't know . . . I'm trying to work all the time to keep my mind off all the shit. What are you here for, anyway?"

"To talk with George Cloud."

"About me?"

"It's not always about you, okay?" I said. "I want to find out about some other guys. You know I'm not supposed to talk to you without your lawyer being present."

He sighed. "You don't seem to like me that much."

"No, I like you just as much as I like the other criminals I've met. Justice is blind."

He walked away to his trailer, his head down. Everyone on the set ignored him.

After Sky left, George Cloud came over, introduced himself, then apologized. "Don't mind Sky. He can be a little bit of a prick."

Dora had said that, too.

Cloud shook his head and spit into the dirt. "If you'd gotten here right at noon, you wouldn't have had to wait so long. What happened?"

"Traffic was a bitch."

"Tim Robbins in *The Player*, right?"

"No, it really was a bitch. A hazardous waste truck went down."

Cloud shrugged and hustled me through the set back to his trailer. He was in his early forties, one of those actors you know you've seen before but can't remember the name. He wore a black hat, boots with spurs, and a pearl-handled peacemaker in a leather holster. He kept digging into the big wad of chewing tobacco and spitting out the juice.

"I'm usually the first guy who gets killed," he said when I asked him about his credits. "If I could have been on *Star Trek*, I'd be the guy in the red who gets turned into a dust cube."

"Who are you in this one?"

"I don't even have a name. I'm listed as 'Right Hand Man' in the credits."

After more small talk I asked him about Sky.

"We knew he had a problem, but generally he kept it under control. Since this happened, he's pretty much been written out of the movie, but his part was kind of small anyway. We weren't real close because he was supposed to kill me."

"I saw. He didn't seem to be doing a very good job of it."

"The director's being difficult. You know, show biz." He spit out the rest of his chaw, he was the spitting image of the Marlboro Man.

"Did Sky ever hang out with any local people?" I asked.

"He started hanging out with this real pretty blond girl with big hair. Anglo but with a Spanish accent, about nineteen or twenty. He even brought her on the set. She was a knockout, flirting with all the guys."

Dora, of course.

"She brought two other guys with her once. One looked like her brother, another was his friend. Both had a lot of tattoos. They all met with Sky in his trailer on the day before it happened. They friends of yours?"

A mental picture of Joey and Eddie formed in my mind. "As a matter of fact, they are—or were—good people, once you got to know them."

"They the kids that got killed in the ditch?"

"Yeah."

"That's too bad."

"About one of them, at least."

"Anybody else ever come see Sky?"

"Yeah, later that day. A big Anglo kid, looked like a football player. Vince, or Vic, the kid who got killed. They went inside Sky's trailer and had some kind of an argument. They were in there for a while."

"Then what happened?"

"Sky came over to me and said, 'I'm going to kill that son of a bitch! He's trying to jerk me around.'"

Bullseye. That set up the Sky-Victor fight. Now it was time to clear up the gun situation. "You notice anything else about that big kid, Victor? Did you ever see Victor with a gun?"

"Yeah, now that I think about it, he did have a gun. They made him leave it at Security. I was right there at the gate. He wanted to bring it through, but Raphael wouldn't let him."

"What happened?"

"Victor said, 'Everybody here has a gun. Why can't I bring a gun on the set?' Raphael told him in the way that only Raphael can: 'Every gun on the set is fake, except this one I'm pointing at your ugly face.' The kid gave up the gun when he went in to see Sky and I guess Raphael gave it back to him when he left."

"Did the cops ask you about the gun?"

"It was weird. All they asked me about was the two kids, Jesus and Joey. When I told them that it was Victor and not Joey with the gun, they told me I must be mistaken."

There was no mention of this at all in the report. Somebody had done some sloppy police work. Or, as Sandoval had said, maybe they didn't want to find the gun after all.

"You also said that there was another kid with blond hair with Joey, lots of tattoos—Eddie. You said he was with them that day?"

"Yeah. He was about fifteen, sixteen. Raphael almost didn't let him on the set because he was so young, but he didn't bother anybody."

"He ever come here after that?"

"No. Sky wasn't allowed to bring anybody back here after the shooting took place."

"You ever see him again? Someone told me that I should ask you about that."

He laughed. "I'll say I did, the little shit. I was walking my dog out by one of the ditches on the dirt road by Oil Avenue, you know?"

"I know those ditches."

"Well, I figured I could let my dog run free out there, you know, outside city limits. He got about a hundred yards ahead when all this shit went down."

"What shit?"

"That little blond kid, Eddie, shot my dog. Killed him right there in the middle of the desert way out there by this shooting range they got."

"I saw your dog. It was a collie, right? Elwood?"

"Yeah. I don't think Eddie saw me when he fired, but once he heard me, he ran away like a rabbit. I reported it to the police and when they finally got out to where the dog was shot the next day, it was gone. Somebody had moved the body. They never pressed charges or anything. So this officer, Thompson or something, he told me that he was real sorry but there was nothing he could do. You believe that?"

"I sure can. Did you get a good look at the gun?"

"Yeah I did. One of them old Tech-9s. I know a lot about guns since I work with them so much. I'm positive that Eddie had the same gun that Victor had."

"Positive?"

"Yeah," he smiled. "I been around guns my whole life—fake and real."

Another bullseye. Finally someone in Aguilar was positive about something.

"Thanks a lot. You've been real helpful. Will you testify?"

"Sure."

"George, this could be the start of a beautiful friendship."

Chapter 35

Cutting Coroners

February 22

AFTER WEEKS OF TRYING, I finally set up an appointment with Dr. Candelaria, the medical examiner on call with the department. He had returned at last from Texas after cleaning up after a coroner who had screwed up hundreds of autopsies.

Dr. Candelaria, ME, was a tall man in his forties, neatly although unfashionably, dressed in a brown, yellow and red striped clip-on tie. I forgave him the tie; he didn't exactly have to impress his patients with his bedside manner. His office was stuffed with Navajo story-teller dolls, mixed in with pictures of his three kids at various institutions of higher learning.

"How was Texas?" I asked, holding my hand to keep from fidgeting with the story-tellers.

"I left my heart in San Antonio," he said. "But I had some orderlies go to the hospital and Fed-Ex it to me. A little coroner humor. Sorry."

"I suppose you guys have to make jokes like that to keep the horror at bay."

"No we're just naturally humorous people," he said. "Sorry about taking so long before I could see you. I was stuck over there for weeks, redoing all those autopsies. Up to my eyeballs in corpses, so to speak."

I was a little worried about having a funny coroner on the stand with my client's life on the line. But this one was the best in the business.

"Well, doctor, what happened with Victor?"

"To put it in simple terms, the victim was killed by being thrown down and his head hitting the curb. There was an involuntary movement after that. But the kick, looking at where the impact was, would not have had any effect."

"So that means that the victim would have died anyway, kick or no kick?"

"All the kick did, really, was scuff up the ear. It did no damage to the brain."

This was good. That meant that the actual killer was neither Latino nor female. It was a washed-up male Hollywood actor with a drug problem who frequently appeared in exploitive, violent, and sexist TV series. This would be a politically correct case after all. Still, something bothered me.

"I don't get it. Why are they even charging my client with murder if the medical report says it had no effect?"

"Well, now, you have to understand, that's merely my professional medical opinion. The state had someone else perform another autopsy. That one will show that it was the kick that did it, not the head hitting the pavement."

"So, essentially, it's your word against his."

"That's right. And since I'm a more experienced medical examiner than Dr. Goldfarb, their expert, hopefully my opinion should be more believable than his." He picked up a story-teller doll on his desk and grabbed it around the throat."Unfortunately, I know my part and the other doctor knows his. He gets questioned, I get questioned. He gets cross-examined, I get cross-examined. It all evens out but it depends on the lawyer asking the questions to make the case."

"This other examiner," I said, "he didn't by any chance botch a hundred autopsies or anything like that?"

"No, Dr. Goldfarb is a professional. He even teaches up UNM Hospital in Albuquerque. But I must say, he has been known to be open to, shall we say, alternative viewpoints?"

"He can be bribed?"

"No, I wouldn't say that, but sometimes he gets an idea of what you want to find, and then finds it for you. That's why he's one of the highest paid experts in the nation. He's much better now but I'll always remember what happened when he was called over to testify in that case over in the Middle East."

"What happened?"

"As I've said, he does get around. This story is top secret. I found out about in Texas last week when I was interviewing the guy I was cleaning up after. He was Goldfarb's assistant when this happened over there."

Candelaria leaned in closer. So did I.

"Goldfarb testified that the victim was killed by a gunshot to the brain, therefore the killing was the work of anti-government terrorists."

"So?"

"Unfortunately, the victim had been found in dumpster and Goldfarb never actually bothered to examine it, even though he was being paid a thousand dollars a day to testify." Dr. Candelaria hissed the amount.

"How do they know that?"

"Think. Goldfarb had testified under oath it was a bullet shot to the brain? How could he know? The body in the dumpster had already been beheaded."

This was funny stuff for coroners.

"And the funny part was, this being the Middle East and all, is that the judge still convicted the supposed terrorist on Goldfarb's testimony."

That night I called Dora at the Princess club. "I told you I got the gun," I said. "Well, I got a guy saying that it was the same gun that Victor had. And I got a medical examiner who can say that it was the throw rather than the kick that killed Victor."

"So?"

"So you can bring Anna Maria home already."

"I already know you got those things," she said. "But do you know what to do with them?"

Chapter 36

Trials and Tribulations

February March

FOR THE NEXT FEW WEEKS, Pete made me go to almost every trial in the New Mexico. I saw a burglary trial in Carlsbad, a murder trial in Las Cruces, even an insanity trial in Roswell where the client claimed the aliens made him break into a convenience store in order to get the grain alcohol to fly their space ship. That defense didn't fly.

Pete made me take every case of mine to trial I once had three DWI trials in a day. I lost them all of course, but got better with every "we find the defendant guilty." By the third one, the jury actually stayed out over an hour, a personal best. The next day I had my first partial victory when I managed to get his "resisting" dropped down to a "disorderly." Somehow I used my charm to get the guy, one Lorenzo Lozano, eligible for work release.

But the battle was far from over. I then had to get Lorenzo a job or it would all fall apart. In the jail's multi-purpose room, Lorenzo at my side, I talked on a borrowed cellphone with the owner of the carwash. I was a little surprised that the owner did not ask why a lawyer was calling him. Apparently this happened a lot in Aguilar. I even used my charm to negotiate an extra dollar an hour for Lorenzo. As I hung up I had to laugh. It had been easier placing a convicted felon than it had been placing myself for legal jobs after graduation. The carwash didn't ask about grades.

Many of my usual suspects came back again sometimes on multiple counts. I started to get a reputation. I had Heidi Hawk's "projection of missiles" (throwing rocks at a window) dismissed when the witness didn't show up with the broken window.

This was such a coup that Heidi referred me to Stephanie Yi, her friend/co-defendant who had once hired a private attorney rather than a lowly PD. Stephanie was accused of battery, shoplifting, curfew violation, and possession of alcohol all on separate incidents in one bad week. I won the battery, the shoplifting and the possession and lost on the curfew. Or did I win on the curfew and lose on the battery? All the hearings blurred together after awhile.

"I'll just try to do one crime at a time," she said at the end of the hearing to the chagrin of her parents, upstanding Korean immigrants. Then she smiled. "Just kidding. I won't do any crimes at all. I saw how hard you had to work."

Pete let me second-chair one of his cases, but I wasn't allowed to open my mouth. In one I had drunk too much ice tea, and I had to excuse myself into the second hour of Pete's blistering cross of Officer Diamond.

Every night I rented a courtroom movie. If they didn't have *Playboy*, I might as well rent something useful. I was becoming a lawyer in spite of myself.

Chapter 37

Billy the Kid Suite

April 1

THE CASE WAS NOW AS good as I could get it before the battle began in earnest. I called Dora again.

"We're hearing some good things about you," she said. But that was it.

It was time to open a new front. I asked Jesus if he wanted to be interviewed by Amanda.

He looked at me for a second. "I don't know. What should I say?"

"The truth," I said. "Well . . . just that you're confident about the trial."

"So you want me to lie?" He laughed. "Actually for some reason, maybe it's prayer, maybe it's I don't know what, I really am confident and shit. Can I talk about finding God in jail?"

"Did you?"

He nodded. He really meant it.

I had to set it all up with Clint, of course, and that took some doing. I met with him in his office, which was in a little control booth right next to the entrance. His eyes were intent on monitors with displays of the entire jail, except for the interview room. One monitor showed the reception desk where Veronica valiantly fended off Pete's advances.

"I need a favor," I said. "Can Jesus give a TV interview?"

Clint glanced over at another monitor that showed a work party outside picking up weeds. "Hurry it up out there!" he yelled into the radio. "Tell Jones to move his big ol' butt." Within an instant, a guard on the screen got in the poor worker's face.

Clint didn't look up. "That's most unusual, son."

"You allowed the movie people in here," I said.

"But that wasn't real." He turned to a screen of the kitchen. "Tell Sanchez not to put so damn much pepper in the spaghetti sauce, will you?"

"It will only take five minutes, max."

"Go ahead, then. You've got it. But I want it in the holding cell, the Billy the Kid Suite, so we can monitor what's going on. And one more thing. Make damn sure you shut the door on the way out."

Amanda wore the Santa Fe outfit when she arrived that afternoon, dragging heavy lights along with her camera and sweating slightly through her clothes. Apparently she was human after all.

The Billy the Kid suite was across from the interview room, down a short corridor. The rest of the jail had been built around it, but it still had the same adobe bricks from territorial days, and even a few stray bullet holes, with smoke burns and eerie shadows on the bricks. All it needed was a skeleton chained to the wall to complete the image.

Sky Roberts must have freaked when they brought him back for real after filming a scene here. If you were inside the cell, the view outward was a hallway, a video camera, and the booking desk. As Veronica had said, a cell was still just a cell.

I helped Amanda carry the stuff into the interview room. I almost dropped the camera on the floor, so I stayed out of her way as she set up the lights.

Clint brought Jesus down, freshly shaven and his hair neatly combed. Amanda went over to him, belatedly thanked him for saving her during the dance. He whispered something in her ear and she nodded.

"Remember," I told Amanda when she came back, "don't ask him any real specific questions. Just ask him how he feels, things like that."

"If you want me to stop," she said. "Just signal me."

I suddenly had a vision of her cross-examining him and me jumping up and down shouting, "He doesn't have to answer that!" like every lawyer representing a mobster.

Before I could say anything, she began the interview. The light had Jesus silhouetted against the uneven bricks.

"How are you feeling, Mr. Villalobos?" she asked.

"Fine."

He sounded calm. I nodded to him.

"Are you worried about the trial coming up?"

"No."

"May I ask why, considering that you could end up spending much of your life behind bars?"

"Because I believe." Jesus nodded at her and she nodded back. "I have faith."

"Did you kill Victor?" she asked before I could say anything to stop her."

"Not even."

"So who did? Any ideas?"

I gave the cut-off signal by running a hand violently across my throat. They both looked over at me, then Amanda turned the camera in my direction.

"That will all come out at trial," I said.

She turned off the camera. "That was great. Thanks, everyone."

"You weren't supposed to ask him that," I said.

"A girl's got to try."

She started to pack up. I walked over to Jesus. "Tell your girlfriend, that it's as good as it's gonna get," I whispered to him. "Tell her to get her skinny ass up here."

He stared at me. Had I really said that? To him?

But he smiled after a moment. "Her ass is pretty skinny . . . I'll call her, but her family, especially Enrique. . . ."

"Make sure she's got a lawyer." I said. "If she does, no one will mess with her, not even her brother."

I said that with some kind of authority as if it was true. Jesus nodded, as if he actually believed me.

"Yo Clint," he yelled. "Hurry up. I got to make a call."

Clint clicked open the doors, and waited as Pete rushed in, fuming. "Don't ever let your client do an interview without permission from me. You do that shit again, I'll have your ass fired."

I looked at him. "You keep out of my case, remember? My dealings with my client are my business. If I screwed this up, I screwed it up on my own. Got that?"

Jesus gave Pete the mad dog look. Pete just laughed, but there was something about Jesus's stare. Just as Eddie had done, Pete turned around walked out.

I was sure glad that Jesus was on my side. He signaled to Amanda, motioned her to come over to him. He whispered something in her ear. She nodded.

He followed Clint out the door, it clicked shut behind him.

"Alone at last," I said to Amanda.

Amanda smiled at me."That was great. By the way, do you ski at all? I have some free passes for Sierra Milagro, compliments of the station."

"Yeah, sure."

"Any good?"

I sighed. "It's probably the only thing I do well."

"I wouldn't say that. How 'bout this weekend? They're closing after this."

"By the way," I asked. "What did Jesus just say to you?"

"Your boy just told me I should 'go for it,' and ask you out."

Chapter 38

Obligatory Sex Scene

STILLDARK WHEN I PICKED Amanda up at her rented Victorian house off Santa Fe Avenue on Saturday morning, there was a strange car in the space by her house. I almost turned around and left. I took a deep breath, knocked anyway.

She emerged dressed to ski in a black jacket, tight ski pants, and a red baseball cap with a "C" on it, her auburn pony tail falling through the back. Her bedroom door was shut, barricaded behind her TV.

"I've got a new cat," she explained. "I can't let him out or he gets into everything."

I helped load her skis and boots into my car.

"I'm stuck with a rental," she said. "My car's in the shop."

"I don't have much room in mine," I said. "I hope you're not bringing your camera."

She smiled. "I have to confess. Sometimes I feel like I'm not really alive unless I'm getting it on tape."

"I feel the same way. I love it when you get my back on camera at docket calls. If it's on tape, it's important."

She grinned. "I have a feeling today might be an exception to that rule."

We took Oil Avenue westbound, toward Sierra Milagro. The small white pyramid barely visible at the edge of the horizon was a bona fide ski area operated by the Capitan Apache Tribe. We headed toward sacred ground. Soon the plains loosened up, grew hillier, but still utterly barren. There was actually something you could define as "terrain." The only sound was the wind out in the open range. It was totally exposed out here. Neither of us said anything until we went down a steep incline and left the wind behind us.

"I hate it here," she said.

"Me, too," I said. "But at least you were getting laid. Imagine living here without sex."

"I don't know what you've been hearing, but I've been living pretty chaste as well. Dating a lot. I've gone out with that Kid Coyote guy a few times but that's not the same thing."

"What about you and Pete?"

"What about him?"

"But I thought. . . ."

All of a sudden she grew very edgy. "What has he been saying about me?"

"Nothing. I just took it for granted that you and he were—"

"Having sexual intercourse within the confines of a monogamous relationship?"

"Well?"

She mimicked Dora. "Not even."

I was so relieved that I jerked out of my lane and almost crashed into an oncoming semi.

"Don't you know about Pete?" she asked.

"What about him?"

"Did he ever tell you about his mission in the National Guard?"

"I remember him bragging about it. He got a purple heart or something, and a bad scar, though I've never seen it."

"Well if you had, you wouldn't have asked that question about having sex. Pete hasn't been able to have sex since the accident."

"So his bragging is all bullshit?"

"If you'd paid attention, you'd know that all his stories happened a few years ago. All that old stuff is true."

"Even so, doesn't talk about all his women bother you?"

"I said it before: I kinda like people who like themselves. Opposites attract. And he's safe. And different. I needed safe and different."

"And what am I? Dangerous and the same?"

"You remind me too much of the guys at Cornell who considered themselves failures unless they conquered the world by the time of their first reunion."

"I guess I am one of those failures."

"And you came on way too strong. I mean, you called me every day at work."

I sighed. I had come on strong, okay, but did I ever cross the border into obsession? There was a fine line between ardent pursuit and a temporary restraining order.

"What can I say? There's a special spot in my heart for you and it seems to cut off the flow of oxygen to my brain."

She looked out at the mountains. We had gone over a ridge, descended into a small river valley of piñon and spindly cypress groves. A few scattered junipers dotted the south slopes.

"It's good to be somewhere else for a change," she said, leaning back and stretching like a cat.

"It sure is." Blood kept flowing away from my brain toward somewhere else.

After an hour we passed through a small resort town set in the tall pine trees and entered the Capitan Apache Reservation. We turned up the steep winding road and climbed to the Sierra Milagro base, feeling the air pressure dilute with every switchback.

"I'm getting a little lightheaded," she said.

"So am I."

We didn't see the base of the Sierra Milagro until just before we got there. It was the only snow-capped mountain with a rocky peak far above the timberline for hundreds of miles around. I could see why the Apaches considered its summit to be sacred.

We parked, bought our tickets, then hit the fresh powder. Their accents and turns exposed skiers from Odessa or El Paso. All of the lift operators were members of the tribe.

We took the gondola to get out of the wind and felt the altitude even more. At the summit, we looked out over the white sands to the west, past the piñons to the great llano to the east. After a few runs, without a word spoken, we began holding hands on the ride up. After a few more, we were arm in arm. We both skied like experts. Amanda was fun to watch as she went up and down on the bump runs. She had an amazing rhythm in those tight black pants.

"Great form," I said, which despite my best efforts still came out with a smirk. I expected a rebuff but got a smile.

"You're not so bad yourself. Where'd you learn to ski?"

"I trained all one fall with the ski team. Got in amazing shape and learned all about technique during dry land training."

"Then what happened?"

"Then it snowed and I got my ass kicked."

She laughed a gentle laugh.

I touched her mitten for a moment and she smiled back at me. "You know," I said, "I'd really like to have consensual sex with you within the confines of a monogamous relationship."

She didn't respond, by word or look. "Are you nervous about the case?"

"Why'd you have to bring that up? For the first time since I've been here, I'm finally relaxed."

"Well, are you?"

"As long as I'm with you, I have nothing to fear," I said.

"I know I'm supposed to be the impartial, unblinking eye of the press," she said, "but I really do hope you win one. I like your client."

"So do I."

"You're kinda likeable, yourself."

We skied all day. I felt like I was going to collapse from the altitude, the fatigue, the exhilaration, the beating of our hearts in the thin air. Maybe it was the excitement of being in Indian country. I knew from my one class in public land law that reservations were technically sovereign nations.

It was Amanda who suggested we spend the night at the Milagro Valley Inn on the reservation, then drive back on Sunday.

"It's not like either of us has anything waiting back in town," she smiled. "I told my landlord to feed the cat just in case. And as you said, we're in a whole other country."

The inn, a dramatic adobe structure a few miles below the ski area, was reminiscent of the Taos Pueblo. Its five stories of square adobe building blocks nestled against an iced-over lake.

We walked over to the desk, past large exotic Native American sculptures from all over the country. The concierge, a Capitan Apache with a long black pony tail, asked our names.

"Jesus Villalobos," I said, "and this is my wife." I was about to add "Anna Maria," but Amanda had already whipped out the credit card and presumably signing her real name on the slip. The desk man took the card, then said, "Enjoy your stay in our homeland."

I showered first, then Amanda. She left the door slightly ajar as she changed, as if daring me to glimpse in. Somehow I resisted the temptation, but barely. She emerged dressed in a denim shirt and a vaguely Southwestern vest.We went down to the bar, which had a superb view of the sunset. The snow at the summit glowed an unearthly red. I bought a bottle of red wine which we shared as we watched the sunset.

"There's one thing I really want to know about you," she said, putting her hand on my arm.

"Shoot."

"I checked up on you."

"What?"

"Through Nexis. And I had a friend check you out in Martindale-Hubble, the lawyer's guide. You were at a big firm. Why are you here in Aguilar? Really."

It was time to tell someone. "My mommie fired me." I laughed after a few moments. "Didn't think so at the time, but it was probably the best thing that ever happened to me."

She stared at me. I felt self-conscious. "Is something wrong?" I asked.

"No. You just look great."

"Thanks. So do you. So how about you? Why are really here?" I touched her vest and ran my finger down to the denim of the shirt.

"Long story."

"I like long stories."

She smiled. "I got fired from the internship I had in L.A. I had an eating disorder and general mental stress and was going up and down so much with weight that I pretty much had a nervous breakdown. I had to go away for treatment to this amazing place called the Gardiner Center out in Scottsdale."

"Drugs?"

"No. All of my mistakes have been made without the benefit of drugs or alcohol."

"Same with me. So what happened?"

"You should've seen me—I looked terrible. And it wasn't good to have the star reporter spending a few weeks in treatment. You can do that when you're older, like Elizabeth Taylor, but not on your first job. I was at the Gardiner Center for a couple of weeks and got my act together. One of the other girls in the program told me about Aguilar."

"She knew your station manager?"

"She knew Pete Baca."

We drank the wine and sat without saying anything for a while, as though each of us was scared to say something stupid. In my case, always a very real possibility.

We went back to our room. I stripped down to my underwear, she slid into something silky. We kissed, lowered the lights, and in four or five seconds we were lying on the bed. I was excited and nervous, afraid I'd forgotten what to do.

I got her sweater off but I had so much trouble with her bra, she had to unhook it for me. I looked at her body. Wow . . . It had been a long time.

"You're beautiful," I said.

"No I'm not. You're just horny."

"I am. But you're still beautiful." I ran my fingers over her erect nipples. I sniffled for some reason.

"Do you have something to tell me?" she asked.

"Trust me on this. My list of partners for the last six months can be counted without using your hands. Actually, speaking of hands, do you have any, uh, protection?"

She pulled something out of her purse. "A good reporter is always prepared."

I slipped a hand under the waistband of her panties. "May I?"

She nodded.

"Please respond, for the record." I was still fearful that she might disappear at any moment.

"Yes," she sighed. "Oh, yes!"

As I pulled the panties over her long, smooth legs, I noticed a mark at the edge of her panty line. She had a tattoo, a small snake coiled in a figure eight, devouring its tail.

"It stands for infinity," she said, kissing me again.

"You're huge," she said as I entered her.

Oh God, did she really say that?

The first time was too fast, of course. But the second and third times were almost out of body experiences. I felt like I was watching it on my VCR, except that the top part wasn't distorted. After a final explosion I looked down at her and smiled. "I love you, Amanda."

"I love you, Dan."

I woke up in the middle of the night, probably to make sure she was still there. For an hour I watched her breathe in and out.

We held hands on the way to the car the next morning. We kissed tenderly, passionately, then I got behind the wheel. She ran her fingers through my hair and then briefly down to my crotch as I drove.

"Please," I said reluctantly, "I've got to keep my mind on the road."

She didn't stop until we left the reservation and officially reentered America.

Chapter 39

The Little Death

AFTER I DROPPED HER OFF, kissed her goodbye one last time, I finally made it home. My door was open, there was a light on inside. Cautiously I entered, prepared to use my ski boot as a battering ram. Inside Pete sat facing me, Dora sat next to him on one side, Anna Maria sat on the other. She wore a sweat shirt a couple of sizes too big, as if she had borrowed the first available clothes and snuck out in the middle of the night. I didn't ask her. For a moment, I half-expected to see Jesus and Joey seated in the remaining ones. I finally had people in my chairs. Certainly not the people I expected.

"So how was it?" Pete asked.

Dora smiled. "We been waiting here all weekend till we put two and two together."

I resisted half a dozen easy punchlines. "A gentleman never tells." I looked over at Anna Maria. "So?"

"My brother Enrique—" she spat out his name as before. "I would have got here sooner, but he said he'd kill me if I came back here to testify, so I got this lawyer Ricky Clark."

Pete smiled at me. "You know the guy—"

"I saw him on TV talking about some murder up north," I said. "They got a soundbite saying 'it wasn't murder, it was the day God abandoned Espanola.'"

"That's the one," Pete said. "Best lawyer in the state after me. I already sent him the subpoena and added her to your witness list."

"But how?"

He didn't answer, kept on going. "So you ready for trial tomorrow?"

"As ready as I could get." I gave him a look. "You said yourself that sex is an amazing stress buster." He didn't laugh. Dora did.

Anna Maria stared at me. "I just had to tell you something, before

I can't talk to you no more."

"What's that?"

"Remember your promise."

Pete smiled at her. "Now get the hell out of here, girls."

Dora and Anna Maria got up. "You better not fuck her over," Dora said. "Remember what happened to my brother." She slammed the door behind them.

Pete laughed it off. He looked over at a stack of files laying on the ground. "You know I should have taken over this case from the beginning. Even if it was a juvie starting out. . . ."

"But you told me the rule about getting a case for life."

"I just made that up," he said. "There's also a rule against taking a case when you're over your head."

"So am I over my head? Isn't that up to the client to decide?"

I couldn't read Pete's face. He handed me a handwritten letter, "Please keep Dan Shepard as my lawyer." It was signed Jesus Villalobos and addressed to the chief public defender up in Santa Fe. The letter was post-marked early January, right after I got back from Mexico.

I looked at Pete again. Why would a scribbled letter from a juvenile in a nowhere part of the state bother him in the least. I'm sure the chief public defender got those letters all the time. Hell one of my clients—I think it was Oswald Thomas—even wrote one about me.

Then it added up. He knew about Anna Maria. "You were there, weren't you? At the party?"

"This is a small town, you know that."

"Were you—"

" No, I wasn't a witness. No, I didn't do drugs. I was long gone before any of the bullshit went down. No, I don't have any confidential information that I'm failing to disclose . . . but the chief public defender doesn't need to hear about shit when I'm up for district defender next year and your little client knows that."

"But why would Jesus want me instead of you—"

"I sure as fuck don't know," he frowned. "But in light of the competency hearing, he's competent to make his own fucked up decision."

"But what does that mean?"

"It means you got a case to win."

I stared at the stacks of files; he hummed a Willie Nelson tune.

I smiled at him. "Could you give me a hand—"

"Hey—you don't have to be the Lone Ranger."

Part III

Chapter 40

Voir Dire

April 8

TRIAL DAY AT LAST. SIERRA Milagro was still white with record snows, but here in the valley, spring came early. The yucca were in bloom. Hot already when I arrived at the office at seven-thirty, Pete was in his office, the door closed. Female laughter echoed from inside the room.

A moment later the door opened and a group of high school students filed out, Pete's mock trial team. They were here to observe.

Pete came out wearing a conservative polyester blue suit and a green tie with brown paisleys. I wore my double-breasted suit from Bloomingdale's in the White Flint Mall in Rockville. I added my beat-up pair of cowboy boots so as not to look too slick.

Jesus's mother, Senora Villalobos, showed up a few minutes later laden with homemade breakfast burritos. "Morning, Daniel," she said. "Thank you for the suit." In her other hand, she held up one of my old suits that I had given her to take in for Jesus. "I had to really use the scissor, but that's what I do for a living."

My neck remembered the last time I'd seen her use her scissors. My hair had finally grown out and didn't look half bad. "I just hope it fits," I replied.

Today was voir dire, the picking of a jury. On the windy walk across the street to court, I asked Pete about the game plan.

"The usual."

I didn't press. I was putting myself in his hands for voir dire. This is what he did for a living after all.

Outside the courtroom, the media was in full force. Amanda waited by the balcony, wearing the same blue blazer she'd worn the first day I saw her. She still had the same intoxicating effect on me.

She turned her camera on when she saw me approach with Pete.

"Any comments before trial, Mr. Shepard?" she asked.

I looked around at Pete, who kept looking ahead. "No comments at this time." I said.

Jesus waited with Clint in a room behind the jury box. My old suit now fit him perfectly after some drastic snipping. The zipper even stayed up. Clint kept him handcuffed.

I was about to shake his hand, then noticed that was my hand dripping with sweat this time. I wiped it on my pants, then shook. I still felt Senora Villalobos's tamales warring with my digestive system. Perhaps I wasn't as acclimated as I'd thought.

"You okay, bro?" asked Jesus, matter-of-factly. "I'm the one who gets sent up to the pinta for life when it's over, not you."

I noticed that he didn't know how to tie his tie. I got behind him and tied it for him.

"What are you trying to do?" he protested. "Choke me before trial?"

As we passed her in the hallway on the way to court, Jovanka approached me with my absolute last-chance plead: second-degree murder plus conspiracy for twelve years. "I'm doing you a favor, because I like you."

I didn't even turn to face Jesus, "No deals."

"Damn right," he whispered.

• • • •

Judge Perez banged the gavel hard, and asked Amanda not to photograph any of the potential jurors. Merril and Smith sat at the table on the other side of the courtroom, both of them in their blue blazers with the little eagle patch.

After he sat down, Jesus reached for the tissue to wipe his glasses. I wiped mine as well, what the hell?

The judge then ran through a few preliminaries, and Socorro, his secretary, called thirty-six names from a glass bowl. The pool came from voting rolls and drivers licenses—no felons, who couldn't vote; nor drunk drivers who had lost their licenses. The pool was also more female than male, average age about fifty.

Damn, no young drunk-driver-murderer-drug dealer jurors to be found in this bunch. I did recognize Deb-the-Deb, but she quickly waived out because she knew me. Seeing a familiar face in this foreign land, was a good feeling, if only for an instant.

Merril gathered up his extensive files, then rose and began his voir dire. It was slow and laborious until he got to a Mr. Sanchez, an elderly gardener.

"Sir, you just indicated that you have some familiarity with Mr. Villalobos?"

"Just what I know from the papers," said Sanchez. "Not really that much, so I still think I can be fair." He paused. "Wait—I saw him on TV."

"What do you remember about that?" asked Merril.

"I remembered he was a religious boy and that he found God while he was locked up. I kinda liked him."

I smiled. One for us.

"How do you feel about that? Him being a religious boy—I have a son whose been in trouble, much like him, and he's finally turned his life around."

That was like music to Merril's ears. Without missing a beat. . . ." So then you might have some trouble passing judgment on this fine, upstanding boy, who reminds you of your own son?"

Sanchez sighed. "You know, now that I think of it, I don't think I want to be on this jury after all. I'd get too wound up. I'd think of my own boy. . . ."

Shit. Three other people said the same things and excused themselves. Merril gave me a wink, sat down.

Pete rose. He too spoke in a folksy voice like Merril. "Anybody nervous about being here?" he asked. "I'm nervous, I'm sweating like a pig under this jacket, so I'm sure some of you are a little nervous too."

An old lady in back nodded her head.

"Well ma'am, let me explain how it all works," Pete said. "Do you have any kids ma'am?"

"Yes, I had two boys. They're grown now."

"Did they ever get in any fights with each other growing up?"

She smiled. "Like cats and dogs."

"Well, when they explained their stories to you, you listened to both sides didn't you? You didn't just take one's word, and not listen to the other at all?"

"Of course, I listened to both sides."

"And both of them turned out okay, of course." That was not phrased as a question.

"Yes sir."

"Sounds like you were a pretty good mother. So today, are you willing to listen to both sides and not jump to any conclusions?"

"Of course."

"Then I think you got nothing to be nervous about. Being a mother is ten times harder than being a juror. You'll do just fine."

He asked a few more questions of other jurors, then sat down. They all smiled back at him with approval.

After the judge excused the jurors, we retired to his chambers. Pete had already crossed out Ms. Scott, the juror who said she wanted to listen to both sides.

"I thought you liked her," I said. "Why nuke her?"

"Because she wants to hear both sides of the story, and your boy Jesus ain't gonna be testifying. The whole time she's going to be wondering what he's going to say."

"Then why that whole routine?"

"That routine is to show that I'm a nice guy. I'm doing it for the rest of them." He pointed to a juror's name, Theresa Rodriguez with the seemingly unsympathetic-to-defendant job of insurance investigator.

Pete continued, "This woman here, her brother testified for the defense in my last trial over in Crater. The DA there cross-examined him, called him a liar. Merril wouldn't know that, and I didn't want to alert him by asking her questions about it. So the whole time I was doing my voir dire for her."

While we talked, I nervously fingered one of the judge's story teller dolls. The judge would read the names of the potential jurors and then we'd say "take," "pass," or "excuse for cause." Whenever I tried to get any of the people I had questioned excused for cause, Merril said, "Your honor they said they could be fair." None of them got nuked. The judge noticed my distress with each of his decisions. He took the story teller doll away from me before I squeezed its head off.

Back in court—as the final jurors sat, Jesus scanned them. "You know I don't know none of those people."

Neither did I. I put on a brave face. "Well we got our crowd, they got theirs."

Chapter 41

Inmost Cave

When I got back to the office, my only message was from Ricky Clark, Anna Maria's attorney. He would meet with me during the lunch recess tomorrow out at the stables by the zoo.

I went to the jail one last time to check on Jesus before the trial started in earnest. I wouldn't have much time after this.

Clint greeted me. "We're shorthanded today, thanks to the security for the trial. Why don't you just go back over to the juvenile wing and meet Jesus in his cell? Just go 'six on one, seven on one' and through the tunnel. It's the first door on your left."

"You mean you're going to let me go through alone?"

Clint laughed. "What are you going to do, not leave?"

I said the magic words and passed through the tunnel over to the juvenile wing. The other side of the tunnel felt newer, cleaner, almost like a clinic with its antiseptic white cinder blocks.

Jesus was the only resident in juvenile wing today, the others were on the annual field trip to the joint as part of a "scared straight" program. Through a small window I saw him alone inside his cell.

I pressed the intercom and the cell door swung open. His cell was immaculate, though a little sweaty smelling. He'd probably just come in from exercising. He stayed on his bed. I sat in his one chair. I looked around. The block walls were covered with pictures of Anna Maria. One was a nude I couldn't help glancing at. According to the picture she had this one tattoo right by her. . . .

"Hey man, that's private," he said.

"They told me I could see you here," I said, averting my gaze.

"They must like you. They never do that."

"How's it going?"

"Jail's jail, bro. You deal with it. Que paso?"

I went over the various strategies for the case with him. He offered his own suggestions—most of which were on point. Then it was time to head on out.

I turned as I called for Clint to click me out. Then for some reason I thought about Joey's funeral. I turned back to Jesus.

"Jesus," I said. "This isn't just a case for me. You're not just a client. I hope I can say this: I consider you a friend."

"Yeah, same here."

Chapter 42

Another Opening, Another Show

April 9

AMANDA HAD PERMISSION TO BRING her camera into the courtroom once the trial began the next morning. She didn't make eye contact with me. Her boss, the old cowboy, hovered a few feet behind her.

"Break a leg," she said, nearly under her breath.

"Isn't that what you say to actors before a show?"

"Isn't that what this is?"

Judge Perez called the court to order and I joined Pete at counsel table. He gave a few standard comments to the jurors on opening statements, then asked if all were ready to proceed.

"The state is ready, Your Honor," said Merril.

"Jesus Villalobos is, uh, ready, Your Honor," I said.

The state went first. Jovanka rose, slowly walked toward the jurors in a simple two-piece navy outfit. She stood directly in front of the picture of her late husband, the farmer turned judge.

"Ladies and gentlemen of the jury, I'm going to tell you a story about a boy named Victor who was an honor student right here in Aguilar County. His teachers will say that Victor wanted to work for the FBI when he grew up. He played football—wide receiver—and was good enough to get recruitment letters from Eastern New Mexico University, just down the road in Portales.

"Over the course of the next few days, you will hear why Victor will never get to play football again, why he will only appear in the FBI building as a statistic on a chart, a statistic of one more life snuffed away.

"Victor was not an angel, I'll tell you that right away. He associated with known drug dealers, in particular, Mr. Guillermo Juarez, a witness here today. Victor was the type of boy that a drug dealer like Mr. Juarez just loves to corrupt: the honor student, the good kid. Victor was first tempted when he met the people who came here from Hollywood to make the movie, *Snakeskin Cowboy*.

"Ladies and gentlemen, this is a story of a good boy from Aguilar who got mixed up with the wrong crowd and got in too deep. You will hear how Victor was invited to a party where drugs were being consumed and sold. Victor, perhaps thrilled with having movie stars and 'cool people' as friends, went outside with the Mr. Juarez and Mr. Roberts and somehow things went wrong. Officer John Diamond will testify that he saw a figure in a dark jacket with letters on it. The letter spelled a name, Jesus Villalobos. You will hear how Victor and Jesus did not get along all their lives here in Aguilar. You will hear from our medical expert, Dr. Goldfarb, how that kick was the proximate cause of Victor's death."

She kept going. The jurors listened with rapt attention.

"Shouldn't we object?" I whispered to Pete. "Isn't that uh . . . argumentative?"

"Of course it is. Welcome to Aguilar, America."

As Jovanka had talked, my mind raced to figure out what to say in my opening. Staring at my three pages of typewritten notes and reading them word for word wouldn't cut it in Aguilar.

"Ladies and gentlemen of the jury," I began when it was my turn, speaking without notes. "Our case today is a simple one. Jesus Villalobos is innocent of the crime he is accused of, for a very good reason: he was not there. You're going to hear from some people in the next few days who will tell you that Jesus left the party before the incident took place with Guillermo Juarez, Sky Roberts, and Victor Slade. Dora Lilly will testify that Jesus indeed left the party and that Victor Slade had a gun. Our experts will confirm this. Lee Yazzie from the forensics office will talk about Victor's gun and Dr. Candelaria will testify that it was the throw, rather than the kick, that killed Victor."

I paused and felt the twisted knot in my stomach. "And, uh, hopefully we will hear from Ann-uh- someone, who . . . uh . . . can say what . . . uh . . . really happened that night."

Someone in the back of the jury box snickered. I put the notes aside and faced the jurors.

"Mrs. Smith talked about a smoke screen of misinformation and conclusions but, ladies and gentlemen, where's there's smoke, there's reasonable doubt."

I sat down, mostly pleased with myself. At least the last part sounded good, and a couple jurors in the front were nodding. Amanda had taped my entire opening. And my zipper was zipped up as well.

After court adjourned for lunch, I went to the stables to visit with Ricky Clark, Anna Maria's attorney. He wore a green and blue striped brushpopper shirt and a large white hat. His face looked like a mosaic of New Mexico—he could have been Anglo, Latino, or Native American, or a little of all three. After we introduced ourselves, he mounted a magnificent white stallion and motioned me to mount a small gray mare.

"The world always looks so much clearer from the top of a horse," he said. "Know what I mean, son?"

I nodded blankly, uneasy on my mount. The world wouldn't look so clear laying face-first in a pile of horse shit.

"I was finally able to come down and help out on this case after I finished that case up in northern New Mexico," he said.

"How'd it go?"

"Not guilty on six of the seven. You can't win them all."

"So how'd you hook up with Anna Maria?"

"She helped me out on another case so I'm doing this one as a favor to her."

We rode a little further and he took out a chaw of Skoal.

"Is she going to testify or will she take the Fifth?" I asked him.

"That pretty much depends on what you're going to tell me right now." He slowed his horse down to my pace. "I often have these little conferences out here when I'm in town, so it's understood that nothing said between us goes anywhere else."

"I understand. So what was going through her head?"

He laughed. "Who knows with women? Her and Victor—"

"What was that all about?"

Clark spit into the dirt. "That dead bastard raped her—after they broke up and she started going out with your boy. Raped her at gunpoint but she was scared to come forward and he never got charged."

I rode in silence for a few moments, not really surprised. "I wouldn't really call it going out," she'd said to me when she grabbed my hand in the cold November air. This time I felt so sad for her there were tears stinging my eyes. I let Clark get ahead of me so I could wipe my eyes with my sleeve in private.

Clark waited for me to catch up. "You know, Victor probably held the very same gun on her that he pulled out that night at the party," he said. "Bet when she saw that gun, she really lost it."

"So I'll put on the gun and that should get her off," I said. "Show that she wasn't thinking straight at the time."

He frowned. "Now, Anna Maria says she saw a gun this time but the cops never did find one at the scene of the crime, did they?"

"Well, this kid, Eddie, Jovanka's kid, he was the one who took the gun away from Victor. He used it to kill himself after he shot Joey Lilly. We've got the gun and we've got Lee Yazzie coming down to testify."

"For you? That's a feat."

"He's not going to say that it was definitely the same gun, but he'll say it was the same type that nicked Diamond. But I got a guy named George Cloud to make an ID. He's an actor."

"An actor? Folks here don't take too kindly to the people who lie for a living. We might have ourselves a little problem. We could be setting that little girl up for a long stay in the women's pen in Grants if we can't prove self-defense or provocation. What else have you got? What about Dora Lilly?"

I pulled the horse's reins to slow it but it sped up anyway. Clark kept pace.

"Nobody knows Dora."

"I don't know then," Clark said. "I'm going to have to watch the trial to see how you're doing before I can really advise her what to do."

"Anna Maria can testify even if you tell her not to, can't she?"

"Oh, she can do what she wants to do." He stood up straight up in his saddle, towering over me. "But I'm a very persuasive man, and I really like that little lady," he said. "She's been through more than either of us can ever imagine. If she loses her nasty little boyfriend to a murder rap, it might be the best thing that ever happens to her because she can get on with her life."

Neither of us spoke for a minute or two.

"Right now she's not facing any charges," he said finally. "I'm not putting her on the stand unless I'm damn sure you're not going to mess up her life. Little girls like her don't have fun up at the women's pen over in Grants."

"I can imagine," I said. "How'd a big-time lawyer like you get involved with her?"

"She's helped me out before."

"How so?"

"Three words—attorney, client and privilege."

Chapter 43

Rope a Dope

WE ARRIVED BACK AT THE courtroom without a moment to spare. Jovanka called Officer Diamond to the stand, guided him through his version of the incident. She would repeat Diamond's last answer before she asked her next question, which made the story sound smoother.

"You got out of the car, then what happened?"

"Then I saw a disturbance in the parking lot."

"After you saw the disturbance in the parking lot, what did you do?"

"I went toward it on foot."

"After you went forward on foot, what did you see?"

It was slow going, but effective. She then asked him how far away he was from the action.

"About fifty feet."

She paced off fifty feet away and held up three fingers. "How many fingers am I holding up?"

"Three."

"Could you identify any of the participants that night?"

"Yes. Jesus Villalobos, who is sitting next to his lawyer."

"Was there anything else about Mr. Villalobos you remember?"

"Yes. He was wearing a sweatshirt with his name on it."

"Thank you. No further questions, Your Honor."

Pete wanted Diamond. "Nothing is more fun than cross-examining the people you went to high school with."

Sounded like fun to me.

After Jovanka sat down, Pete reached under the desk for a large gym bag, set it on the table, then smiled at the jurors. "You're all probably wondering what's in the bag," he said.

For the next few minutes he asked Diamond some technical questions. Diamond responded. Jovanka objected frequently and her objections were always sustained by Judge Perez, but the eyes of all the jurors were on the bag.

Finally Pete opened the bag and pulled out a rope. At the end of the rope was a lariat.

"Officer Diamond, I want you to grab one end of the rope." Diamond took hold of his end and Pete gave the other end to a juror. "Officer," Pete said, "I know that you, like me, have done some roping professionally. I guess we were both a lot thinner back then."

"Right. That was about a hundred and fifty pounds ago. I was on the Pro tour."

"So you've had a crazy calf running at you that you was trying to rope?"

"Sure. Those calves moved pretty quick."

"If I remember right, it was pretty hard to tell exactly how far away things were, since that there calf was always moving?"

"I guess so."

Jovanka leapt up. "Objection! Relevance! Your Honor, this is not the Pro Rodeo tour."

"Your Honor, Mrs. Smith has raised the witness's ability to judge distance. I am ascertaining the extent of his depth perception when the target of that perception is in motion."

"I'll allow this line of questioning," the judge said, "but please be brief, counsel. Mrs. Smith is correct: this courtroom is not the rodeo grounds, though it might seem so at times."

Pete then had the other jurors grab the end of the rope until the lariat made a circle about ten feet in diameter. "This loop is big enough to contain all the participants, right? You could fit all of them inside here?"

"Right."

Now, how easy would it be to throw the rope all the way to the gentlemen and rope something inside? It would be tough to spot it exactly?"

"Yes, but—"

"That was a yes or no question. It would be tough to accurately gauge all the distances in that circle?"

"Yes, but—"

"Thank you. No further questions." Pete sat down quickly, leaving Diamond and the jurors holding the rope.

On redirect, Jovanka firmed up the identification. Diamond swore again and again how good his eyesight was. She made him demonstrate his visual acuity by reading various signs around the courtroom. She finished by having him read the lettering over the exit sign which said "This way to jail, authorized personnel only."

Pete came back hard on re-cross. "In addition to being a rodeo star, you were a football hero. Correct, officer?"

"Hero?" he laughed. "I wish. Played right here, for the Eagles. You remember those days."

"Did you letter?"

"All four years."

"So you received a letter jacket?"

"We got sweaters in those days."

"You ever lend that to your girlfriend?" Pete asked before Jovanka could get to her feet.

The jurors looked puzzled for only a second, then several of them nodded. Jovanka started to rise.

Pete withdrew the question and sat down. I hoped that someday I'd be able to cross-examine my classmates, just like him.

Dr. Goldfarb, the state's medical expert, was a tall man with a regal bearing, the kind of witness jurors believe before they even open their mouths. He wore a conservative but expensive-looking blue suit with a black and blue rep tie. None of the TV stations stayed for his testimony.

Dr. Goldfarb spoke in a monotone, very deliberately. Merril had him first testify in technical terms, then explain the terms "for the laymen." Merril went through every line of his twenty-page report, discussed every diagram, then passed the witness.

After he sat down, I looked around the courtroom. There was still no sign of the media. I turned to a page of his report.

"A 'strong possibility' is different from 'absolute certainty,' isn't it, doctor?" I asked.

"Yes, but my studies indicate that—"

"So there could be a 'reasonable doubt' on whether it was the kick or the throw?"

He waited for a moment. "Not in my mind," he said. "I'm positive that it was the kick."

"Doctor, have you ever testified as an expert in foreign countries?"

"Yes, I have. I've testified in Latin America and in the Middle East."

"About the Middle East. Didn't you once testify that a person died of a gunshot wound to the head, when that person was, in fact, beheaded? Wasn't the body missing its head when you supposedly saw it?"

He frowned. I had done my homework. I beat the expert.

But the jury kept it's eyes on Goldfarb, who didn't miss a beat. "Not exactly. This is how these rumors started. I was able to testify about the man's gunshot wound and I was able to examine the body. It's just that the court over there had already beheaded the defendant before I got to testify."

He paused for dramatic effect. "I'm glad I'm back here where the process of justice is shall we say more enlightened."

"Don't be too sure about that," I said, without thinking.

Too late. Both judge and jury shot me a dirty look.

Chapter 44

Prior Bad Acts

THE NEXT DAY, MERRIL AND Smith called a few more witnesses, mainly cops and other investigators. They were all well prepped and boring. Even Pete couldn't lay a glove on Thompson this time. In the afternoon, Merril called Paul Celestino to talk about Jesus' reputation for violence. By that time Amanda had returned.

According to Pete, Celestino used to be a gangbanger. Now in his black suit he looked like a young divinity student. Celestino testified about Jesus' prior bad acts. He was repeating some of the insults that Jesus had said to him in a previous fight. Before Pete could stop me, I was on my feet. "Objection, Your Honor! Hearsay."

The judge didn't even look over at Merril. "Statements of a party opponent are, of course, admissible. Proceed, Mr. Merril"

After a few more minutes Celestino testified about things that Anna Maria had said.

Pete elbowed me. "She's not a party opponent. It's hearsay under Rule 801. Object!"

I rose, but Merril beat me to the punch before I could say anything. "Your Honor, these statements are not being offered for the truth of the matter asserted."

Judge Perez sighed. "As long as no one in the jury thinks those statements are being admitted for the truth of the matter asserted, I'll let them in."

Merril asked Celestino whether Anna Maria had told him about Jesus' feelings toward Victor.

"She told me that Jesus had always hated Victor."

"Why was that?"

"She never said. I guess her and Victor used to go out or something. She said Jesus got jealous."

"Did she say anything else about what Jesus had told him about Victor?"

"She said that he was always bragging that one of these days he was going to kill Victor."

"He said he would kill Victor. Nothing further, Your Honor."

Ricky Clark sat in the front row of the gallery. He eyed me intently. I decided to take a big gamble with Mr. Straight-Laced. "Did Anna Maria ever tell you that Victor had raped her?" I asked.

Merril leapt to his feet. "Objection, Your Honor! Lack of proper foundation. Lack of any foundation. Mr. Shepard should be held in criminal contempt for even suggesting that."

All jurors eyes focused coldly on me, as if I'd kicked Victor right there on the courtroom floor.

"Mr. Shepard, that is a strong accusation," Judge Perez said over his banging gavel. "A strong accusation against a boy who is unable to come here and defend his honor. Can you back it up?"

"Your Honor, Anna Maria Arias is on our witness list. We'll know at that time."

"Then I will not allow the question until I have more foundation. I am also prepared to hold you in criminal contempt if you attempt any such stunts in the future. The witness may be excused."

Celestino got off the stand. He shook his head, as if he'd been offended by my horrible cross examination.

I looked at the jurors. Every one of them glared at me

"Well, you just about pissed everybody in the whole room off, including me," Pete whispered. "Check with me first before saying stupid shit like that."

Ricky Clark gave me a wink as he put a chaw in his mouth. At least I had made one person in the room happy.

I walked out for some air during the recess and stretched against a saber yucca outside the courthouse door. When I got back, Merril was ready to begin.

"We call Guillermo Juarez to the stand," he said after court began again.

Guillermo was dressed in a suit, possibly the same one Celestino had worn, I couldn't tell for sure. Next to him an interpreter, Monica Romero, Dr. Romero's younger sibling, who shared her regal bearing. On the other side, his lawyer Woodford, who looked like a potted palm in his green and brown outfit. As for Guillermo, in his suit and with glasses, he now could pass for Keith Richards' accountant.

Merril now drew Guillermo's attention to October 6—after a few more questions, Merril took Guillermo to the moment of Victor's death. "Who kicked Victor?"

No hesitation whatsoever. "I know that it was Jesus Villalobos who kicked him."

"Can you identify this person here?"

"That's Jesus Villalobos, the one who kicked him."

"And was Victor alive or dead after being thrown down by whomever?"

Romero looked at Guillermo as he strained to remember. "Yes, I think Victor was still alive."

"Nothing further. Pass the witness."

I could feel sweat staining my nice shirt all the way down to my suit as I stood up. I didn't know what I should do now. Merril had just made this crazed child molester look like a Mexican Norman Rockwell.

Ricky Clark shook his head from the gallery. Anna Maria would not testify if I didn't do something with Guillermo.

I could attack on vision, memory or the hood, but when I looked over at Guillermo I knew I would never shake him, especially now that he was the picture of respectability in that black suit. The tears on his face were dry, he was now back to his tough old bastard self. Back in the joint he ate guys like me for breakfast, literally. I might as well be crossing Charles Manson.

I went though some inconsistencies in his testimony then asked, "You are absolutely positive that it was Jesus Villalobos?"

"Yes he is."

I hammered and hammered on every point, but he was too good. He'd been cross-examined by the best and I couldn't break him.

I sat down, utterly exhausted.

When he rose, he looked over at me and smiled, whispered something to the interpreter.

"He told me to tell you, 'I enjoy our visits,'" she said.

The State's next witness was a paramedic, a woman named Edith Lomas. She was a late addition I hadn't had a chance to question. I had read her statement and it wasn't that damaging. So why was she so near the end?

Jovanka asked her a few questions describing the scene when she arrived. Lomas was able to paint a picture of a body laying on the curb, blood rushing from its head.

"Was he still breathing?" Jovanka asked.

"Yeah. He was still alive when I arrived. Just barely."

"You said in your statement to the police that you heard him say a few words?"

"Yes, I did."

There was something about that in her statement, but nothing in specific. I looked up the reference: "The victim said a few words before losing consciousness." If the victim had said anything important, Lomas would have put it in her statement. I stood up to object.

Jovanka anticipated and kept going. "But you didn't relate those words to the police at the time, did you?"

I was already halfway up so I objected anyway. "Objection. Leading the witness."

"Your Honor, I am merely laying a foundation."

"Proceed."

She gave the jurors a smug look, then turned back to face the witness stand. "Please tell us why you didn't tell the police about these words."

"I didn't understand the . . . the . . . ah, context of what he was saying. I didn't realize they were so important at the time. But then when I found out who the defendant was, it all made sense."

"What were those words that were said by Victor in what he thought were his last moments on earth?"

I was about to stand up, but Pete whispered in my ear, "Dying declarations are admissible if someone thinks they are dying, regardless of whether they actually die. Sit the fuck down before you make a fool of yourself again."

"He was whispering, 'Jesus, why have you forsaken me?'" she said, pronouncing the "J" in the Spanish style. "'Why did you kill me?' At first I thought he was just being religious and I wanted to respect the dead. But now that I found out that the defendant's named Jesus—"

"Thank you, Ms. Lomas. No further questions."

Pete whispered in my ear. I stood up and did exactly what he said. "You've talked to the police since then?"

"Yes."

"And you've talked to the district attorney? To Mrs. Smith?"

"Yes."

"Were they the ones who helped jog your memory?"

Before she could answer, I withdrew the question.

Jovanka had expected that statement as well. "Why have you come forward today with that new information?" she asked on redirect.

"I see death everyday in my job. But I'll always remember that poor boy, Victor, lying beaten against the curb, bleeding and whispering the name of his killer. Victor's last words were, 'Jesus, why have you forsaken me?'"

It worked. The old ladies in the back row of the jury box had tears in their eyes.

Jovanka knew she had them in the palm of her hand. "Your Honor, members of the jury, the state rests."

The judge then asked me if I had any motions, after the jurors had left.

"Directed verdict" Pete whispered in my ear. "Say something. Anything."

"Your Honor, on behalf of my client, I ask for a directed verdict on the grounds that my client is innocent."

"Judge Perez looked at me. "Come on now, son. You'll have to do better than that."

"I intend to," I said, then took a deep breath. Amanda was right. This was a show.

"Your Honor, my client was not identified by a witness. The witness only said he saw a sweatshirt or a jacket and we have established the likelihood that such an item of clothing could have been lent to another person. We have also established that it might have been the throwing down, rather than the kick, that killed Victor. We have a dying man saying the name of the Son of God while gasping for breath, which the state would have us interpret as a positive ID of my client.

"There are many scenarios that play better than the one the state would have you believe. There is more to this case than meets the eye."

That last bit put me close to the contempt line, since I had indirectly referred to my question about the rape that had been thrown out. I knew the story about sticking a skunk in the jury box and asking the jury to disregard the smell. To my surprise, the judge nodded.

"And so, Your Honor, I ask that you direct a verdict for the defense."

When Merril started to stand up, the judge waved him down. "That's much better, son. Court is adjourned until ten on Monday." He rose.

"Your Honor? Your ruling?" I asked.

"The motion is denied, of course. But good job, nonetheless. Defense begins Monday at ten."

That afternoon I ran along acequia trail. Because of spring runoff from the mountain, water flowed at a steady pace. Water was soothing in the desert, even if muddy and brackish and only a foot deep.

While running, a real live rattlesnake startled me in the middle of the path. I stopped dead for a moment, then walked gingerly around it. It let me go past. I thought of the old joke . . . professional courtesy.

That night Amanda came over to my crappy apartment. She looked different. Her hair was a short bob and her highlights were gone. I had cleaned and cleaned, put up a few Western paintings I'd bought from Wal-Mart. For the first time ever, it looked like an adult lived there. It was even better this time, now that I knew what made her happy. She knew things that I hadn't known that made me even happier.

But at the end of the night, utterly spent, I kissed her forehead.

"I've got something to tell you," she said.

I didn't like the sound of that.

"I'm moving," she said. "I've got a job offer to move out to L.A., to work for one of those trial networks."

"How'd you—"

"I sent them a few of my tapes. The ones about Jesus."

I froze.

"Is that what all of this was," I shouted. "Using me, using Jesus, so you could get a better job back in the real world?"

"Dan, it wasn't about that at all." She kissed me again, grabbed me down below, "Maybe you can come out with me in a few months. Besides, there are things that I would never lie about to get a story."

Chapter 45

Red Sky At Morning

"I CAN'T TELL WHETHER YOU'RE up or down today, bro," Jesus said as I sat down next to him at counsel table Monday morning. "What happened?"

"Hey man I don't know everything about you," I said. "You don't get to know everything about me."

I called Sky Roberts to the stand. Sky had tried to weasel out, of course, based on the deal with the state and was disappointed that he'd have to testify anyway. I'd like to take credit for getting him on the stand, but it was all Pete's doing. Pete hated big time lawyers even worse than I did. He had raised such a stink, even calling the New Mexico State Bar to get Rose's pro hac vice admittance revoked, that Rose finally cried wolf. Rose knew when he was being hometowned by the hillbillies, so he had to cut his losses. Sky would testify for the defense after all. Rose's only condition—the questioning would be done by little old me rather than big bad Pete.

Rose stood next to Sky, glaring at me as he battled his allergies. I took Sky through the preliminaries, then moved to the night of October 6.

"Tell me, Sky, what happened when you, Victor, and Guillermo were out there in the parking lot?"

"Victor said some things to me. Then I saw him pull out a gun."

"How did you feel when he pulled a gun on you?"

"I didn't feel nothing. I was just kind of pissed off a little."

I frowned. "So you were real scared when he pulled a gun on you?"

Merril jumped up, "Objection! Leading."

I looked at the judge "Laying a foundation?"

"No you're not," he said with a glare. "I don't see anyone or anything getting laid here." He lifted his gavel, started to bring it down.

Pete nudged me. "Witness's state of mind," I offered.

The judge stayed his gavel in mid-air. "Continue."

"I didn't quite catch your last answer. How did you feel when Victor pulled a gun on you?"

"I was scared when he pulled a gun on me," Roberts said. "Real scared."

"Why was that?"

"I don't know."

I frowned again. "He had a gun, a gun that could kill you." As Merril rose, I continued. "How did that effect your judgment?"

"I was real scared that he was going to kill me, 'cause of the gun."

"What happened after you saw the gun and were real scared that he was going to kill you?"

He looked over at Rose, who nodded. "That's when I threw him down."

Rose then gave me an anxious look, I had to protect Sky right now, just in case. . . .

"You didn't intend to kill him, of course?" I asked.

"Uh. . . ."

This guy just didn't get it sometimes. I had to spoonfeed him. "You were just protecting yourself," I said. "Right, Sky?"

Merril stood up again.

"I'm sorry, Sky," I said, "I'm afraid I asked the question incorrectly, as Mr. Merril is about to point out. What exactly were you trying to do when you threw him down?"

"I was just trying to protect myself." he said at last.

Rose nodded at me—nicely done. But by being nice to Sky, was I harming my own client? No time to think, had to press on.

"What happened after that?"

"Victor lay still for a second, then he jerked around. He still had the gun and it looked like he was going to fire it at someone."

"Then what happened?"

"Then somebody kicked him."

"Who kicked him?"

Sky was confused, he looked over at Rose. I half expected him to yell "line?!"

Finally he spoke. "I think it was the little Mexican kid that's at the table."

Shit. "But last time you said—"

Merril stood up "Your honor, we'd really appreciate it if Mr.

Shepard will continue this line of questioning. If he can ask the witness to identify his client for the record, it will save us the trouble of doing it on cross-examination."

I paused—I considered going into his eyesight, state of mind, state of sobriety, but I decided to cut to the chase. I looked Sky right in the eye. "Are you sure it was Jesus that did the kick?" I shuddered when the words were halfway out of my mouth. This was the same stupid question I had asked the officer in the first hearing on Jesus.

Sky didn't even blink. When it came right down to it, he just wasn't all that bright. "I'm not sure. Like I said, I was pretty fucked up at the time. It could have been anybody under that hood. And the face did kinda look funny—with all the drugs, I sometimes have problems with my memory."

Even I knew enough to sit down after an answer like that. Rose shook his head.

"What a dumb fuck," Jesus whispered in my ear. Merril stayed seated. You don't ask a question when you have no idea what the witness is going to say, one way or the other.

Rose was halfway out the door before the judge banged down the gavel excusing his client for good. He had a plane to catch back to civilization. If he stayed too long he might end up like Sky, or worse yet like me. . . .

After testimony finished for the day, I approached Amanda, who whispered with a young woman I'd never seen before. This woman could have been in beauty pageants. Amanda excused herself and we walked outside to the courthouse grounds.

"I'm out of here tomorrow," she sighed. "Miss Teen Congeniality over there is my replacement."

"How does it feel?"

"Great. Can you help me move?"

"Sure."

"I've got a lot of stuff, so I'm getting Pete to help, too."

"All right," I said. "I'll miss you."

"I'll miss you, too."

"But what about that news magazine show? Aren't you going to film the trial for that?"

"No. There's some big murder out in L.A., the big racial one. They want me to get there and cover it this week. I've already got video of all the principles on this one. We can pretty much make it up from here. And besides no one out on the coast is really going to care about a murder in flyover land."

Off in the distance, I could see Victor's mother. She cared. I looked at the empty seat where Jesus had been sitting. He cared too.

Chapter 46

Last Supper

THE AFOREMENTIONED MISS TEEN CONGENIALITY did the news that night, so at six-twenty-two we were deep into chips and dips at Rosalita's.

"Mr. Clark says I shouldn't talk to you unless he's there," Anna Maria said when she brought us our tea. "My family is letting me stay on here 'cause they know I'm under a court order, but they don't want me talking to you, either."

She looked like she had lost some weight off her already thin figure—but she was a survivor. She kept moving as quickly as before.

"Mr. Clark told me I might have to take the Fifth," she said.

"Can we talk about green chile chicken enchiladas?

"Sure."

"Green chile stew for me," said Amanda. "Vegetarian this time, okay?"

"Have you seen Jesus?" I asked Anna Maria.

"Not even. My lawyer won't let me talk to him, either. But at least my lawyer told Enrique to mind his own damn business."

"Lawyers can get in the way of true love," Amanda said.

"Either way I'm going to marry him," Anna Maria said. "No matter where they send him."

I stared at Amanda—would she stick by me after she went away? I didn't have to think about that too hard. Our dinner was excellent, of course. For dessert we went back to her rented Victorian.

While she undressed, I scanned her aerobicized body, my eyes following the curve of her legs and back, perhaps for the last time. "I hate to say this but I'll never look at you the same when you say, 'Sports is next, stay with us.'"

I woke up at her place the next morning and felt something warm and soft and furry in my face. I heard Amanda's voice. "I love you," she said.

The cat darted off my face. Amanda picked it up. "I love you," she said again.

"Meow," I replied.

Chapter 47

My Turn

April 14

PETE AND I HELPED AMANDA move her stuff into a rented U-Haul on Saturday. It only took a few hours, she hadn't really put down roots. After the last item was loaded, there was a moment of silence. She shook our hands and then drove off.

"I already have a date with the new girl," Pete said. "Did you know that she was. . . ."

"Well, aren't you the lucky one," I interrupted.

"No, she is."

I went to the office several times over the weekend, tried to concentrate on the case. I failed. Amanda was gone. I wouldn't be famous after all. Fuck it! That's not what this case was about anyway.

On Monday afternoon it was my turn at last. I called Dr. Candelaria to the stand and had him discuss the uncertainties of Victor's cause of death. He used a rubber skull as a prop.

Merril then cross-examined Dr. Candelaria slowly and distinctly as he took the expert through a guided tour of brain injuries. When it was over, Merril put the skull back on the prosecution table. Dr. Candelaria had the embarrassing chore of walking over to the table and asking "Can I have my skull back?"

My next witness was Lee Yazzie. The forensics expert was a short, heavy-set man with long black hair tied in a pony tail but he still looked every inch the cop.

I'd read the chapter in the judge's book about qualifying experts and introducing evidence. There was a section that described using multiple witnesses to get evidence admitted. Sometimes you then had to call the first witness back again. It sounded confusing.

I floundered at first with Yazzie, but Pete whispered some encouraging words in my ear.

"Your Honor," I said, "we ask that this gun be admitted for demonstrative purposes only."

"So admitted," he said and the bailiff put a blue defense witness sticker on it.

"What type of gun is this?" I asked.

"A Tech-9, an older model."

"Based on your expert opinion, was this the type of gun that was used to shoot Officer Diamond?"

"Yes."

"Based on your expert opinion, was this also the type of gun that Eddie Smith used to kill himself?"

Jovanka jumped up. "Objection! Lack of proper foundation. I must point out to Your Honor that you have already warned counsel. Once again I ask that you have him held in contempt."

The judge looked at me and banged his gavel, "Son, I am rapidly losing my patience with you in this courtroom. Please lay the proper foundation or I will see to it that you will never lay anything in this town ever again."

He banged his gavel down. I knew what that gavel would be smashing next if I didn't shape up.

"Yes, Your Honor. Mr. Yazzie, I've given you the police reports, both of Victor's death and of the investigation into the deaths of Eddie Smith and Joey Lilly?"

"Yes. I've read all of them."

"You are aware that the gun that I have shown you was found in a ditch a few hundred yards downstream from where Eddie Smith and Joey Lilly were found dead?"

"Yes, I am."

"Based on your expert opinion, is it possible for that gun to be carried downstream in the current after a heavy rain?"

"Yes. Especially if there's a sudden gush of water coming down from the higher elevations when they let the floodgates open."

"What was the weather that night in Aguilar?"

"Objection! Lack of personal knowledge," Jovanka said. "Your Honor, once again I renew my standing objection and once again I ask you to hold Mr. Shepard in contempt. I ask that you strike all testimony about this gun from the record on the grounds of relevance and lack of proper foundation."

"I'm stopping you here, son," said the judge, still holding the gavel. "I will allow you to try again, once you have provided proper foundation. Are you prepared to do so?"

"Yes, Your Honor. I call George Cloud to the stand—" I looked down at my little cheat sheet, "provided you will allow me to recall this witness after Mr. Cloud testifies."

"I will hold the motion to hold your contempt in abeyance until after that," he said.

Cloud wore his Western costume from the movie set. I showed him the gun.

"Have you ever seen a gun that looked like this?"

"Yes, I have."

"Where was that?"

"On the set, when our security guard removed it from Victor Slade."

"Did you ever see a gun like this again?"

"Yes, I did."

"When was that?"

"I saw it a few weeks later, when I was walking out on the mesa."

"Who had that gun?"

"Eddie Smith."

"How did you know Eddie Smith?"

"I was introduced to him on the movie set."

"What happened on the day you saw Eddie Smith out on the desert?"

"He stood a short distance away from me and shot my dog. He didn't see me at first, until I yelled at him, and then he ran away. But I was able to get a pretty good look at the gun. And I know a lot about guns from work. I'm positive that it was the same gun."

"Let the record ref—"

"I'm way ahead of you Mr. Shepard," the judge said, motioning the bailiff to put a defense sticker on the gun.

I smiled, continued with Cloud. "Were you here New Year's Eve?"

"Yes, I was."

"How was the weather that night?"

"It was raining like . . . the end of days. The power went out at the crew party, it was so bad."

"Thank you, Mr. Cloud."

I looked down at the sheet again, excused Cloud, and recalled Yazzie.

"Mr. Yazzie, could this have been the gun that Eddie Smith used to kill himself, or may have been used to kill him?"

Jovanka stood up again, this time pounding her hands on the table. "Objection!"

"No, I'll allow the question," said the judge. "I think we've heard sufficient foundation."

Yazzie nodded his head. "Yes."

"And could this be the gun that some witnesses have testified to be on Victor Slade?"

"Yes."

"The same gun that shot Officer Diamond?"

"Yes, it could be."

"Your Honor, I'd like to move this gun into evidence."

"Objection?"

"None."

"So admitted," the judge said. "I'm glad we already had it marked."

Ricky Clark smiled.

The cross-examination of both Yazzie and Cloud was ferocious. Jovanka proved that there were a million Tech-9s, and no indisputable evidence linking the gun that killed Eddie with the gun that shot Officer Diamond. But the jurors kept their eyes on the gun on the table.

After a recess, I called Dora Lilly to the stand. Her mother sat in the rear of the room. I could feel the weight of her gaze on the back of my neck. Neighbor or not, she didn't want me to mess with her little girl now that her son was gone.

Dora wore a long-sleeved blue turtleneck that hid her arms.

"Would you please state your full name for the record?"

"Dora Deanna Lilly."

"Was Jesus involved in killing Victor?"

"I don't know nothing about that."

I was expecting her to say no, but that was close enough. I didn't say anything and pressed on. "So who went outside with Guillermo and Roberts?"

She smiled at me and flashed her braces. "I don't know nothing about that."

I stopped for a moment, stunned. She kept smiling at me. She wasn't going to rat out Anna Maria after all.

"So what knowledge do you have about the death of Victor and the shooting of Officer Diamond?"

"I don't know nothing about that."

I sat down, shocked.

Needless to say, there was no cross.

"What happened?" I asked Jesus at the recess.

"I guess she didn't think you'd done enough to save Anna Maria yet."

"Why would she do that?"

Jesus shrugged his shoulders. "Nobody knows Dora, ese."

I went into the gallery and talked to Ricky Clark. He spit into a plastic cup. I asked him what Anna Maria was going to do.

He shrugged. "You know women."

"Not lately," I said. "So what's up?"

"It can go either way, is the way I see it. I'm giving her a form to sign telling her that I advised her that she had a Fifth Amendment right not to testify. I don't know if you really did enough to show self-defense or insanity."

"Could I talk to her, at least to find out what she's going to say?"

"I rather you didn't do that. Her family is after her again, you know."

"They are?"

"Even after I talked to them. Remember, they hate Jesus, especially her brother Enrique. So I've got her staying up at my ranch. She's not talking to anybody until tomorrow."

That was great. I calling my last witness with no idea what she was going to say.

The outcome was truly in los brazos de Dios.

Chapter 48

Don't Cry For Me, Anna Maria

April 15

I DIDN'T WATCH THE NEWS that night, I didn't want to watch someone I didn't know. I tossed and turned, which left me tired Tuesday morning for our final witness. . . .

Anna Maria came to court with Ricky Clark. She wore a long blue peasant dress. I was reminded of Amanda's Santa Fe outfit, but Anna Maria had no adornments on hers other than a simple black belt. She was the real thing after all. But in contrast to her outfit's simplicity, she wore a little too much make-up, especially around the eyes.

"Well?" I asked Ricky.

"She's going to testify until you get to certain questions. Then I'm going to advise her to take the Fifth. You better make damn sure that you've set it up correctly, so she's not looking at any charges."

"What you mean?"

"Basically, you better prove that she didn't do it before you ask her if she did."

"Like how?"

"You better show either self-defense, insanity, battered woman's syndrome—anything—before you have her saying she kicked him. If I'm not totally satisfied, I'll persuasively advise her to take the Fifth."

"How do I—?"

"You got to show that she was scared or that she didn't know what she was doing, or she was provoked suddenly. One of those."

He handed me copies of NMSA 14-5140, excusable homicide; 14-5171, justifiable homicide; and 14-5102, insanity.

"Read these to get an idea of what I would have to show if I had to defend Anna Maria at a trial for murder," he said. "Try to get in the magic words."

"Magic words?"

"Just read them."

I spent a few anxious moments reading over the law and learning what to say. The judge arrived, called court to order. I called Anna Maria Arias to the stand. Ricky sat right next to her, dwarfing her. I hurried through the preliminaries and got right to the money questions.

"Anna Maria do you know the deceased in this case, Victor Slade?"

"Yes, I do."

"How do you know him?"

"He went out with me a while, before I started going with Jesus."

"Could you describe this relationship?"

"Objection," Jovanka said. "Relevance."

That got me for a second. "Your Honor, it goes to her . . . state of mind and it, uh, shows bias she might have toward the defendant."

The judge looked down at me. I tried again before he could tell me I had to do better than that. "Your Honor, opposing counsel brought this up when she questioned Paul Celestino."

"She did indeed," the judge said. "You may continue."

"Anna Maria, you may answer the question. Tell us a little about your relationship with Victor."

"He beat me a lot. He raped me once, after I broke up with him and started going out with Jesus."

"What happened?"

"Objection again, Your Honor. Relevance."

"Your Honor, may we approach the bench?" I went up with Jovanka. "Your Honor, you held the contempt in abeyance until I proved my point. Well, Your Honor, I'm ready to prove it right now."

Jovanka glared at me. "Your Honor, it's still not relevant if it doesn't go to the defendant's state of mind."

"Your Honor, it goes to the state of mind of the person who actually kicked Victor. I would assume you want to find out who that is?"

"I'm going to allow the questions, but please be brief."

I walked back to the podium and flashed a quick smile at the jurors to let them know that I had won the last battle. "Anna Maria, you may answer the question."

"A couple of months before this all happened, after we broke up, Victor held a gun to me and raped me. He said if I ever told anyone he'd kill me. He meant it too."

I picked up the Tech-9. "Was this the gun?"

"I think so."

"Were you at the party the night of October 6?"

"Yes, I was."

"Why were you there?"

"My boyfriend, Jesus, was going to be there."

"What were you wearing that night?"

"I wore Jesus's old sweatshirt for wrestling because it was kind of cold out."

"Would you describe that sweatshirt?"

"It's kind of dark and it has a hood."

I produced the sweatshirt and had her put it on. She drew the draw-strings closed tight. With all her makeup and eyelashes, she still looked like a girl wearing a sweatshirt. Shit.

Suddenly the lights went off. . . .

"Sorry your honor," Pete's voice echoed from the back. "I must have tripped."

"Turn them back on this instant!" The judge yelled.

"Give me a second your Honor," he said. "It's kinda hard to see in the dark. I can barely make-out the witness's face in this kind of light."

There was laughter from the jury, then the lights magically came back on. Pete gave me a wink. I nodded back to him.

Time to keep pressing on. "Was Jesus there that night?" I asked.

She took the hood off. "He was there earlier, but he left with Joey."

"Did he come back?"

"No."

"Was Eddie Smith, also known as Aryan Eddie, there?"

"Yes, he was."

"What did Eddie look like back then?"

"He was kind of thin and had real long blond hair."

"Did you see Eddie with a gun prior to the incident?"

"No, I didn't."

"Did you see him with a gun after the fight?"

"Yes, I did."

"What was he doing?"

"He was firing the gun, all crazy like."

Now for the big questions, and whether the case was won or lost. "Where did he get the gun?"

"Objection!" Jovanka jumped up. "Lack of personal knowledge."

The judge gave her a dirty look. "That's something I'd expect from Mr. Shepard, not from you, Jovanka Smith. We'll know about her level of personal knowledge in a minute. Mr. Shepard, you better ask a foundation question first, just to be safe."

I froze for a moment like the judge had handed me a gift and I didn't know how to unwrap it.

But only for a moment. "Anna Maria, do you have, uh . . . personal knowledge of where Eddie got the gun?"

"I don't understand."

"Did you see him get the gun?"

"Oh . . . yes. I saw him take it from Victor's body while Victor was lying there."

All right, we're almost there. Get the gun in now. "Did the gun look like this one?" I asked, still holding the gun.

"Yes, that's it."

"How did you feel when you saw Victor there that night?"

Anna Maria took a deep breath, then started talking rapidly. "It brought back all the bad memories. I hadn't seen him in a while and I just lost it. I didn't know what came over me."

I aped Jovanka's style, repeating the last answer for emphasis before asking the next question. "You don't know what came over you, so then what did you do?"

"Like I said, I was crying and that's when Jesus left and Dora was supposed to give me a ride home, so I was outside waiting."

"After you went outside, what happened?"

"There's some people outside in the parking lot of the high school."

"What happened in the parking lot?"

"I saw Victor."

"What was he doing?"

"He held that gun there."

"How did you feel when you saw Victor outside holding that gun?"

It made everything even worse. I was all crazy."

Ricky Clark was now on his feet. This was the moment for the magic words. I had to show some variant of temporarily insanity.

"Could you tell right from wrong at that time?"

Ricky gave me an anxious nod.

Jovanka jumped up. "Objection! Leading. Your Honor, could you please instruct—"

"Withdrawn," I said and tried again. "Anna Maria, what were you thinking at the time?"

"I didn't really know what I was doing. I couldn't tell right from wrong. I was, like, all confused. . . . "

"How fast did everything happen?"

"Everything happened real quick and all of a sudden."

That sounded about right so I continued. "What did Victor do?"

"Victor pulled a gun and then got pushed down by Sky Roberts. When he was down, I don't know why but he pointed the gun right at me, then pointed it toward the ground. I was just terrified. I wanted to get him before he picked it up again and raped me again. I didn't totally know what I was doing then. I just lost control. . . ."

"What did you do?"

"Your Honor," Ricky was on his feet. "I must advise my client that she has a Fifth Amendment right not to testify on the grounds it might incriminate her."

"Do you wish to take a short recess to confer with your client?"

"I do, Your Honor," he said.

"Five minutes."

"Your honor," Anna Maria said as she got up. "Do you mind if I take this sweatshirt off? It's really hot in here."

The judge nodded.

I sat with Jesus who looked downward at the oaken table, his head held in his hands.

"Do you think she loves me?" he asked the table.

I glanced back out the reinforced pane of glass in the door. Anna Maria argued with Ricky Clark, tears in her eyes. It was hard to tell, but Ricky looked like he was demanding that she not testify, that she protect herself. Enrique and the rest of her family stood nearby. He wore that "Shut up bitch" shirt again. He pleaded with her as well, as did the rest of the family. But she wouldn't listen to any of them. She stood firm, wiped away her tears.

"I think she loves you more than any woman has ever loved a man," I said.

"Sometimes I wonder if that's a good thing or not."

Ricky signaled to the judge. "The witness may answer the question," the judge said. "Unless. . . ."

Anna Maria looked at Ricky, then at Jesus, then over at me. "I was the one kicked him. It looked like he was going to pick up the gun and aim it at me again. It made me all crazy."

She told the whole story in a high-pitched voice, the sentences tumbling over each other. Anna Maria fought back tears until she lost the battle. Somewhere in there, she got all the magic words of the statute. I sat down, profoundly relieved.

Jovanka rose. "He's your boyfriend isn't he?" she asked.

"Yes, he is."

"So you'd say anything to keep him out of jail, wouldn't you."

"Not even." Anna Maria looked up and smiled. "I testified so bad for him at his last hearing when I told the truth, I was the one who got him locked up in the first place."

"But why didn't you tell anybody after all this time. Didn't you tell the officers when they arrested you?"

"I told them alright. I yelled and screamed that night. But Officer Thompson said—"

"Objection" Jovanka yelled.

"Not being offered for the truth of the matter ass—" I tried.

"You may answer the question young lady," the judge ruled.

"Officer Thompson said that you guys wanted Jesus so bad, that he didn't care."

"Your honor I ask that the comments be stricken," she said, incensed.

"I agree," the judge said, before I could protest. "Those were indeed being offered for the truth of the matter asserted after all. Officer Thompson is not on trial here. Move on counsel."

Jovanka said nothing as she caught her breath. Even though the statement had been stricken, the damage had been done, like offering a skunk into evidence and telling the jury to ignore the smell. She looked over at her husband's picture for a moment, as if she had let him down. She swore something under her breath in her native tongue, then pushed on. "You're sure it was you who kicked him?"

"Yes, I am."

Jovanka looked around. There was nothing more to be gained by badgering Anna Maria, but she couldn't resist.

"You're really sure?"

"Yes." Now it was Anna Maria who sighed. "Do you want to ask me again? I'll tell you the same thing then, too."

"Nothing further."

I stood up. "Your Honor, the defense rests."

Chapter 49

Closings

JUDGE PEREZ WANTED TO GET it over with that night. He gave us fifteen minutes to argue jury instructions, then another hour for preparation then boom, boom, boom, it was time for closings. This ended tonight one way or another.

In chambers, there was an argument about jury instructions. I quickly glanced over the jury instructions and submitted 14-5150, the instruction for alibi.

After glancing through the bulky orange volumes of the New Mexico Statutes Annotated, Merril made a few technical objections. A few months ago they'd filed a "Demand for a Notice of Intention-to-Claim-Alibi" that I had never responded to after Joey had died. These guys just didn't quit.

The judge looked at me and asked simply, "Mr. Shepard, did you know for sure what that last witness would say?"

"No, Your Honor. I hoped, yes, but I wasn't sure." I was very careful. "Once she returned to the United States, I didn't talk to her about her testimony without talking with her attorney, Mr. Clark, first."

No one caught the implications of my statement. Before anyone could say anything more, Ricky Clark handed the judge a fistful of New Mexico Supreme Court cases supporting that position. The judge reviewed them, then overruled the objection.

After a few more minutes of arguing about the instructions, the judge made up his mind, recalled the jurors. He then read every single one himself to them, line by line. . . .

Reading jury instructions proved even more boring than medical testimony, so I stared at the pictures of the judges on the wall, who glared right back at me, especially Jovanka's late husband.

"Madam Prosecutor you may begin," the judge said at last.

She rose and walked over to the podium. Starting slowly and distinctly, she kept it pretty matter-of-fact, with just the slightest touch of her foreign accent to make it sound like she was a visiting professor. She went through the elements of each of the crimes and said how the defendant satisfied each of the elements. There was no emotion, whatsoever. She drew a checklist on a big sheet of paper under the heading of First Degree Murder, NMSA 30-2-1A. Then she drew a diagram for Second Degree Murder, NMSA 30-2-1B. "These are the elements of the crimes charged. . . ."

She kept on with conspiracy, and all the way down the five or six other charges that the state had filed. I wondered if I was the only one bored out of my mind.

No . . . the jurors looked bored. The judge looked bored. Even the picture of her husband looked bored. This wasn't the fire and brimstone close they all had expected.

Merril rose, told the jurors that he would be doing the rebuttal. Judge Perez nodded. Merril turned, smiled at me. He had something up his sleeve. Perhaps he had learned a trick or two from Pete.

Then I looked behind him—Officer Thompson and Officer Diamond sat in the gallery holding all of the pieces of evidence. I think they even had a video of Victor's football exploits that I had mistakenly stipulated to somewhere along the line.

Both of them smiled at me with evil anticipation.

"Merril saves it all for the rebuttal," whispered Pete in my ear. "He gets fucking sadistic and these redneck juries love it. He didn't have to remind me that this was Aguilar after all.

"Remember, I'm still your boss and I want you to say these exact words. Just remember, all they've said in closing arguments about your client so far is a boring chart listing the elements of the crime. This is going to seem like a risk, but what the fuck. . . ."

After he told me what he wanted me to do, he added one last instruction: "You gotta pull it off like you mean it or it won't work 'cause this is something that takes a lot of balls."

When I told Jesus what Pete suggested, he nodded and smiled at me. "Yeah, I know. That's pretty much what you do in my dream."

I stood up and walked to the state's diagram that showed the elements of both first- and second-degree murder. I looked in the gallery until I spotted Anna Maria at the back of the room. I nodded.

For a brief moment I wished Amanda was there—but I supposed

it didn't matter anyway. This wasn't about her anymore.

Jovanka scribbled down notes on all the points she wanted Merril to make. Thompson and Diamond pointed out various items in the bags that would drive those points home. Merril kept one eye on them, the other on me.

I took off my glasses and focused on Jesus. He nodded. I had become the Man of Steel in his eyes. I then looked at each of the jurors in turn. It was totally silent, except for Jovanka's furious scribbling.

"Your Honor, we waive closing argument." Keeping my glasses off, I negotiated my way back to the table and sat down.

Merril stared at me, shocked. Jovanka's pen stopped halfway through a witness's name. Thompson and Diamond practically dropped their bags.

Pete laughed.

Jesus nodded.

"Good," the judge said. "In that case, we don't need to hear from the district attorney's office. Jurors, you may retire to the jury room and begin your deliberations."

"But!!!" shouted Merril and Jovanka simultaneously.

The judge banged the gavel "No rebuttal when there's nothing to rebut. You know the rules."

The jurors went out, their eyes down. If they don't look at you when they're leaving, it's bad. Or maybe that meant it was good. I didn't know either way.

While I waited, I paced a few laps around the outside of the courthouse. A beautiful sunset out against the mesa, the last snows of Sierra Milagro shined pink in the light, then turned dark. Not wanting to get poked by one of the saber yuccas in the night, I hurried into the multipurpose room of the main jail, to wait with Jesus.

• • • •

As the new guard looked at us both, trying to figure out which was the lawyer and which was the criminal, I scrounged for my bar card for proof. I tried to joke about it, "All lawyers are really criminals," or something like that, but the new guard was still too nervous to laugh. Hell, so was I.

I followed behind as the new guard dragged Jesus toward the door. Jesus stopped suddenly, as if he'd seen his own ghost in the bulletproof glass. “I don’t know if I want to go back in there.” he said.

“I don’t think you got a choice,” I told him.

Now that reality was about to bite, his confident mask crumbled. “You’ll come visit me up in the joint, won’t you?” he asked. “I heard you got that guy out on work release. . . . Shit what do I put on my resume for the next thirty years for when I finally get out?”

“Don’t worry.” I said. “Don’t worry.”

But I was as nervous as he was.

The new guard stared at the mysterious door, forgetting something

I laughed. “One on the one, two on one.”

The doors clicked open. . . .

• • • •

Back in court, we waited. All the jurors stood outside, waiting to go to the bathroom one last time. Was going to the bathroom a good sign or a bad sign?

They filed back in, their heads still down. The foreman gave the piece of paper to the judge, who then gave it to his secretary, Socorro, who finally read the verdict. “We find the defendant, Jesus Villalobos, not guilty.”

The judge smiled for a second when he heard that. “Son, you’re free to go.”

Jovanka rose, but the judge preempted her. “I’m sorry,” he said. “Son, you still have to be sentenced on your other charges. I believe there is still a probation violation. But you’ll be free to go at the completion of your sentence.”

He smiled. “I hope your time up there is good time, and then vaya con Dios.”

Pete shook my hand in his vice-like grip. “Ese, look down. You got shit on your boots.”

I was stupid to enough to look down.

“It’s from kicking their asses so hard.”

Jesus gave me a hug, his face teary. Then Clint had to drag him away from his mother, who cried with joy.

Senora Villalobos then hugged me, almost with the same fervor with which she’d hugged her own son. Somebody’s mother liked me.

Jesus practically dragged Clint over to Anna Maria. He kissed her one last time. “Anna Maria, I love you.”

"I want to marry you right now," she said without a moment's hesitation.

He looked over at me. "Can you set up a wedding?"

I looked over at Clint. "Not before they send him up to the Boy School on the probation violation," he said, almost as disappointed as they were.

Just like I told Jesus that one time, love wasn't going to be an alternative sentence.

Clint had to pry the two of them apart with a billy club, then handcuffed Jesus, led him back to jail.

Anna Maria's elation turned to sadness as the door clicked behind them. She hurried outside to the courtyard to try to get a last glimpse of Jesus through the barbed wire before the doors shut.

Jovanka sat still, staring at the papers on her desk.

"What about Anna Maria?" I asked her.

"She's got either self-defense, justifiable homicide, or maybe even insanity. She'd walk so we're not going to file on her, either. Hell, I don't know. Ricky might even say it wasn't murder. It was the day God abandoned Aguilar. Meanwhile I have to crucify Officer Thompson."

"Well I hope he doesn't ask me to defend him." I smiled. "I'll tell Ricky about Anna Maria."

"And by the way, I'm taking back what I said about you. You did a damn good job."

"Thanks."

"About the wedding. . . ." I said.

"I'll think about it," she said, closing her notebooks. "Who am I to stand between true love? But I've got another trial tomorrow. It might take awhile."

I rushed home to my apartment and ran joyfully out to the Acequia Madre to hunt for rattlesnakes again.

I didn't see any.

Epilogue

Later That Year

ROBERTS VIOLATED HIS PROBATION ON drugs a few times, and Judge Perez finally gave him the gift of time—thirty days in jail. It worked. After his release, he stayed clean and started telling kids about the dangers of drugs and eventually snagged a recurring part as a goofy neighbor on a hit sitcom.

"Other than the week I spent sharing a cell with a serial killer from Albuquerque, I'd say this whole thing was a pretty good career move after all," he told *People* magazine when he was interviewed for their cover story on comebacks.

Guillermo went back to the penitentiary, of course. With all the various enhancements, he'd be there for the rest of his life. A news show raised publicity about his artwork—his paintings and carvings were shown in galleries in New York and Los Angeles, where he was hailed as a "primitive genius." His work can still be purchased at the penitentiary gift shop in Santa Fe and off the world wide web. Older pieces may even be available at the prison craft shop at the federal penitentiary in La Tuna, if you want to make an afternoon of it after visiting the water slides.

I never saw Dora again, which was probably just as well. She supposedly moved in with a famous Tejano singer and moved to Austin. One rumor had that the singer was another woman, but that was never proved one way or the other. I had always wondered why she'd been so protective toward Anna Maria, but I certainly never brought that up to Jesus.

Pete took over Woodford's "conflict attorney contract" and did such a good job of it that a few rich defendants actually declared bankruptcy just so he'd represent them. His life story was optioned by Amanda's cable network, but never produced. He did get to do a stand-up gig on a contest for *America's Funniest Lawyer* and had a chance to go big time. The night of the finals was the same week as a death penalty trial out in Crater. Despite the chance for fame and fortune, he went to do the voir dire. That's what he did for a living after all.

I kept in touch with Amanda for a few months by phone and e-mail. She was a producer most of the time, off-camera, but every once in a while I'd see her on a national story. When they changed the time for her show so that it was up against one of my favorite new shows, I didn't watch so much. She e-mailed me that she had started dating some big time lawyer-novelist whatever the hell that meant.

While we were still in contact, she e-mailed me that I should consider writing a screenplay about my experiences. "You're a funny guy," she said, "and I have a few good contacts in Hollywood. I could help you out here."

I was tempted, but ultimately decided I didn't want to see my private neuroses on the screen for all to see. The prospect of some young asshole fresh out of film school, skimming through my scripts and bitching about "character arcs" and "plot points"—who needed that shit, anyway?

We lost touch after that. I think she got married moved someplace like Santa Barbara and had a couple of kids. As Amanda's image began to fade, I decided to stick it out and make the best of things in Aguilar. I even turned down a chance to make it Shepard, Shepard and Shepard back home. I sure thought about it, especially if I could do some criminal law on the side, but my mom made it clear that the big Florida municipal clients certainly didn't want "those people" coming into their same waiting room.

I politely declined. I told her that I was one of "those people" now.

I got to know Veronica at the jail better with every "one on one, two on one." Her old boyfriend, the felon, had been sent up for good and she dropped him like a bad habit.

"I usually give a guy one felony but once he does a second, it's hasta la vista, dude," she said with a smile on a sunny Friday afternoon when I went to visit an aggravated batterer. "Two strikes and you're out with me," she said.

"I'll remember that. Now what?"

"I'm finally done with my degree over at the Satellite campus. Maybe I'll go to law school. I want to be a lawyer who helps people. Like you."

"Thanks."

I couldn't sleep that night, and suddenly it dawned on me. The perfect woman had been sitting in front of me for over a year and I had never noticed. The next day I stood outside her office with the jail windows holding a big sign reading:

VERONICA, LET'S DO LUNCH

She smiled when she came out. "I'd love to. Anna Maria told me to give you this. We can go together."

It was an invitation to the wedding of Jesus Villalobos and Anna Maria Arias.

It would be the social event of the century for Aguilar. Jesus certainly had his notoriety. Anna Maria did as well. After some posturing for the press, the state never filed charges on her. She quit Rosalita's and became a star of sorts, as if testifying in court had helped her over stage fright. She did a few spots a month as a spokes-model for a chain of used truck dealerships, sang a few nights at the Tumbleweeds with the surviving members of Joey's band. But despite her fame, she stuck by her man.

Jesus had to serve his probation violation of course, but on top of that he had to serve a few more months on the heinous charge of "talking back to a teacher" of all things. The teacher happened to be a nun as well. He wanted to take it to trial, but I reminded him "Who they gonna believe, you or the nun?"

The violation made it a tough sell on getting the furlough, but Jovanka finally relented for a beautiful late autumn afternoon.

"Wedding and reception. Two hours max." She told me, giving her telephonic approval.

"We'll live with that."

Jesus and Anna Maria's wedding took place at the Aguilar Activity Center by the zoo. Anna Maria wore white with a train, Jesus a white tux. I took it to him in jail the day before. Clint and Yvonne did the alterations in the Billy the Kid suite while Jesus tried to hold still.

The activity center was packed. Even though Jesus had been away for awhile, far more people came to his wedding than ever would have come to mine. They even ran out of chairs, so I hurried home and added my six.

Because of all the security concerns, Judge Perez did the wedding.

He joked to me that marriage was the only life sentence he liked to hand down.

The squad car carrying Jesus was late of course. They had to stop at Chaves County Detention Center to transport a convicted burglar for a "Motion to Reconsider" along the way. It was nearly dark when Jesus arrived in the car with Clint. Jesus had to wear shackles with the tux but he still looked the perfect gentleman.

As a precaution, Clint had to walk down the aisle with Jesus as a sort of a best man. Clint pretended not to notice when some friends of Jesus put cans on the back of his car during the ceremony.

Veronica and I sat next to a friend of Jesus he had met up at the Boy's School, "You on the bride's side or the groom's side?" he asked.

"She's on the bride's, but I'm on the groom's, I guess."

After the judge finished the ceremony and they kissed at last, the crowd rushed out to the reception in the grassy field. There was a mariachi band on one side and Kid Coyote the disc jockey on the other. He actually wore a tux in honor of the dignity of the occasion. Dancing began right away under the torchlight and full moon.

I danced a few with Veronica. When the light hit her just right she looked a bit like Anna Maria.

There was some rough looks on the dance floor on the other side—apparently Anna Maria's brother Enrique didn't get along with a few of Jesus's cousins. I politely took Veronica for some punch.

After looking into Veronica's eyes and talking a bit about Rashomon, I went over to congratulate Jesus. Jesus whispered to a young man wearing a shirt reading "New Mexico Boy's School Print Shop." Jesus held up a finger before I could get too close. "Do not disturb." They huddled together as if he and Mr. Print Shop were closing the subsidiary rights for a movie and sequel.

Anna Maria came over to me, still radiant in her white wedding dress. "Give them a minute. They haven't seen each other since Isaac left the Boys School a few months ago." She gave me a big hug. For a moment, I wished I was the groom. But when I looked over at Veronica, who was asking the judge to write her a recommendation to law school, I was more than content.

Mr. Print Shop got up. "Buena suerte," Jesus called out to him.

I pulled up a seat, gave Jesus and Anna Maria my present—a hand crafted turquoise and silver rattlesnake from another trip to the Capitan Apache Reservation.

They both thanked me. Anna Maria took it and brought it back to the table piled high with presents. On the other table, a veritable feast of chicken and turkey.

Jesus and I were finally alone for a moment, although Clint stood a few yards away, eyeing us carefully.

"I just want to tell you that I'm real proud of you," I said. "You've come a real long way since I first met you."

"You, too," he said.

"You know, at first I really believed that you killed Victor," I said. "I was scared shitless of you."

He looked around. There was some kind of disturbance on the other side of the building, but he turned his attention back toward me.

"It took awhile, I suppose."

Suddenly more people headed over to the far side of the building. Something was definitely going down. Clint perked up. We could hear shouting in the distance. . . .

I looked at Jesus. He shrugged. It wasn't a party until there was a fight. . . .

"One thing that always bothered me," I said over the rising noise. "What's up with those tears under your eyes?"

He smiled. "We still attorney-client?"

I nodded. "Friend-to-friend."

The first one was for Jovanka's old man," he said. "But that was a long time ago.."

I went numb, but had to ask the next question. "The second?"

"I ain't saying nothing." he said. "Privilege or no privilege . . . maybe it's something you don't need to know about. There are a lot of unsolved mysteries around here."

"What about the third," I said after a long beat. "The one that isn't filled in yet—"

As if on cue. . . .

Bang! Bang! Bang!

I jerked my head up. What just happened? People ran in all directions.

"Enrique's been shot!" A female voice yelled from the other side of the building. Was it Anna Maria? It was impossible to tell from this far away. More shouting, more screams.

Clint drew his gun, stood ready, but he couldn't leave. He had to guard his prisoner.

My eyes tried to make out the people scattering into the darkness. Which one of them would be my client?

I looked over at Jesus. He stayed calm, somehow this was no surprise to him. My mind raced.

Didn't he say something once about killing Enrique?

What had he just said to Mr. Print Shop?

And if he had Enrique killed, could that mean. . . .

"Jesus!" Clint shouted sharply, stopping my train of thought before it could get out of the station. "Get the fuck in the car!"

Jesus smiled a Cheshire grin, dragged his shackled feet into the squad car, then closed the door behind him.

"Who do you think—" I asked. For some reason, my eyes went back to Jesus, who sat serenely in the back seat

Clint gave one last look around. The party had already cleared out. Ambulances and still more squad cars raced to the scene.

He pointed towards Jesus. "Stay in the car!" He looked over at me. "Don't you go anywhere either! We're going to need you."

"As what?" I replied. "A lawyer? A witness? A suspect?"

"Maybe all three."

FINITO

Acknowledgements

I could not have written this book alone. It goes without saying that the following people named on this list do in no way endorse anything written here within. Some of the people might not have realized that they have had a positive impact on my career. First, my family, who are far more supportive than poor Dan Shepard's family. Words cannot express my gratitude for sticking with me during this long ordeal.

There are several attorneys I wish to thank for being positive influences on my career. In no particular order: Robert McDowell, Joe Shattuck, Jiff Rein, Charles Plath, Gennanne Anderson, Jess Cosby, Mike Stout, Ted Lautenshlauger, Gary Mitchell, Calvin Carstens, Ray Twohig, Mark Jaffe, Albert Lassen, Ahmad Assed and the late Christopher Hassan who I had the privilege of doing a trial with and was destined to be better than all of them. Salaam Ali cuum, Chris.

I'd like to thank my English teachers at the Albuquerque Academy, especially FX Slevin who is probably spinning in his grave. Also Art Kellner and everybody else in that fateful Creative Writing Class. At Cornell University and the University of Colorado, I'd like to thank all my friends and teachers. A special thanks to the horny Boulder Betas (RIP), Heidi Hawkins, the "Boys of Summer" in Ithaca, Eric Goldman, Anne Kelley, the staff of the Colorado Advocate, my roommates on the east side and the west side, especially Sam Ventol and Frank Rybalid and all those big law firms that didn't hire me because of my grades. Who knows where I'd be, if they had.

From my Washington DC days, I'd like to thank Jenny Koos, Paul Whitely, all roommates, the Solicitor's Division at the Department of Interior, all the people I worked with in my temp jobs, and the Washington City Paper for publishing my first professional article, entitled appropriately enough "I Fought the Law and the Law Won." I'd like to thank my first agent Ron Goldfarb and his staff who took a chance on some crazy kid from New Mexico. I'd also like to thank Nick Goldfarb who never hesitated to tell me when something wasn't working.

In Chicago, I'd like to thank Lane and Wilma Kendig (RIP) who encouraged me to return to New Mexico. Also all the good people at the ABA and YLD, especially Cie Armstead who unleashed some of my mad rumblings for a national audience.

A lot of people helped me with editing at various times—Rennie Brown, Dave King and Marilyn Pesola all took a stab at helping me tame this beast. But all fault rests with me.

In Roswell, I'd like to thank all the people working in the Fifth Judicial District, the judges, their staffs, the public defender's department (especially Rebecca, Rich, Paula, Sharon, Lucy, Lloyd, Scottie, and everyone else I can't remember lo these many years later) and District Attorney's Office, the probation officers, the therapists, the correctional officers, and the police. As for friends I'd like to thank Laura Gardiner, Tia Bland Douglas and Henry Douglas, Mike Anthony, Chip Sutton, Rozan Cruz, Monica Baca, Todd Holmes and all my clients who I hope have gone on to bigger and better things. There are a few clients who are no longer with us, and I hope they know they are in my prayers.

In the Seventh Judicial District I want to thank all the good people in Estancia, (especially Viola and Anita), Moriarty, Socorro and of course Truth or Consequences. Maddie Melka, Mark Taujillo and the rest of the Prosecutors were all worthy adversaries. I met a lot of good folks in Los Lunas, Las Vegas (NM), Bernalillo and Santa Fe along my legal travels and travails well. I'd also like to thank the folks at BCJDC, BCDC (Main and Satellite), and Western New Mexico in Milan. When I go to jail, I'm sure you'll give me a warm welcome.

In Albuquerque, I'd like to thank the juvenile division of the Public Defender's office, in specific Diana Garcia, Connie Keegan, Mike Sousa, Mark Van Leit, Louise Sauer and all the contract attorneys. To everyone in the Death Penalty Division, keep fighting the good fight. In the prosecutor's office I'd like to thank Judy Faviell, Todd Heisey, Nancy Neary, Almarosa Delgado, Jacqueline Medina, and Gloria Lucero. Judge Tommy Jewell and staff, Judge Michael Martinez and staff, Judge Geraldine Rivera and staff. I'd like to thank all the folks at the state bar, especially Cheryl Bruce, Joe Conte, Maggie Gombos, Brian Jaramillo, Diana Sandoval and all my friends who I met through the NM YLD. Some other friends and/or lawyers—AC Carpenter, Sandra Gardiner, Marianne Romero, Norma and family, Lora Lucero, Stan Chandler and family, Brady Lovelady, Julie DiTucci and family, Gianna Mendoza, Ruby Silva and family, Lydia Montes all the folks at Midtown especially Lizzard and Lewis S, Nelson Franse, Becky Branch, Donna Dodd, Melanie Homer, Kathleen Lebeck, Mike Hacker, John Utton, Active 20-30 club, especially Garret Hennessy, the New Mexico fantasy football league especially Jeff and Glen, and of course Jill Woodford whose undying faith has changed my life. Jill always told me that God has a plan for me. I finally believe her.

In Los Angeles, I'd like to thank Josh Frey and family, the Wootton family, Laura Wolfe, Veronica Kume, Margareda Meranda, Joelle Sellner, Jay Tannenbaum, Stacy Zackin, Erik Bauer at Creative Screenwriting and all the good folks at Bet Tzedek Legal Services and everyone I met through Friday Night Live who provided spiritual guidance when I was down. At AFI—Jean Firstenberg, Sam Grogg, Sheila Sullivan, Willie Tucker, Lynn Mezzuchi, Stan Brooks, Natalie Perkins, Megan Kennedy, Terrie Thrush, Nakwoi Sung and of course Seth Winston, Barbra Adams, Scott Barkman, Vita Galvan, Clay Haskell, Natalia Lusinski, Lee Metzger, Dax Phelan, Nathan Skulnick, Brian Smith, Shelly Smith, James Thompson as well as Mike Ellis and Karen Janszen.

Finally I'd like to thank all the people who didn't believe in me. You know who you are.